BY LAW PROTECTED

By Law Protected

a novel by Alistair Campsie

CANONGATE – Edinburgh 1976

*First published in 1976
by Canongate Publishing Limited
17 Jeffrey Street, Edinburgh,
Scotland*

© *1976 Alistair Campsie*

ISBN 0 903937 27 1

*Printed and bound in Great Britain
by Robert MacLehose & Co., Ltd.,
Anniesland, Glasgow*

For Robbie,
in mitigation . . .

A fig for those by law protected.
Liberty's a glorious feast.
Courts for cowards were erected.
Churches built to please the priest.

Robert Burns: "The Jolly Beggars"

Author's Note

As no divorce court exists in Glasgow, it must be clearly understood this book is fictional, and the situation imaginary. What is not imaginary is that, while England and Wales have been permitted to modernise their divorce laws, Scotland has been forced to struggle on, using the distasteful methods outlined in this novel. Acknowledgements and thanks are due to F.S. for legal checking, and to J.R. for help in constructing a group of academic sentences.

Avizandum

Glasgow Divorce Court, Scotland
Closed Record (as amended)

In causa

The Most Hon. Bodkin Stuquely Vane Strummet, Marquis of Strummet, of Strummet Castle, Drumshire,   *Pursuer*

against

Jayne Marie Fitzgerald Pinwheagle or Strummet, Marchioness of Strummet, his wife, of 59 India Street, Edinburgh,   *Defender*

1. Summons.

Elizabeth II, by Grace of God, of the United Kingdom of Great Britain, and Northern Ireland and of Her other realms and territories, Queen, Head of the Commonwealth, Defender of the Faith, To the said Jayne Marie Fitzgerald Pinwheagle or Strummet, Marchioness of Strummet:

Whereas by this Summons the pursuer craves the Lord of

our Court to pronounce a decree against you in terms of the conclusion appended hereto, We therefore charge you that, if you have any good reasons why such decree should not be pronounced, you cause appearance to be entered on your behalf in the Office of the Court, High Court Buildings, Glasgow, on the calling of the summons in Court, which calling will not be earlier than the Fourteenth day from the date of service upon you of this Summons; and take warning that, if appearance is not so entered on your behalf, the pursuer may proceed to obtain decree against you in your absence.

Given under our signature:
M.M. Odhar, solicitor, India Lane, Edinburgh.
G.S. Murd, solicitor, Jail Square, Glasgow.

Conclusion

For divorce of the defender from the pursuer on the ground of the defender's adultery.

2. *Condescendences for Pursuer*
and
Answers thereto for Defender.

Cond. I   The parties were married at Martha Street Registry Office, Glasgow, and an extract certificate of the marriage is produced herewith. There are no children of the marriage.

Ans. 1   Admitted.

Cond. II   The pursuer was born in Scotland of Scottish parents. His home is in Scotland and he is permanently resident there, apart from occasional trips abroad and to England. His domicile is Scottish.

Ans. II   Admitted.

Cond. III   After the marriage the parties resided together at Strummet Castle and in Edinburgh and London. The marriage has been unhappy from the start, and two years and nine months later the parties separated and they have not cohabited or had sexual relations with each other since then. Admitted that the pursuer went to Kushta City, Kushta, to meet the defender but it is denied they spent the night together or had marital relations. Explained that the pursuer went there to plead with the defender to cease from her libidinous behaviour in respect of public scandal already caused.

Quoad ultra the averments in answer are denied.

Ans. 3 Admitted that after the marriage the parties resided together at Strummet Castle and in Edinburgh and London. *Quoad ultra* denied. Explained that the marriage was unhappy from the start because of the pursuer's sexual impotency and his continued and frequently expressed desire for the defender to have sexual relations with other men, and other habits. The pursuer arrived at his own wish at Kushta City and forced the defender to have marital relations against her wishes.

Cond. IV Subsequent to the separation of the parties as aforesaid, the pursuer believes and avers that, while engaged in raising recruits for the pursuer's private regiment, the Strummet Foot, she committed adultery in a moveable recruiting tent variously situate at Motherwell, Wishaw, Craigneuk, Bellshill, Mossend, Hamilton, Uddingston, Rutherglen and Whifflets in the County of Lanark; at Paisley, Milliken Park, Barrhead and Newton Mearns in the County of Renfrew; and at Glasgow Green in the City and County of Glasgow with the following men:—

2nd Battalion (Derry Mutineers) The Strummet Foot: Peter Acheson, Walter Cosket Adams, George Addyman, Reginald Annett, Robert Archer, William Arlow, Adam Auld, Jack Bailey, Adam Ball, John Balmer, Gilbert Banford, Jack Barfoot, Jack Barton, Alexander Begley, Robert Bellingham, George Bellshaw, Jack Best, James Bleakley, Patrick Breaden, Robert Breenen, George Brolly, James Brock, Lancelot Brush, Noel Bryars, Dennis Burke, David Burnside, James Cameron, John Calvin, John Campbell, William

Capper, Frank Caren, Edward Carrol, John Cartwrite, Simon Caskey, David Catherwood, David Chapman, Ronald Clague, Henrey Coole, Ian Colhoun, John Conaty, Harold Coppel, Norman Corr, Hamish Corry, Peter Craig, Ben Crawford, Patrick Crowe, Tom Crowley, Gerald Curren, Hugh Daly.

John Davey, John Davin, John Devine, Joseph Devine, John Dicky, Samuel Dixon, William Dobson, James Doig, Michael Donnan, Anthony Doolan, Richard Dowey, Jack Drain, James Drummon, Joseph Durkin, David Early, Maxwell Edens, David Elwood, Henry Earskin, John Evans, William Ewig, James Farnan, Basil Fay, Claude Fisher, Henry Ford, Rodney Flack, James Fink, Joseph Fosey, Hugh Fulton, Alexander Gaff, Robert Gallery, Wilson Gaston, Andrew Getty, Joseph Gildea, William Gilliland, Walter Ginn, Thomas Glover, Alan Gorman, Bertie Graham, Ralph Guiney, Harry Hamilton, Eric Hamill, David Hanna, Hugh Hanthorn, Patrick Hartley, William Hartsag, John Hasteings, George Hegarty, George Hendron, William Heron, Hermann Heron, James Higginson.

Norman Hobson, Barry Hoey, Jackson Hoey, Thomas Horner, Samuel Hough, Kennedy Huston, Douglas Hutton, Herbert Ireland, Edward Irvine, Terence Jack, William Jennings, Stanley Johnston, Frederick Kelso, Tom Kernohan, Samuel Lemon, James Liggat, George Long, Hugh Love, Michael Malloy, Gerald McCarton, Harold McAlmoan, Stanley McConkey, Robert McCully, Ronald McDade, William McDivot, Wilson McElhinnie, John McIlroy, Donel Leaky, James Knipe, Dickson McGettigan, James McGonigal, Patrick McGowan.

Patrick McHaffie, Thomas McIlwane, Andrew McKenna, Alexander McKeown, Peter McGibbon, Ernest McLeer, Frederick McLaw, Frederick McMaw, David McMullen, James McRandle, Daniel McSorley, Brian McWilliams, Arthur McGurran, Patrick McCrimmon, William Mast, Clifford Mayne, Vincent Mercer, Gerard Mills.

Ralph Moffatt, William Molloy, John Moors, James Morgan, Stanley Mulhern, Hugh Nabney, Thomas Niblock, Fred Nutt, Michael O'Hare, Robert O'Rowe, Robert Orr, William Payne, George Peel, Bobby Pepper,

Hans Ploughman, Ernest Poots, Andrew Posnett, Ernest Prier.

Thomas Quin, Ven Raffo, Hugh Rammit, Trevor Rea, Hugh Rennie, James Ride, James Riddle, Peter Rock, George Roe, Peter Rowan, Stanley St. Clair, John Sallons, James Semple, Shaw Sheriff, William Shilcock, Stewart Sinton, Leslie Sroggie, John Service, Robert Skelton.

David Smith, Albert Smythe, Albert Sprott, Albert Sheather, Alfred Stanley, George Stitt, Richard Sturgeon, David Teelan, Thomas Todd, Fred Tomelty, Peter Trainer, Patrick Tremble, Robert Twyford, Henry Uprichard, David Vernon, Kenneth Welsh, Ebenezer Yarr, Alfred Zebedee.

3rd Battalion (Lady Jayne's Own) The Strummet Foot: Richard Addie, Jeremy Alhern, John Alpine, Denis Appleyard, Frank Arthur, Leonard Alymer, Eric Baldwin, John Barron, Anthony Barrie, Luke Beamish, Nigel Bell, Thomas Beuly, Geoffrey Birch, Peter Black, Lawrence Blondel, Stanley Bohill, John Bollins, Alexander Brook, William Boylan, Michael Brady, Noel Brean, Christopher Brazell, Peter Briscoll, John Brogan, Edward Burchapel, Liam Burgess, George Butterley, Barth Burn, Patrick Cahal, Kenneth Callaley.

Bernard Campion, Daniel Caplin, John Carloss, Edmond Cartey, Brian Casserley, Barry Cavanagh, Percival Chambers, Leo Chapman, Eustice Clancy, Austin Claxton, Bernard Colgate, John Collins, Brendan Condon, Simon Considene, Aldan Cooke, Dick Corr, Augustine Cowie, Frank Craddie, Thomas Cronan, Timothy Cuddlehy, Donal Cunningham, Dermot Dagg, Henry Daly, William Darent, Mathew Daunt, Thomas Davison, Alfred Deany, John Dellany, Brian Dempsey, Fred Dodd, Brendan Dolan, Charles Donaldson.

Basil Donahue, Patrick Donavan, Anthony Doolan, Roy Doron, Jack Downes, Leslie Doyle, Gerard Drea, Donald Drew, Derrick Drumm, Thomas Duckle, Andrew Duigan, John Dunnett, Frederick Doire, Patrick Ebbs, Arthur Eagerley, Martin Elcans, Eric Ellis, James Fagan, Bryan Fannin, Vincent Faulkner, Hubert Fennel, Daniel Fish, Danny Finn, Kevin Fitztipper, Gerald Fitztimmons, John Fitzowen, John Flannigan.

Maurice Fleet, George Flood, Gerard Foggerty, Patrick Forde, Henrey Fox, Francis Fuller, Gordon Gaffney, Eugene Gayne, Paul Gannon, Patrick Garland, Patrick Garvey, Richard Garrity, Patrick Gernon, Robert Ging, Thomas Glee, Denis Goggin, George Gooch, Oliver Gough, Basil Graham, Graham Grant, Philip Griffon, John Grouse, Hugh Holpin, Ivan Hanlon, William Hardon, Peter Harrington, Joseph Hayden, Hugh Heffear.

Benny Hennessey, Frank Heuston, John Hickey, Timothy Hoey, Francis Hogan, Colm Holder, Donald Hooper, Ivor Hope, David Huggard, Shaw Hurley, Henry Hines, John Ireland, William Inglis, Anthony Iremonger, Hugh Ivory, Basil Ignatius Jackson, Patrick Jones, John Jordan, Sean Duhal, Eamonn Davannah, Luke Petine, John Kelly, William Kelly, Gerald Kenny, Kenneth Kent, Aloysius Kettle, Christopher Kilbryde, John Kilmartin, Henry Kinseller.

Patrick Lacey, John Lalor, Joseph Latchford, Robert Lawless, Eugene Lemass, Eamonn Lett, Harold Liddy, David Loftoss, David Luke, Robert Lynan, Timothy McAdam, Owen McCarry, Hugh McCabe, Barry McAuley, Duncan McCormack, George McDermott, Desmond McDonall, Donald McDyer, Andrew McAvoy, John McEntee, Bernard McGilloway, Brendan McGrottie, John McInnes, Hubert McKenna, Eamonn McKay, Eamon McLochlie, Patrick McManus, George McNamarra, Kevin McNicholl, Gerald McSweeney, Thomas McMattigan, William Madigan, Joseph McGinn.

Finton Mahoney, Timothy Malone, Edward Mangin, Francis Mansefield, William Martin, Richard Matthews, Colin Mead, Peter Meehan, Patrick Melon, Douglas Merrigan, Thomas Monks, Arthur Mowbray, Sean Mulcahy, Shawn Milgrow, Brendan Murphy, Kevin Murphy, Michael Murphy, Leo Murphy, Nelson Murphy, Neville Murphy, Robert Murphy, Zebedee Murphy, Vincent Malley, Harry Neary, Neil Neilly, Daniel Neville, Richard Nicholl, John Nixon, Noel Noonan.

Anthony O'Brien, Thomas O'Brien, Colin O'Callahan, Thomas O'Connel, Edward O'Connor, Godfrey O'Donnell, Charles O'Driscoll, Dennis O'Dwyers, Godfrey O'Flanahan, Mortimer O'Mara, Eric O'Neill, Brian O'Reilly,

Mortimer O'Rourke, Martin O'Shea, Gerard O'Sullivan, Dermot O'Toole, Peter Palmer, Hubert Parrott, Bartie Plant, Patrick Pitcher, Lawrence Prendergast, Samuel Pryal, James Purfield, Patrick Quin, Gerry Ralph, Thomas Reyle, Owen Raymond, Patrick Raymond.

Eugene Reccia, Ben Reagen, Eamonn Reldy, Austin Rice, James Riggley, Brian Roach, Stanley Rowe, John Ronan, Sheamus Rubenstein, Bertie Bush, Aloysius Ryan, Henry Sargent, Lawrence Scott, Edward Scully, Thomas Sexton, Daniel Shanaghan, Bartholomew Sharkie, Owen Shirran, Frank Sinnott, John Smiley, Miles Smythe, John Sodden, Peter Sparkes, Cecil Squires, James Stanley, Harold Staunton, Dennis Stevens, William Stokes.

Richard Stuart, Patrick Sweeney, Colm Swords, Vincent Talbot, Talbot Tarpy, John Teeling, James Telfor, Frederick Francis Tiernan, John Toman, Edward Tracey, Raimond Traciey, John Trotters, Dennis Tucker, Dan Toobig, Patrick Underwood, Ivor Ure, Henry Verso, Patrick Wayne, Joseph Walton, Alan Watchorn, William Wick, John Wine, Pat Woodcock, Kevin Woolfson, Patrick Yonge, Robert Zechart, Bartholomew Zuvus.

Ans. 4 Explained that the defender interviewed recruits in a tent at the above-mentioned places at the urgent request of the pursuer and Her Majesty's Government. On no occasion has the defender committed adultery with the aforementioned men.

3. Pleas-in-law for Pursuer.

1. The defender having committed adultery as condescended on, decree of divorce should be pronounced as concluded for.
2. The defender's averments in answer (apart from her denials of adultery) being irrelevant, they should not be admitted to probation.
3. The defender's averments in answer of marital relations between the parties since the date of their

separation being irrelevant, they should not be admitted to probation.

In respect whereof:
    M.M. Odhar, Solicitor, India Lane, Edinburgh.
    G.S. Murd, Solicitor, Jail Square, Glasgow.

4. *Pleas-in-law for Defender.*

1. The pursuer's averments being irrelevant and unfounded in fact and in corroboration to support the conclusions of the Summons, the action should be dismissed and the defender should be assoilzied.

2. The defender not having committed adultery as condescended upon, Decree of *absolvitor* should be pronounced.

In respect whereof:
    B.F. Rapport, St Andrews Square, Glasgow.

5. *Interlocutor.*

The Divorce Judge having heard the solicitor for the Pursuer and solicitor for the Defender, allows the Closed Record to be opened up and amended in the terms of the Pursuer's Minute and Defender's Answers thereto, nos. 1048 and 1049 of Process, this having been done of new closes the Record; appoints the Pursuer to intimate a copy of the Record so amended to Alain Seymour Grant Gerontian-ffylde, and allows him, if so advised, to apply to the Court for leave to appear as a party within fourteen days after such intimation.

Ebenezer Divot.

Minute of Amendment for Pursuer *in causa* the Most Hon. Bodkin Stuquely Vane Strummet, Marquis of Strummet, of Strummet Castle, Drumshire, *Pursuer,* against Jayne Marie Fitzgerald Pinwheagle or Strummet, Marchioness of Strummet, of 59 India Street, Edinburgh, *Defender.*

Lorimer for the Pursuer craved and hereby craves leave of the Court to open up the Closed Record and allow the same to be amended by adding a new Article 5 of Condescension as follows:—

Cond. V The pursuer further avers that the defender associated with a man named Alain Seymour Grant Gerontian-ffylde, described as an Army Press liaison officer, hereinafter described as the Party Minuter, The Defender accompanied the Party Minuter to Kushta City and stayed at the St Andrews Hotel there with him for one night. It is averred that the Defender and the Party Minuter spent the night together in the Defender's bedroom and further averred that the Defender committed adultery with the Party Minuter during their visit to Kushta City, and thereafter of new to close the Record.

In respect whereof

J.B. Lorimer.

Ans. 5 Admitted that the Defender went with the Party Minuter to Kushta City. *Quoad ultra* denied. Explained that the Party Minuter spent the night in question in another hotel. On no occasion has the Defender committed adultery with the aforementioned man.

1

The Minister of Aggression's personal heliplane, a revised and sophisticated version of the jump-jet of the seventies, hovered and settled over the Castle home park, the down-draught from the compensatory rotor moulding the brilliant green tussocks of grass over the hummocky ground and alternately puffing out the shiny black bikinis from the bronzed Nordic bodies, and flattening them again. The Minister was unable to tear his eyes away.

He had been in the midst of one of his interminable questions about whether the marquis would suspect anything, when he caught sight, beneath him, of the two lines of half-naked ash-blonde girls, dressed in the thin satin costumes and obviously there as a welcoming party.

He said in a strangled voice to Basil Makebelieve, "I suppose this is another of your little frolics?" His hand went automatically to his right-hand jacket pocket.

The naked and slim brown arms were outstretched and waving like a bosky thicket of birch saplings dancing in the wind. *"Hyvaa paivaa?"* the girls called above the blast and roar of the dying engine. *"Hyvaa paivaa? Mita Kuuluu?"* To his astonishment, he saw they were waving little twig brushes. Laughing and smiling, they uncoiled a long canvas streamer, and two of the girls each took an end and ran in opposite directions, tautening the canvas and revealing its inscription.

"Strummet Sauna," it read, in immense capitals, and underneath, "Scotland's tourist attraction of the Century."

"God almighty," said Tony Pleasance. He took his hand slowly from his jacket pocket and stood up, his legs quivering, ready to disembark, and the little party stepped down from the heliplane and disappeared into the breathless huddle of near-nudity and shrill and excited voices. Basil Makebelieve was saying something behind him, but he could not make him out, nor did he care.

High in the turret room of Strummet Castle, the Marquis of Strummet, standing on a velveteen hassock to gain the necessary elevation, had the visitors under continual observation through a ship's telescope, mounted on an elongated music stand. "One, two, three, four, five . . ." he counted out to his valet. "Five of them. I take it we've enough to go round, Cinnamon." The valet said in a strong Irish accent, "Quite enough, sir. I took the liberty of purchasing another half-dozen copies from the book boutique in Edinburgh." He indicated with his hand the pile of paperback volumes, entitled *The Psychopathia Sexualis*, by Baron Richard von Krafft-Ebing, the famous Viennese professor of psychiatry, who was noted for his studies of sexual aberrations.

"Excellent, my boy," said the marquis. "We must complete our little joke. One on every bedside table, remember, and especially on Mr Makebelieve's . . . We really must whip up his interests." He went into a spasm of laughter, through which ran another and colder note. "We must whip up Basil's interests at all costs."

Basil Makebelieve was the Cabinet minister responsible for the flight north by the five-man committee. In his official capacity as Minister of Redeployment he was considering—along with Pleasance, the Minister of Aggression; a civil servant of permanent under-secretary rank; and a consultant sociologist—means of countering the disastrous fall in recruiting figures for the Army. There was also a certain urgency, for the world situation had made it essential to form a new brigade, but the fall in recruits which had followed the continual scrapping of regular Army battalions had made it difficult, if not impossible. The Territorial Army, once a customary and traditional source of men, had long since been abandoned. It was, as Basil Makebelieve pointed out, only possible for units which had retained their regimental identities and *esprit de corps* to attract recruits. He had been bored by London in an already dusty May and had added that it was a formation like the Strummet Foot, one of the two private regiments left in Britain, which was the model they sought. The other private regiment was owned by the Duke of Atholl, he said, and was rightly regarded as a joke, but the Strummet Foot, although promotion was technically controlled by the Marquis of Strummet (who could also convene courts martial), was a highly professional combatant unit. "If you're worried about recruiting," Makebelieve had yawned, "you should all go north to Scotland and find out how Bodkin does it . . ." His fellow members had looked puzzled. "Bodkin Strummet," Makebelieve yawned again to hide his intense pleasure. "The Marquis of . . . He's an old friend of mine. In fact I think these cavemen would be eminently suitable for what we have in mind."

They had then called in Eoian Lorimer, Minister for Internal Security, Scotland, as a fifth member, because they intended acting on his territory, although they told him little of what was planned. The urgency had arisen after certain classified information had been leaked through sources in Cyprus and Edinburgh that nationalist elements in Russia, tired of remote-control government from Moscow, had grouped under the slogan "Devolution before Revolution", and were in the process of planning a breakaway state composed of Eastern Siberia and Northern Mongolia, with a new capital at Irkutsk. The new formation was to be capable of "fire-brigading" any outbreak of traditional military ground action. But instead of "taking out" nuclear weapon sites, especially in Eastern Siberia, by modern methods, the brigade was to "break in" the bases, using the non-traditional methods of criminal-type entry and destruction.

"In other words, they've to be a suicide brigade," said Makebelieve on the way north. "Expendable and preferably with criminal tendencies. I don't think we could do better than recruit in Scotland." A servant in R.A.F. uniform brought him his tumbler of warm milk. He extracted the silver nutmeg grater from the fob pocket of his waistcoat and floated almost a salt-spoonful of the hallucinogenic powder on to the surface of the milk. He stirred it and drank it quickly.

"I don't think we should use the word suicide," said Pleasance. "It has unpleasant connotations."

"Why don't we call it the Atomic bracket S-bracket Brigade?" Makebelieve stared fixedly at the ashtray in front of him. "We could say the 'S' stood for Scots."

"That's rather a brilliant idea, Basil. I never thought of that."

Makebelieve looked over his shoulder. Lorimer was deep in conversation with the permanent under-secretary and would be unable to hear them. "It's rather a paradise up here, you know," he said to Pleasance. "The judiciary has the Press by the throat; authoritarianism keeps the people down; there's none of this rubbish about treating workers like princelings. Up here, by God, the local rag used to advertise for males and females . . ." He choked with laughter. ". . . males and females, indeed. Makes it sound like a concentration camp lavatory. And there's positively no problem about recruits, especially if you invoke the cry of the clan and all that rubbish. There must be thousands of them baying around the labour exchange doors." He drank the few remaining blobs of cinnamon-stained milk. "They're perfectly all right when they escape. Half of London's run by Scots, but what flops they are at home."

Pleasance grunted and stared pointedly through the window. Makebelieve, noting his discomfiture, decided to prolong it. He added didactically as the hallucinogenic drug began to affect him, "It's as if the Scots have gone slow on us. I was reading somewhere recently of a condition called 'synthesised environment' which roughly means that if you put a peasant, or a crofter, into a successful factory in the Midlands, in no time he'll work as efficiently as the rest of them, but if you keep him at home among people lacking in confidence, they infect him and, between them claiming he can't do it, and the mental hurdles he sticks up, he can't even screw on a nut properly. Perhaps the Scots have synthesised the environment of failure."

Pleasance looked at him suspiciously. He always distrusted

Makebelieve when he started this intellectual patter. "I thought you said Strummet was a friend of yours." He wondered if Makebelieve was drunk.

"He is." Makebelieve's eyes were slightly filmed over. "A great friend."

"How sharp is he? Is he sharp enough to spot what the 'S' would mean?"

"Old Bodkin? The only thing he's sharp enough to spot is any hint of insurrection among his bloody natives," said Makebelieve as they touched down. Pleasance was staring out of the window, wide-eyed and palpitating as the half-naked girls swamped his vision. "You'll have to be careful, though," Makebelieve stressed. "I told him we only wanted his advice on recruiting. He'd go mad if he knew we were turning his regiment into a suicide squad." Then Basil Makebelieve, too, caught sight of the girls and sat entranced, watching them cavort in golden and graceful near-nudity around the heliplane. He felt a delightful shiver go through him. What had Strummet in store this time?

Makebelieve first discovered what country-set life had to offer when he was staying in a house in the West Country for the week-end and had noticed a bent hunting horn over the front door. "Bodkin Strummet bent it over his darling's head last Christmas," his host had explained in a high voice.

"Was he drunk?" Makebelieve had been fascinated by the thought of actually bending a hunting horn over a girl's head.

"No, he was jealous. He found his darling kissing me."

Basil tried to be risqué with a social superior for the first time. "I didn't know you kissed girls?"

"I don't," said his host, giggling.

Makebelieve had then begun to develop a large circle of semi-deviate friends, enjoying their company and their swift if spiteful wit. When he was warned about the security risk, he used to claim he would openly admit to being homosexual, although he claimed he wasn't, and then proceed to compromise the accuser. He also began to develop a reputation as a dandy, wearing lustrous grey suits with mother-of-pearl buttons and black brocaded collars and cuffs. He threatened to re-introduce dove-grey gaiters. The nutmeg grater was his latest device for attracting attention, and he used the excuse of the hallucinatory power of nutmeg for his daring remarks to ambassadors when their wives were present. He hated drabness. He also hated the memory of his early life, which was tough and hungry. He was a Bermondsey boy and had fought to rid himself of his accent, his background, and finally his parents. After considerable and diligent work at nightschool and two years at a Workers' Educational Association college, which he never spoke about, he entered politics in the Birmingham area, where his academic veneer was considered to give tone to the junior section of the Party. He was in the Commons within five years as yet another boy-wonder, and figured largely as the MP who, during his party's stay in Opposition, brought to light the Turgenev political scandal, when it was revealed that a game of strip poker had degenerated into a card game for State secrets, which later proved valueless but were of great assistance in overthrowing the Government.

Tony Pleasance, on the other hand, was determined to get into the county set by more straightforward means, and he continually resented Makebelieve's social success and rapid wit. Sleek, dark-moustached, with almost vermilion lips which he constantly wet in a nervous reflex movement of his tongue, Pleasance was a committee man. His first move when he had achieved junior rank in the Government was to put his son down for Eton, possibly to compensate for being unable to rid himself of his slightly flattened and intrusive A's, which survived from his lower middle-class upbringing in County Durham, despite intensive speech therapy. His greatest secret had developed during his days at grammar school, when he found himself incapable of resolving satisfactory relationships with girls, and he took to carrying a yo-yo in his jacket pocket. Its convex sides brought him sexual comfort when he clenched it, and it had developed into a fetish. His personality changed when he was given psychometric tests at Durham University and it was discovered that he had a massive reservoir of unsublimated aggression. He entered university politics and was successful, his hand thrust forcefully forward in his jacket pocket giving him an air of maturity, and he was even compared to Prince Philip. His most significant political remark was made at University when he said, "We may produce a lot of loud-mouthed surgeons at Durham, but we've got some of the finest left-wing Nazis in the world." His skill with committees brought him early promotion, and he was considered more reliable than Makebelieve, which was not necessarily true. By the time he rose to the Cabinet, he insisted that his children were taught to ride to hounds. He had also made a study of Evelyn Waugh, and refused to have fish knives in the house.

Basil Makebelieve was saying to him, "So flatter him, dear boy." Pleasance was oblivious to him.

"Is that Gaelic?" he asked, as he walked trembling down the steps of the heliplane into the welcoming ranks of the girls.

"*Suomaleinen,*" said the tallest, playfully slashing his behind with her twig brush. "You come, please. Me Griselda. Sow-nah bath . . . Ah, sauna, you say."

To his fury he saw over his shoulder that Makebelieve had instantly mastered the situation, with a girl already on each side, his arms round their naked waists, and their ribbon-decorated hips pressed against his. All three were swaying in unison as they walked across the grass to a wicket gate in the castle wall.

Lorimer was babbling, "I've never seen anything like it. I would never have believed it possible in Scotland." His briefcase was clasped over his chest with both hands. The under-secretary followed, wincing strangely with pleasure.

"*Mita kuuluu,*" said the sociologist, Professor Knapbone, in Finnish. "*Saammeko uida taallaa?*" The girls closed on him, shrieking in fresh delight at someone who could speak their language. "How are you today?" he translated for the civil servant. "Can we bathe here?" His scrawny neck was bulging. "I . . . would . . . like . . . to . . . survey . . . your . . . habits," he said distinctly in English. He offered them a yeast extract tablet, fortified with Vitamin E for fertility. "Go on—have one." He gestured with the bottle towards the girls' full breasts. "I like to take tablets. Make me fit for sauna bath." He pointed to the canvas streamer. "Me take sauna." He made an imaginary gesture of whipping himself, whirling round and round like a top, as if he were already rolling himself in the Arctic snow, the afternoon sun glinting on his spiralling bald patch. *"Kylla, kylla,"* they shrilled. They set on him with renewed vigour, until he ran limping in acute and thrilling pleasure before them into the castle.

Cinnamon, the valet, had appeared and began conducting the Government party through a huddle of tourists who surrounded a guide dressed as an eighteenth-century butler, his diagonally-striped buff and yellow waistcoat showing under his cutaway coat and over the top of his black knee-britches. "My title," the butler was announcing in an authoritative manner to the tourists, "is the Master of the Chamberpot . . ." he glared at a girl from Milwaukee who had read mediaeval English at Cambridge and had begun to giggle. "It is an honorary title, conferred upon the head of the household since the days of Donuil Odhar Strummet, the first chief of the clan—the chief who never slept."

While Cinnamon ushered the Government party through a turret door, the butler led the tourists through the Bluidy Gallerie, where the family portraits hung, Raeburns and Nasmyths mildewing along the gilt beading of their frames. "In this house, it is tradition that comes first. Tradition and the great purity of the Clan Strummet descended from the mists of time, from the very Nordic gods themselves." He regarded them with small, shrewd eyes. "My chief is proud of his lineage. We have no interlopers here, no miscegenation; no pure Highland blood sullied with the taint of lesser races and unspeakable colours . . . 29th chief of his clan, 19th earl and 10th marquis . . ." The Chamberpot stood erect and proud. "A Highland gentleman is my master, indeed."

"Look at his hairy ears then," said a child in a white blouse. He pointed up to the Nasmyth portrait of Rufus Strummet, the 11th earl, who had bushy clumps of red hair growing from and on his ears. The Chamberpot's face twisted in rage. He looked as if he could have squashed the child beneath his buckled shoe. "You are observing the portrait of Lord Rufus, who was born in Japanese waters in the early 1800s," he hissed. "A man of dash, of daring, a man of action."

Hurriedly he shepherded the tourists towards the Martyr's

Gate, an opening at floor level, only nine inches wide and eight inches in height. "The dimensions of the person," he said, confident his next remark would evoke the horror which he found so satisfying, "determined the degree of martyrdom. Some of them had to be helped through by us with a trusty pike, while we recited all the while from the good book to ease them in their distress." In a final blasphemy, he pulled a soiled and tattered copy of the Bible from his britches pocket. The book sprang open at the accustomed place, and he began to intone, with appropriate gestures, "Matthew, chapter nineteen, verse twenty-four: 'It is easier for a camel to go through the eye of a needle than for a rich man to enter the Kingdom of Heaven.'" He snapped shut the book and stared into their silenced and horrified features. A pert grin appeared on his face. "Or as the marquis says, 'Easier for a dromedary to get into heaven than a Campbell to get through the Martyr's Gate.'"

On the top step of the turret stairs, the marquis stood listening, and smiled his appreciation. He turned back to his guests. "I must confess I like that line. We always did a major piece of surgery on the Campbells, you know. It almost makes up for having these tourists marching about my home. If I hadn't had eighty thousand out of them last year, I'd kick their arses down the driveway."

Tony Pleasance, sinking into the luxurious circular divan in the turret room and drinking a glass of exquisite sherry, said, "I quite agree, Lord Strummet." He gave the impression of understanding only too well the problems of intruders from the lower classes. "We sometimes have trouble with them on the Terrace." He was going to add, "I suppose it's a price we pay for having to control the masses," when Basil Makebelieve broke in, "No-one fallen through the mirror yet?" He was lolling back on the black velvet divan and staring up at the ceiling, which was composed of a gigantic circular mirror. In compensation Pleasance's hand slipped into his jacket pocket. Makebelieve went on, "I don't think I'll ever forget that pantomime man whatsisname who took off his trousers and chased that actress girl round the bloody divan three times." He shook with laughter. "I almost fell through myself. It was the first amusing act the fellow had put on in years."

They all craned up at the ceiling. Cinnamon, the valet, seated above the two-way mirror, obligingly took a series of group photographs with his Polaroid camera, and three minutes later, came down to distribute them to the party. "Don't poke your fingers over them," warned the marquis. "They're still a trifle sticky . . . but aren't they good?"

Tony Pleasance's lips were engorged and almost wetly ruby with excitement. He tried to appear laconic. "That isn't a two-way mirror, is it?" His hand had moved uncontrollably towards his pocket again. His thumb nail entered the delicious bisection of the yo-yo. "These girls . . ." His tone was lascivious.

"Yes, Bodkin; these girls," echoed Basil Makebelieve. His intensely white teeth were bared in a cat's grin, the points separate and sharp. "Where did you get all the girls from?"

"Haw, haw," roared the marquis. "I knew I'd fool you."

"Come on: tell us," said Basil impishly, "or I'll have you investigated by the Special Branch."

"They're *au pair* girls," shouted the marquis in triumph. "They're Finnish *au pair* girls. I got them for £3 a week and their keep so they could learn English and English customs . . ." The divan was shaking with his laughter. "Habits, more like it. They run my sauna bath for me."

He stared at Basil Makebelieve. "You're so deviated you can't see it. You've come so far back in full circle you've gone normal again." He trumpeted, "Sauna baths . . . Steam whipping, you bloody fool. What a tourist attraction *that's* turned out to be . . . I even got a Government grant for it."

*   *   *

In the red sandstone stables, which were built behind the castle, and were reached through the arch to the east of the turret, the marquis's son, Torquil Strummet, lay on a pile of meadow hay. He was chewing a stalk of sweet vernal, the delicate grass tasting like caramel in his mouth. Half-hidden on the far side of the hay was his elder sister, Sheila. Torquil Strummet, Earl of Pumphrey and heir to the marquisate, was forced to work for four hours every day as a stableboy in the belief that manual labour would cure his strange malaise. His hours of work were accountable to the Chamberpot who was authorised to chastise him physically. The treatment had been prescribed for him by the local doctor, a typical general practitioner in his fifties, who informed the marquis peremptorily there was nothing wrong with his son. He had in fact thundered at Torquil, "Pull yourself together, boy. You're only imagining you're sick. In the army you'd be jailed for malingering." He had shaken slightly at his impertinence to the laird's son, but just as quickly recovered his omniscience and aplomb, and advised the marquis, "Put him to work. A good day's manual work will do him more good than any of these modern potions they're handing out. Don't believe in them myself. And punish him if he won't."

Although he was a finely-boned boy with the long wolf-hound face of the Strummets, Torquil had started to run unaccountably to fat. His concentration had vanished, and he could stare at a page in a book for hours without a word making sense. He had also, by his own admission, become lazy, and he felt physical pain acutely. Even his sister, Sheila, five years older than him, could not rouse him from his torpor, although they had been close from child-hood, and she, at least, wanted to continue the affectionate relationship. "I just can't seem to feel," he protested to her. "My emotions seem to be withheld from me. I imagine I'm one step from reality." The silence dropped again for several minutes. She did not disturb him. "Ever since I found that old bastard on the day of the funeral." He turned his head away. On the day of his mother's funeral he had walked, unbearably lonely and a little afraid, into her bedroom, and had discovered his father, apparently writhing in un-controllable grief on her silken bed. At first he thought he could hear his mother's ghost when a woman's voice rose huskily towards him, then to his ultimate horror, he saw the marquis was straddling his new stepmother; or at least the woman who became his stepmother a month later. After his initial and hysterical rage, he had become withdrawn and reserved, rarely wishing to speak. "If only I could get away somewhere," he told Sheila, darkly beautiful in her skin-tight jeans in the dusty stable. "If only I could get away, even to a technical college, where I could use my hands and my brain together, I would be happy. But this . . ." He waved a limp hand around the stables, the trevisses obscured with cobwebs and the harness turning green on the wall pegs.

Sheila said, "Don't worry too much, darling. I made a plan today. I phoned somebody who might help." They were disturbed by a fierce pawing of hooves over the cobbles in the stableyard. Their stepmother dismounted from her immense black hunter, *Hon dhu*, his flanks striped with great suds of foam and his barrel heaving.

"Rub him down," she shouted at Torquil, as if he was distant. "You'd be sweating too if you'd been between my legs for three hours." She threw the reins at him. "Come to think of it . . ." She turned towards him, a curious expression on her face. Sheila Strummet sat bolt upright. "Oh, it's you," said the marchioness. "Have the guests arrived? I'd better go up and change."

2

Gerontian-ffylde felt his skin contract in embarrassment as he stood wedged into the far corner of the narrow L-shaped bar of the Chromatic Club and was forced to overhear the conversation which the homosexual major-general was conducting. "Disgusting habit, sauna bathing," the general said loudly. "Type of thing which corrupts entire countries if it goes unchecked. Young men completely nude together in a hot steamy room, indeed. I'd like to know how many of them keep their virginity after a thrashing over the bare behind in those conditions, uh?"

Gerontian-ffylde tried to edge past the general but his back, wedged between the mahogany counter of the bar and the row of heavy bar stools, was as immovable as a tank-trap made from an upended girder sunk in cement. "Done by one of their own sex, what? Libertinism, nothing but damned libertinism."

He looked over his shoulder and saw Gerontian-ffylde whom he vaguely recognised as coming from the Ministry of Aggression. He lowered his voice, and became reflective. "There isn't one opening round here is there?" To his continued and total embarrassment, Gerontian-ffylde could still hear. "Aren't thinking of joining, are you?"

The junior Government minister, to whom he was speaking, blushed and replied, "I would, but I'm afraid I wouldn't know what to wear."

Gerontian-ffylde realised he had to get out, even if he had to touch the general in passing. He reflected how odd it was that people thought you odd if you didn't like touching queers nowadays. He coughed, and pretended to brush against the homosexual major-general's shoulder. "I do apologise, sir," he said. "I'm most frightfully sorry . . . do you think I could get past, now that I've disturbed you?"

"See what I mean?" The major-general moved fractionally closer to the bar to allow Gerontian-ffylde to squash between his back and the bar stools. For some unknown reason, the committee had ordered stools with seats so wide that it was impossible to walk down the space between them and the white-painted wall, especially if a member had pushed out his stool so that he could lean against the bar. "See what I mean . . . ? The whole damned country's corrupted already."

Gerontian-ffylde found himself in an ambivalent state of revulsion. He decided to return to the Ministry of Aggression and have a meal sent down quietly from the canteen rather than lunch at the communal table at the club, where he would feel even more exposed. The contents of his briefcase seemed more unpleasant than ever. He wondered how he could explain them away if he was knocked down by a bus. A taxi came sweeping past. He managed to attract the driver's attention and he ran after the taxi as it slowed, in case the driver changed his mind and accelerated off again. They drove down the Mall.

"Eighty pence, guv," said the driver as Gerontian-ffylde got out. The clock read fifty-five pence. "Extra for the briefcase, see. It's a new rule." Gerontian-ffylde gave him £1. He climbed the marble steps of the new building and took the express lift to the sixteenth floor, where his office faced a white-tiled ventilation shaft. He locked the door and opened his briefcase.

The first pamphlet showed a stereotyped, brutally-pretty girl with brunette hair caught in a ponytail and brushed forward over her left shoulder. She was wearing an indeterminate short garment, elasticated and ruched around the upper curve of her breasts. Her inner thighs were exposed and apart. She was seated on an uncomfortable wooden bench and appeared to be stimulating herself with an electro-

23

massager. On her right was a sort of wall electric heater, while a wooden milking pail, which he recognised from his boyhood summers in Scotland as being called a luggie, was on the floor beside her.

Overprinted in dense black capitals was the super-scription: "Your own log sauna for £500." Under the figures, in much smaller type, it added in lower case, "plus erection."

He dropped the pamphlet into the waste-paper basket, then realised the implication of its being found there. He put it back in the briefcase and took out the confidential memorandum for which he had signed in the late morning. "Proceed immediately to Strummet Castle, Scotland, for high-level conference on forthcoming recruiting campaign. Arrive in advance of Friday a.m. initial conference. Be prepared to stay in vicinity for resumed meeting on Sunday p.m. Grateful if you would bring information on sauna baths, Finnish methods." It was signed by the permanent under-secretary with the party, a man called Babcock, and had obviously been radioed from Strummet Castle over the transmitter in the Minister's personal heliplane.

Gerontian-ffylde raised his head to call through to the ante-room and summon Angela Proof, his secretary, before he remembered she had asked for the afternoon off to see about her stepfather again. He looked at his watch. It was 1.45 p.m. Thursday. He re-read the signal. He decided to leave a note for Angela Proof, and drive north. If Saturday and Sunday were free, she could fly up and join him at Breacogle for the week-end.

He lifted the telephone, in what he incessantly described as the first neurotic link with his house in the Highlands of Scotland, left to him by an aunt who had bought a small castle there to put on plays on the green with local villagers. She had died soon after the first open-air production of Othello, in which she had taken the part of Desdemona. The tired voice of the switchboard operator drifted towards him. "Not another personal call to Scotland, Mr Gerontian-ffylde . . . ? I'll have to put it in the book, Mr Gerontian-ffylde . . . It causes a great deal of trouble passing these calls at peak hours . . . We're not supposed to pass personal calls at peak hours, Mr Gerontian-ffylde . . .

If there was a four-minute Mr Gero . . ." A series of haunted clicks eddied into his mind. Disembodied vowels approached him. A choked double ring, splitting hollowly in the middle of the fifth concatenation, reassured him that it was his number ringing out. In the Cairngorm Mountains, the receiver lifted.

" 'Allo."

"Is that you, Emilio?"

"*Si*."

"I'm coming north for the week-end with Miss Proof. Tell Mrs Emilio to get the mistress suite ready, will you? Tell her I'll take my usual room. Is Mr Carberry still there?"

"Mr Carberry 'as gone to Africa to shoot ducks."

"Gone to Africa to shoot ducks?" shouted Gerontian-ffylde. He was so astonished that he sounded incensed. Carberry was supposed to be holidaying at Breacogle. What was more important was that ever since his schooldays he had amassed an encyclopaedic knowledge of the Scottish aristocracy and their habits, and could have enlightened him about the Strummets. "What do you mean: gone to Africa to shoot ducks? What for?"

Emilio was saying in his implacable and sombre Italian voice, "Because the season is closed in Scotland during May and does not re-open until the first of September and goes on until January the thirty-first unless the tide is out when the birds are shot until February the twentieth."

"Where in God's name did you find all that rubbish?"

"I read it in a newspaper."

"A newspaper?" His voice was cracking in astonishment.

"*Si*. There is another letter from three people saying they do not care if the tide is in or out. The whole thing is a *canard*."

"Oh, go to hell," bellowed Gerontian-ffylde and slammed the telephone back on to its cradle.

A high-pitched metallic shriek emerged. The tired voice of the operator emerged and climbed robot-like towards him. "Did you call, sir? I seem to have been cut off, sir. Is this the end of your personal call?" The metallic shriek began again and grew louder. "Are you THERE?" It stopped so suddenly it was frightening.

In the emptiness, the scuffling of his feet on the cheap

Government carpet seemed noisy. He crossed to his bookcase and took down *Who's Who*, flicking over the filamentous pages, which had always reminded him of lavatory paper, until he came to "Strummet". He carried the squat, over-thick, red book to his desk. The entry read:—

STRUMMET, 10th Marquis of; Bodkin Stuquely Vane, D.S.O. 1944, bar 1945; T.D.; Earl of Pumphrey, Lord Macfugel; Baron O'Reilly and McEntee, 1688; 29th Chief of Clan Strummet; Her Majesty's Keeper of the Druids in Scotland; Lord Comptroller of the Northern Lights; Counsellor of the Royal Privy; Water Captain of the Strummet Gate; Hon. Colonel-in-Chief The Strummet Foot, his private regiment; formerly Lieut. Strummet Foot, War of 1939–45; *s.* 9th Marquis; *m.* 1st Francoise Poincaré (who obtained a divorce) 3rd daughter of Emile Poincaré, Lille, France; 2nd Millicent McNaught, only daughter of the Rev. Michael McNaught, D.D.; *d.*; one *s.*; one *d.*; and 3rd Lady Jayne Marie Fitzgerald Pinwheagle, 7th daughter of the 7th Baron of Pinwheagle. *Educ.:* privately and the Sorbonne, Paris. *Heir:* s. Earl of Pumphrey, q.v. *Address:* Strummet Castle, Drumshire. *T.* Dunstrummet 1. *Clubs:* Chromatic, Poops. *Hobbies:* 19th century French literature, timetables.

Gerontian-ffylde closed the volume. He pinned a note for Angela Proof on to her typewriter cover and left, carrying his briefcase under his arm. He re-entered the express lift, and shuttled between the seventh and twenty-second floors for several minutes, then emerged unaccountably at the mezzanine floor. He walked two floors down to the basement car park. He began to whistle the impossible first *arpeggio* of the *Zigeunerweisen*.

His Maserati crooned to him from behind his seat as he swept up the dark alleyways of the motorways into Scotland, the twin exhausts bubbling like an enchanted river. The wheels hit the rough transition between the surfaces as he sped across the border, and accepted the change with nothing more than a hissing of undisclosed effort. Gretna Green swooshed away from him in his mirrors, the blacksmith's shop and anvil almost obsessively labelled for tourists. White faces glowed in the darkness like expectant globes. Long slats of yellow light came from the sprawling transport cafe. He wondered how many runaway couples were still being fleeced by the wedding industry, as they waited for the registrar's shop to open . . . So Strummet was a flagellist? Carberry had come into his flat in St James to apologise for leaving Breacogle so abruptly, and had caught him packing. "They do say he's very odd," said Carberry. "He's made a life study of the Marquis de Sade; that's what accounts for his entry in *Who's Who*. I rather gather he's made a practical study of his habits, too. So keep your hand on your penny, dear boy, if you venture within his walls and all that, or at least wear a pair of cast-iron britches."

Carberry reflected. "He married again after his second wife died. This time he married the only daughter of Bertie Pinwheagle, the glassware king. Seventh daughter of a seventh something or other. She's raving, apparently. There's also a couple of children left over from the previous marriage, a boy and a girl. She must be twenty-two at least, but I've never met her. I've never seen the boy either, come to think of it. That's odd, isn't it? He must have done something wrong." He assembled the likely reasons in his acute mind. "He's probably in a dungeon somewhere. You know what the Scots nobles are like about their children.

"Or locked in a stable, eating turnips and imagining he's a horse." He picked up his canvas gun cases. "Off to Africa, old boy." He said it as casually as if he was going to the lavatory. "Ta ta".

The darkness was intense now, enveloping the dazzling white barrels of his headlights. He turned his left wrist inwards and glimpsed the radio-active numerals. It was thirty past midnight. It was always mysterious, this coming back to Scotland. It was as if he were coming home. He could never fully explain the feeling, which recurred whenever he felt the Maserati pull slightly and the engine note sink into a bass diapason of power on the long slow curves of Beattock Summit, the road listing steadily higher between the bare slender hills, green to their rounded summits, and still silhouetted against the luminous and delicate ribbon of the night sky.

Alain Seymour Grant Gerontian-ffylde was in reality one of the stateless people created by modern, upper-class society. He had wanted since boyhood, desperately, to be a writer, which had been denied him. All he remembered of his childhood was a series of long and incredibly taxing stays with relatives in Scotland, schools, and a few terms at university before final rebellion against the feelings of deprivation which had merely enhanced his insecurities.

Then his Aunt Dolores died, leaving him Breacogle and a suitable legacy to run the open-air arts theatre, with the condition that if it folded, the remaining money was to finance a project somehow bringing Art direct to the people. Among the hangers-on at the theatre, who knew of the terms of the legacy, was a typical member of the Edinburgh artistic set: a woman entrepreneur, whose major contribution to the arts was to wear a reversible, rust-brown and jet-black gypsy skirt which she liked to switch round at parties to show her contempt for wearing bourgeois knickers. She also had a vast store of animal magnetism, which she first used on Gerontian-ffylde to make him assume he had fallen in love with her, then to impel him to buy a collection of erotic sculpture which she had found abandoned in a disused sweet factory after an Edinburgh Festival, and which she had stored in a furniture van. "What a charismatic opportunity to take Art to the people. To enrich the quality of their life-style; to raise their work-dazed eyes to the gilded horizon of true intellectualism. . . . I'll even lend you my assistant to get it on the road. Won't I, Angela?" With Angela Proof, he toured the country with the exhibition, but was almost totally ignored by the entire population. Eventually they went broke in North Wales, and the collection was again abandoned, this time in a slate quarry, and Gerontian-ffylde was left with only enough money to buy train tickets back to London for Angela Proof and himself.

"I felt so sorry for the kid, those enormous black eyes staring at me as if she loathed me," he had said to Digby. She had gone home to Sussex while he had gone to camp in the family flat in St John's Wood, which had been stripped of furniture by the trustees before being sold. Three weeks later, he had been walking back from Fleet Street, after drinking with Digby, a reporter who had been investigating the abandoned sculpture exhibition, and with whom he had struck up a tenuous friendship. As he passed through St James's, an elderly, spruce and iron-haired gentleman seemed to bound from a club doorway towards him. "Hello, sir," Gerontian-ffylde said reluctantly. It was General Moffat-Blake, an old service friend of his father.

"The very chap," said the general. "I was saying only last week that if your father had been alive he would have known how to deal with the situation."

"Which situation, sir?" Despite his artistic inclinations, Gerontian-ffylde had never lost the habit of politeness.

"It's these demned Press fellers. We've been having a great deal of bad luck with our Press relations, and we've discovered it's because they've infiltrated us with their own chaps. It's demned discouraging, what. Every time these Press fellers phoned up for information, their chums used to give it to them. They don't think like us." He leaned forward and patted Gerontian-ffylde's shoulder. "I know you were never in the Army, my boy, but I'm sure you think along our lines. I know you're a clever chap. Your father was quite proud of you in a way, you know. He used to tell me about you."

"Did he, sir?" Gerontian-ffylde hid his amazement. He had always thought his father had disliked him.

"Yes, indeed. Why don't you come in with us, in a special post? Handling the Press; a sort of Press liaison officer. You don't have to tell them anything, of course. That's what this new post is all about."

Almost immediately he found himself on a major's pay and allowances. Later he went up to lieutenant-colonel, then colonel, in status and money. The job itself had compensations; short hours and long leaves. Then he found himself devising more and more official trips to Scotland so that he could spend week-ends at Breacogle Castle, in reality, a small, centrally-heated fortalice. In his more serious moments, he realised he had found what he needed most: a home, a piece of territory. "It's my own air space," he told Digby in El Vino's. "It's my own air space and no-one can occupy it without my permission. I'll lend you some. Why don't you borrow it and write that book you always talk about? You're originally Scots. You'd love it."

He had driven through the central belt of Scotland, and was emerging on the forward slope before Stirling where Digby once said his ancestor had initiated the rout of the English army at Bannockburn, for which he had been honoured on the field by King Robert the Bruce and made Great Officer of Scotland. He wondered why Digby was so careless about his ancestry; why Digby was so careless, full stop. He felt a tinge of envy. His own family's earldom went back only to the nineteenth century. He could never understand Digby, nor why he went on working as a hatchet-man for Lord Acarid on that ghastly paper. There must be some hidden meaning, somewhere.

Fumes of orange light from overhead ghostly lanterns illumined the roadway. He changed down, the engine momentarily resenting him, to take the right-angle bridge over the River Forth, and swept onwards through Bridge of Allan, almost ricochetting off a series of broken wooden palisades, guarding long-abandoned roadworks, then he was out into the open country. The car was swimming through the ground mist, layer piled upon white layer, as he sped onwards and into the great fertile plain of Strathearn. On the north-west horizon, he could see the first precursor of dawn, a pollen-yellow thread as fine as a silken filament, forcing the night sky upwards and away. It was three a.m. At six, he was trickling the petrol-blue car over the cobbles of Dunstrummet Village. He passed the castle gates, then the Strummet Cave hotel. It looked too small for breakfast at that time in the morning. A cow stared at him from the pavement and went back to eating a lilac bush in a front garden. His exhaust noise was murmuring off the lime-washed houses. He cut the engine in front of the Strummet Arms, an imposing white building, glittering with Snowcem and black paint lines. A sign read, *"Ceud mile failte."* For those who did not understand Gaelic, it provided an English translation, "A hundred, thousand welcomes." He swung out of the long rakish car and stood up, stretching first one leg, then the other. He knocked on the hotel door. An upper window slid up. "Get away," shouted an angry voice. "Get away from that or I'll send for the police. Go on, get away."

"I only want breakfast."

"It's the police you'll be getting. Come back when the rest of those bloody tourists get here."

"I appreciate I'm a little early, but . . ."

A circular crimson face appeared. There was no hair. It resembled a flesh football. "If you don't go away, I'll have you arrested for breach of the peace."

Gerontian-ffylde wondered how many times the scene had been re-enacted outside Highland hotels. He said, "Oh dear, I'll have to go up and disturb them at the castle. I did think it would cause less trouble here."

The crimson flesh lost its tensility. Creases of alarm appeared and developed into a sick smile. "The castle, sir?" The face withdrew. A few moments later, the bolts thudded back and the owner appeared, either suffering from glandular disease or having totally shaved his head. He was obeisant. "Come away in, sir. A castle guest, if ever I saw one, sir. A truly Gaelic welcome, sir." Gerontian-ffylde was taken to the newly varnished dining room where he sat on a wicker-bottomed chair, and ate bacon and solidly fried eggs. "I thought at first you was one of those bloody tourists we're always getting hereabouts. They're always about here, demanding service and cups of tea and food. I refuse them whenever I get the chance, sir. But castle folks . . . *the gentry*." His fleshy eyes were prescient. "Nothing is too good for the gentry, sir."

In the morning calm, Gerontian-ffylde waited until he saw the marquis's standard being run up the turret flag-staff. It draggled there in crimson and gold limpness. He paid his bill and drove up to the castle.

"Name and business, if you please," said the Chamberpot. He was in full ceremonial dress, with only the black bows at his white hose tops slightly askew.

"I'm expected by Mr Pleasance." Gerontian-ffylde made to move forward, and to his astonishment, found the Chamberpot barring the door with his arm. "You'll wait here," the servant said, "till you're vouched for."

Gerontian-ffylde thought his insolence was matched only by that of the inn-keeper. He found himself wondering how impertinent the garage-keepers were in the district. He supposed all tradespeople became much the same when they found themselves in positions of temporary power. He allowed his eyes to move slowly from the Chamberpot's pompous and authority-flushed face, down over the pouter chest and swelling belly, over the ridiculous knee-breeches, and descend to the buckled shoes. Equally slowly, he began to raise his eyes, pausing in a precision of loathing at a speck on the Chamberpot's striped waistcoat. The servant seemed hypnotised. Gerontian-ffylde took out a monocle and screwed it into his right eye as if he could scarcely believe the evidence which his eyes had adduced naked, and needed somehow to verify it. For a moment, he kept his face expressionless, then in a final and insulting manner, he jerked the monocle from his eye, as if he had seen too much and had been horrified. "Take me to your master," he barked. He wondered why menial people had to strike such poses.

Disordered and shattered, the Chamberpot moved aside to conduct Gerontian-ffylde through the Great Hall, past a star-shaped thicket of pikes, to the door leading to the turret stairs. In the semi-darkness, his trance-like voice even advised Gerontian-ffylde of the trick warning step, raised an inch higher than its fellows, so that an uninvited guest would stumble in the gloom and fall against the upper turret door, warning the occupants.

The first person he saw was Basil Makebelieve, incredible in a black and yellow Strummet kilt and a white sporran made from an otter's head. His legs were grey and scaly. At his side was a smooth, bespectacled and earnestly youngish man, Moral Re-Armament and Oxford written all over him, and looking antiseptic and splendidly germ-free even at that time in the morning. A goat-bearded man, with a scrawny neck and over-bright darting eyes, was also talking to Makebelieve, and appeared to be interfering with his sporran. The group laughed and the word "codpiece" floated in the air. A door opened at the far side of the turret, obviously leading to an even higher room, and from it emerged the Minister of Aggression and a flushed man in a black and yellow Strummet tartan lounge suit. He was holding a malacca cigarette holder, at least three feet in length. They stared around the room with a trace of condescension and appeared to be sharing a joke *à deux*. Once or twice they stared up at the mirrored ceiling. Gerontian-ffylde felt Babcock, the under-secretary, materialise at his side. "You've arrived," Babcock finally said, in a fine Civil Service appreciation of facts which had been established for some time.

Tony Pleasance caught sight of him. "There's our Press man, marquis," he boomed. The antiseptic young man, who was really Eoian Lorimer, the Minister for Internal Security, Scotland, came across to Gerontian-ffylde and said "Didn't I meet you at your Aunt Dolores' once? I remember you: weren't you one of the artistic set? I always hoped you'd come over to our side of the political fence with your talents. I'm so glad you're here. It's so difficult dealing with some of these people: one hardly knows where they've come from." His nose wrinkled. "Or what they've been doing on the way . . . How is your Aunt Dolores, by the way?"

"She's dead, I'm afraid."

"And who has Breacogle?" Lorimer was blatantly inquisitive. "Did she by any chance leave it to you? We wondered if it wouldn't be a perfect setting for putting on some plays we had in mind."

At Breacogle, in fact, the theatrical club had collapsed. The cedar wood half-auditorium was in ruins, shaded by one of the last oak trees in the Highlands. This had escaped the vandalism and opportunism of the nineteenth century because it was said to contain the spirit of a murdered witch, who had been shot not by a silver bullet but by an ordinary lead ball, and could thus be possibly still alive and dangerous. Or so the locals claimed, thought Gerontian-ffylde. At least it would have frightened off Lorimer and his curious crew.

To his relief, he heard the Minister of Aggression, Tony Pleasance, say, "I think we can all begin, gentlemen." As the minister spoke, a concentric segment of the massive circular divan sank to the floor, revealing the centre as a padded table, encircled by a cushioned bench. The marquis cackled at the surprise of his guests and took the seat of honour, lolling over the black cushions in a roman attitude.

"I may say," the marquis began, "that around the original of this table some of the finest and most successful campaigns in Scotland were planned, formulated and carried out. I am greatly honoured that it has again been chosen for a campaign which can redound nothing but good on our country. Around here sat the men who brought civilisation and grace of living to Scotland, but who also ensured the old and sacred order of things would not be lost, while the creeping forces of modernity and permissiveness among the lower classes would never be tolerated by law. It is my opinion that the lower classes feel, work and think better when the great decisions are taken for them. This, after all, is merely an extension of the clan system, which it has been our good fortune to carry on into this century, and which can guide us in an affair no less important to the future history of our country. We can safely draw on the tradition and gallantry evoked by this war-chamber to guide our feet and our minds into the new battle." Tony Pleasance winked at the marquis and gazed knowingly up at the ceiling mirror.

Offended, because he had painstakingly written and re-hearsed the speech, the marquis continued. "I am proud to associate myself, my clan and my regiment with your new venture. You, Mr Minister"—he looked pointedly at Basil Makebelieve, the Minister of Redeployment, in revenge—"have given me an inkling of the project ahead. I can only say that I am a traditionalist, ready to fight to the last drop of blood of my clan against these aliens. I am Nordic, with not the merest genetic addition of the Celt, and I am thus Nordic both by inclination and breeding. My blood is pure and untainted by contact with the, these . . ." He hesitated, not sure for the moment if Mongolians were Chinese. He had intended to say "slit-eyed Chinks". He substituted "inferior races". "Be assured, gentlemen, that I pledge myself, my family, my clan who are my vassals, my regiment which is under my iron discipline, my entire nation of Scotland, to aid you in your endeavours to free us from tyranny.

"My motto is: No miscegenation here. I don't want my daughter raped by a Chinaman." He fell back against the cushions, not appearing to notice the irony of his colour scheme.

Gerontian-ffylde thought how dangerously paranoic the speech sounded, if not megalomaniacal. He wondered why he had been drawn into this curious conference. The heat of the strangely-scented room and his sleepless night began to affect him. He dimly heard his Minister, Tony Pleasance, rising to his feet and speaking about the splendid example the marquis's regiment had set in recruiting, but he did not appear to want the Scots for his new project, only ideas on how to recruit men in England. In his haze, he was vaguely aware that Pleasance repeated several times, almost seeming to stress the fact, "We want to draw our recruits from the cities of technology in the south to give them the opportunity of showing their inherent fighting qualities which seem to have been lost for the present in easy living and affluence." Eoian Lorimer, the Scot, was almost beside himself. Gerontian-ffylde sat bolt upright as Lorimer sprang to his feet, imploring Pleasance so fiercely that his voice began to quiver. "But, minister, you promised . . . you promised to help us . . . to give us the opportunity."

Basil Makebelieve, his eyes wide and apparently un-deceptive, said, "I know you Scots are all glory-seekers, but this is really going too far." He laughed.

"But there's a great chance that most of them would be wiped out, isn't there?" Lorimer's voice had risen higher.

"Oh, I say," said Pleasance, looking protestingly at Makebelieve.

"But you promised to help us. We told you if we even took a hundred of these anthropoids out of the population, we might get Glasgow back under control. The problem is frightening; it's almost out of hand. Thugs roam the streets in broad daylight and absolutely refuse to respond to remedial treatment. We've given them everything we can think of, tried out every new theory, but none of them seems to work. Even at the height of the race-rioting in the States, the Americans were jeering at us. They claimed Sauchiehall Street on Saturday lunchtimes was as bad as Vietnam . . . When night falls, it's worse."

Pleasance said smoothly, "I don't know if this is the approach we had envisaged. We respect the Scots and their fighting qualities. We don't want it held against us that we came to Scotland out of all the kingdom to recruit men who were then sent to their certain deaths."

Lorimer broke in again, his voice savage. "There's a

political reason, too. All the Protestants vote Tory and the Catholics Labour. They just aren't interested in us. If we could get rid of all this fake religious nonsense, they might become enlightened and vote for our Party instead. We'll never do it as long as these thugs are at large in Glasgow."

Pleasance's right hand was deep in his jacket pocket. He looked bland and reassuring. "I suppose you'd say we would be doing you a service, in a sense." His voice was joking. Out of the corner of his eye, he watched the civil servant taking meticulous notes of the meeting to transcribe as eventual minutes. He could hardly believe how easy it had all been. "No returns for such a favour."

Eoian Lorimer burst out, "The Secretary said he would put you up for a Knight of the Grail . . . Once one fell vacant, it would be yours." His voice was vicious, underlying the desperation. "He couldn't be here. He had to go to an important Scout jamboree, but he said to send his apologies." His overt criticism of his political master frightened him and he became more desperate. He blurted, "How about a judgeship? No, of course not, you aren't a lawyer. Chairmanship of one of our advisory boards?" Makebelieve thought he was speaking almost like a huckster. "Splendid fishing and shooting. Lovely holidays for your family and for you. And an extra ten thousand a year never goes amiss. You don't have to do anything. The Secretary would be only too happy to oblige, and it's all in his gift."

He became aware that everyone was staring at him, open-mouthed and astonished by his outburst. Babcock, the civil servant, had prudently laid down his ball-point pencil. Lorimer was still standing, his face reddened and his black, executive spectacles slightly askew. His embarrassment made him flinch, a swift contraction of the nerves in his stomach and back. He suddenly hated them all for witnessing his exposure. He felt himself impelled to tell them, to shout at them, what that evil, sensational newspaper, that rag, of Lord Acarid was doing to him. It wasn't his fault that he was shooting off his mouth. It was Acarid and his henchmen, persecuting him about punishment and retribution; they just didn't believe in modern therapy at all.

They only wanted revenge on criminals. The bastards had no ethics, no standards of conduct, no decency. He thrust away the thought that his bargaining with honours was dubious. If these newspaper people knew how much it was in their power to wound and terrify and bludgeon and force leaders like him into no longer knowing whether they were right or wrong, there would be no halting their filthy influence. God, how he hated them, how he hated every last one of them. "We're very keen," he said lamely.

For a moment Basil Makebelieve felt a pang of pity for the Scots. Instinctively, he suppressed it. If the Scots wanted to offer themselves as partners in a murder pact, it was hardly his fault.

"How do you feel, Lord Strummet?" Pleasance was deferential.

Diagonally across the table, Gerontian-ffylde could see Basil Makebelieve groping for something. On his own left, Professor Knapbone, the sociologist, was alternately looking up at the ceiling mirror and plucking tendrils of grated carrot from a silver salver which had materialised in front of him. "I take it for the carotene," he whispered to Gerontian-ffylde, as if he was disclosing a scientific fact of great obscurity. "It is the precursor of Vitamin A which in turn is the precursor of rhodopsin which occurs in the retinal rods of the eye." Carrot tendrils sprayed on to his papers as he proceeded. "Rhodopsin is a light-sensitive pigment which breaks up in the presence of light of a certain wavelength and intensity, and stimulates the optic nerve." He delivered the punchline earnestly. "It helps you see in the dark . . . Try some; go on, have some." He pushed the salver towards Gerontian-ffylde, his maniacal eyes fluttering and brightly blinking.

"I don't especially want to see in the dark," Gerontian-ffylde said faintly. "I don't even like carrots."

"Don't be so faddy," Knapbone insisted. "It also helps the iodopsin formation which is violet in colour, compared with the purple of rhodopsin. Go on, have . . ." His voice was drowned out by Tony Pleasance, who rose and said, "We seem to have come to a remarkably swift decision, gentlemen; namely to increase the Strummet Foot to brigade strength, adding two more streamlined battalions, each of

300 men, which are to be raised in the Highlands and . . ." he paused for the benefit of Babcock who was falling behind with his note-taking ". . . at the Minister for Internal Security, Scotland's, request and recommendation, recruiting is also to take place in the Glasgow area to help with the almost uncontrollable crime problem. Lord Strummet has pledged his regimental organisation and traditions to spur the recruiting of these men, who may well turn into decent, reliable, dependable and completely useable—no, make that 'acceptable'—citizens. The Minister of Redeployment has come up with another brilliant suggestion and I feel it should be minuted that the meeting feels praise should be apportioned where praise is due."

Basil Makebelieve swiftly added, "I feel that it should be rephrased to ensure the Minister of Aggression is given full recognition for the major part he has personally played in urging the Marquis of Strummet to co-operate and raise these men from Scotland." He sat back satisfied, as Babcock inserted his statement. "I think we should have a celebration cup of tea, or something."

"What an excellent note to conclude on," said the marquis, who had not followed the byplay of apparent compliments. "Let's have a drink." He pulled at a curious, cylindrical bell-rope, which had a protuberance at the base. "Torquil . . ." he shouted.

"There's only one thing," said Basil Makebelieve, again anticipating Tony Pleasance, and nodded across the table to Gerontian-ffylde. "This is where you come in. It's your job to recruit them, bring them in to the colour sergeant, make them take the Queen's shilling. You're the person who's going to have to find the gimmick to attract them . . . Don't be too sharp about it." He grinned, his little white teeth dentate and potentially vicious. "No, don't be too sharp. Let's have your proposals by Sunday tea-time."

The rough sandstone wall of the turret collapsed behind them. From the apparent shambles emerged Torquil Strummet, pushing a drinks trolley. His sister, Sheila, her face hard in rebellion, was beside him. Gerontian-ffylde realised the brother and sister were moving off a steel platform which had the power of rising and falling noiselessly in a shaft. As the trolley came forward into the turret room, the platform descended without a murmur, and the fake sandstone wall rose and clicked back into position. "Splendid trick, what?" The marquis was braying like a jackass. "I didn't tell you chaps about it, did I? It's a water lift which I saved from some vandals in Glasgow and installed in the old disposal shaft." He explained that the soundless water lift, built by the Victorians, took its hydraulic power from a deep well which was sunk behind the water gate of the castle, formerly guarding it from attack by sea. He leered at the girl. "And this is my daughter, Sheila. Isn't she lovely? As for this apparition . . ." He flicked vengefully at Torquil with his malacca cigarette holder. ". . . This is what you might call my dumb waiter. Hurry up, dumb waiter: give the gentlemen drinks." He turned to his daughter. "Sheila, the presents." Torquil was already distributing glasses of a malt whisky, Dunstrummet's Dream, which the marquis received free from the distillers in return for appearing in full Highland dress on the label, a bottle in one hand and a glass extended welcomingly in the other. Sheila, her cheeks white with contempt, began to give away the marquis's gifts: each guest discovered his name neatly printed on a card which read, "Strummet Sauna beckons you to health." To each card was attached a pliant, estate-grown, birch switch.

Basil Makebelieve pretended to croon with delight, bending his besom between his fingers and staring passionately at Gerontian-ffylde. "I've been watching you." He mimicked throatiness, appearing to be joking. "You look terribly aristocratic. I'm sure you'd enjoy it." His eyes assumed a gloating passion. It was no longer possible to tell if he was serious or not. "It's quite the latest kink . . ." He advanced on Gerontian-ffylde, ". . . being thrashed *by* a Cabinet minister for a change."

Gerontian-ffylde could feel the turret door handle pressed against his back. "If you say so, sir." He was as polite as ever. "Excuse me for a moment, won't you, sir?" Swiftly he was through the door and closing it in Basil Makebelieve's face. He found his birch switch was still in his hand. "Faugh," he said. There seemed no other word to express his feelings. He dropped the switch and walked down the turret stairs and went out into the open air.

3

In the home park between the castle and the sea loch, where the twin horns of a spruce forest sheltered the greensward from the west wind, the estate workers had erected two white marquees, and constructed several rough wooden platforms and a many-tiered bank of seats. A banner had been stretched between two oak trees at the lochside entrance to the park, which read, "*Failte* 207th Strummet Highland Games." At the far end of the park, an olive-green Army tent was already in position, with an echelon of the new Skoda-Benz one-man rocket launchers and a troop carrier parked in front. By tradition, the Strummet Foot always sent a weapons platoon to the Games to show the flag and recruit a local or two, when they were drunk enough to sign on, or even to entice a few of the remnants of the volunteer company into the Regulars.

Lieut.-Colonel Robert Ramsay Strachan, commanding officer of the Strummet Foot, thought the exercise was useless, and only made bearable by the drinks situation. The marquis, as honorary colonel-in-chief, always sent down a case of Dunstrummet's Dream which the officers and the pipe major, by right of custom, drank before the day was over.

Through the shading branches, the utterly clear sunlight of the West Highlands suspended the cone buds of the larches into a fret of silver and darted on to the colonel's cap badge, pinned over the blue regimental hackle. The badge, the only one of its kind in the British Army, was of a naked woman chasing a wild boar, which she had already caught by the pin-bones. Underneath was the motto, wryly given them by Napoleon when they were disturbed in a Flanders brothel on the morning of Waterloo and perforce fought in their shirt tails, which was, "Toujours prest". This led to their vulgar nickname, the Tadger Pressers, which referred in Scots to their masculine physiognomy and undoubted habits, and caused many inter-regimental fights.

Col. Strachan withdrew his head from the tent doorway and sipped at his dram of whisky, brimming to the rim of a castle goblet. He made little impact on the contents. "Strummet's coming," he observed to the knot of officers and the pipe major, giving the marquis the courtesy of his territorial title, "with as nasty a collection of poofs in tow as I've ever seen."

At first sight, the marquis's procession resembled a giant, furry, black and yellow caterpillar, using its startling colours to scare off potential attackers, in the way that poisonous insects warn predators of their toxic contents.

Shrilling bagpipes overlaid the fury of the colours. At the head of the procession was the marquis, swaddled in a black and yellow plaid. Rising above it was his sleek, pomaded head, surmounted by his bonnet in which two eagle feathers were implanted, while his right arm rose even higher to grasp the carved handle of his shepherd's crook, the emblem of clan paternity. From behind, and surrounding him, came the scream and roar of bagpipes as Seumas MacPratt, the chief's piper, played the tail of men and women onwards, his glasses lopsided and his calves bulging out dramatically where he had turned his kilt stockings over twice to make his legs look thicker. More figures followed in the hideous tartan, its colours so affronting Gerontian-ffylde's eyes that he put on his sunglasses. From his position in the rear he could see Basil Makebelieve in his borrowed kilt, arm in arm with the marchioness, who wore a loose, pleated skirt of the stuff, and a tartan stole around her shoulders. Makebelieve's arm slipped free and went daringly under the stole. He was waving his free hand. Behind him was Tony Pleasance, right hand thrust firmly into his jacket pocket, and wearing a Strummet tartan tie. Lorimer had almost disappeared inside hairy tweeds. Even Babcock, the civil servant, attempted to look in an outdoor mood and was wearing a Norfolk jacket with patch pockets and a cloth belt, while behind him, there was a scattering of local retired service officers and their wives. Gerontian-ffylde, remaining well in the rear, was apparently the only one to notice the slim elderly man holding a battered Minolta camera, which he raised to his eye. As the official party filled the viewfinder, Vic Ventnor pressed the shutter button. He flicked on the next frame and took another photograph, this time inadvertently showing Basil Makebelieve waving his fingers and screwing up his face at the marquis's back, while he and Lady Jayne snuggled even closer.

Vic Ventnor, who had won an *Encyclopaedia Britannica* award back in the fifties, had retired from Fleet Street to Dunstrummet with his wife, who was a native of the village. To enhance his pension and to please the villagers, and especially the marquis, who loved seeing his photograph in the papers, he occasionally took Press pictures and sent them to the nationals.

Even for the marchioness, thought Ventnor, this was a curious type of romance. Basil Makebelieve's personal life was widely known and gossiped about in Press circles. He decided to phone the Scottish news editor of the *Tentacle*. "This is what you might call really queer," Ventnor told him. "Here's Basil as nutty as a Dundee cake, groping a raging nymphomaniac behind her husband's back. Do you want the pic?" There was a choking, garbled flow of language, and Ventnor gathered that the news editor wanted to send it to London for Lord Acarid, who had issued a confidential memorandum earlier in the week that all society photographs with a potentially immoral connotation should be wired to him for inclusion in a special file he was compiling for what he called Project X.

"It's a funny thing about news editors," Ventnor told his wife as he packed the film into a contract envelope. "They always seem to have difficulty in expressing themselves. It's a damned good job they aren't allowed to actually write anything for the paper."

At the air-strip, fourteen miles up the coast, he put the film safely aboard the plane for Prestwick Airport. The airport at Glasgow had gone on strike again. At Prestwick a fast car waited to drive the film to the *Tentacle* offices, where it was processed and printed. A wet print was wound around the drum of a photo-transmitter, and fifteen minutes later, the photograph of Basil Makebelieve and the Marchioness of Strummet dropped on to Lord Acarid's desk.

"My boys," said Lord Acarid proudly. He ignored the fact that Ventnor was a part-time freelance. "My boys have done it again. I ask for proof of immorality in political and upper-class circles, and here we have, within the week, a picture of seedy little Basil Makebelieve, latest in a long line of suitors, trying to cuckold the Marquis of Strummet in broad daylight behind his very back."

He paused reflectively. "Funny thing," he added. "I didn't think Basil was having an affair with her. I always thought he was a raving old queer . . . but, no matter, one of my men was there to record it. Send the Scottish news editor a bonus for his foresight in having a man posted at the correct place, Peterkin, and file this in the amoral aristo file . . . and find Digby."

Lord Acarid threw the photograph on to his desk. "We'd better get a good man up there right away, and Digby's bound to know all about this. He's Scots, you know."

He groped under his desk, and Peterkin, his personal assistant, hurried forward to anticipate his master's wishes, and switched on the tape recorder.

"Digby, my boy," dictated Lord Acarid. "I want you to return to your beloved and revered homeland and give it the moral spring-clean which it so direly needs. I want you to go back to root out the evil which has beset it in this century of permissiveness. I want you . . ." He was idly gazing at the photograph when he realised that Tony Pleasance was looking over Makebelieve's shoulder. God in heaven. What was the Minister of Aggression doing up there? He looked again . . . and the Minister for Internal Security, Scotland? He had been on TV a week ago, trying to explain away the Scottish crime epidemic. And who was that shifty little man behind them? His withered face made him look like an archetypal civil servant.

"Cancel that message," he barked into the tape recorder. "Digby, apart from finding out what Basil Makebelieve is doing with his hand on the Marchioness of Strummet's bum, uncover the reason for half the Cabinet watching him." In a terrible voice he added, "In other words, find out what the hell is happening at Strummet Castle."

Gerontian-ffylde sidled through the door of the inner room in the marquee, where the official party had been entertained by the Games Committee, scraping in pleasure at such important guests. Apart from the marchioness, who was talking to a bovine officer of the Strummet Foot, her hand delicately poised on his forearm, he was alone. All the other guests had gone out to take seats of honour on the wooden tiers and were watching a constant fusillade of hammers, steel balls and cabers, hurtling and spinning through the air.

Gerontian-ffylde wondered where the photographer had gone. He was suddenly suspicious. He stepped out on to the games field and picked his way through the cigarette packets and empty whisky bottles which were already beginning to litter the grass. He could not see the elderly photographer anywhere. The roar of the bagpipes was almost overpowering. On a wooden platform, Seumas MacPratt, his legs bulging outwards where he had wound his kilt stockings over once more, played a strange piece of music which seemed to have no beginning and no end. His hands were brown and glistening, and when a finger moved off the chanter of the bagpipes, which seemed to be the part of the instrument supplying the different notes, a sticky tendril was spun between the wood and the flesh.

In the scattering of people around the platform, the old man saw Gerontian-ffylde staring puzzedly at MacPratt's hands. He held up a dark-brown bottle and cackled. "It's my patent hand-warmer," he said. "It's to help yon MacPratt break his record. He's been piper to Strummet for thirteen years now, and for twelve years, since the summer he became the old fool's piper, he's happened to win the pibroch competition. That's a pibroch he's supposed to be playing now. He's won the march competition and the strathspey and reel competition for twelve years, too, and if that isn't a record, nothing is.

"He came up to me this morning, rubbing his hands together and complaining of the bitter cold on a fine summer's morning like this. It'll be his nerves again, I thought to myself, so I took out my bottle and told him, 'Just you rub this into your hands half-an-hour before you play and you'll get hot all right, boy.' "

He cackled again. "He's hot all right. It's a mixture of embrocation and joiner's glue. I've got his hands stuck to the chanter as hard as a . . . aye, well; hard anyway. And if that doesn't break the bugger's record, nothing will. Even a Pibroch Society judge couldn't give him a prize."

Gerontian-ffylde wondered what he was talking about. The old man looked triumphantly up. "I got the recipe from a man in New Zealand. It works a treat out there, too." He stared inquiringly at Gerontian-ffylde. "You're one of the gentry," he said. "If you give me the price of a dram, I'll tell you the piper's nickname. Och, you don't need to buy me a dram. I'll tell you for nothing: it's Poodle."

"Poodle?" repeated Gerontian-ffylde, attempting to make conversation. "Isn't that an odd name for a Highlander?"

"Highlander? He's no Highlander. Born in a Glasgow tenement more like it . . . It's his legs, you see. The way he turns his stockings over to make them look fatter, he ends up looking like a trimmed poodle. The Piping Poodle, that's what we call him . . . o, thank you, sir. I'll drink yer health, sir. What did you say your name was, sir?"

"Gerontian-ffylde, actually."

The old man suddenly demanded, "Did you know the marquis sleeps in his coffin every Friday night? He keeps it under his bed. He claims it will get him used to the next world, but he won't be sleeping in a bed in" (he gave the word an initial capital) "Hell."

His voice lowered in a final confidence, intent on giving value for money. "And do you know why those posts are there, standing solitary and mysterious in the park beside the castle? I'll tell you . . ." up soared his voice in a strange chant ". . . in another way on another day. Remember the Brahan Seer, who held the key to all mysteries." He scuttled off into the crowd around the refreshment tent, with Gerontian-ffylde's fifty-penny piece glinting in the sun like a small, silver icon.

"What did that old devil say to you?" The new voice at his elbow was cultivated, almost from Mayfair, but anxious. "You're Gerontian-ffylde, aren't you? I saw you in the committee tent. I'm General Lomax, chairman of the piping judges."

"He seemed rather worried about the marquis's piper. Something about his hands being cold. I don't know if that's the Highland equivalent of cold feet?"

"Possibly is . . . He didn't mention the prize list or the judges, did he?"

"He did give the impression that MacPratt had won the competition for more years than seemed desirable. He said he was going to help him break his record."

Lomax's upturned face, a white moustache floating in the dished centre, flooded with purple. "Impudent scoundrel," he shouted. "He's always nobbling important strangers about our judging and trying to make us feel small. These common people think they own pibroch music. But they don't own it. The music's ours; it's all ours. If we hadn't preserved it, it would have been lost. Of course it's ours."

Gerontian-ffylde began to feel uneasy. To fill in the awkward silence, he asked, "Are you a piper, too?"

"You needn't play the bagpipes to be a judge," Lomax said frigidly. "And if that's your attitude, I can see that old fool has been putting impertinent thoughts into your head. Good day, sir." He stamped off through the cropped grass to the judges' table, which was placed on one side of the platform where MacPratt was producing a curious, rattling sound from his bagpipes. It ceased and comparative quietness crept over that part of the field.

"Bravo, MacPratt," Lomax called. "We'll have to give you first for that. No need to hear anyone else. No one could surpass that." He glared around at Gerontian-ffylde, who decided to walk hurriedly away before Lomax involved him again.

He passed another platform where little girls, crouched forward like crabs in kilts, sprang into the air in time to another piper. Gerontian-ffylde had almost reached the olive-green Army tent. He stepped inside before anyone noticed.

A gale of laughter swept over him. Col. Strachan, tears running down his cheeks, was punching a sleek, dark-haired lieutenant in the back and shouting, "Rossetti, you're a genius; a whizz kid . . ." He caught sight of Gerontian-ffylde. "Puff, my dear chap, you've just made the big feature . . ." He pulled Gerontian-ffylde closer to the trestle table, where the marquis's whisky was stacked along with an assortment of other bottles and soft drinks. "Come and hear this. It's unbelievable."

In the sudden gloom, Gerontian-ffylde could at first make out only the officers and the depressed and saturnine face of McGurk, the pipe major. Then he discerned a matchbox-sized radio receiver on the table.

"Turn it up, Jamie." Col. Strachan prodded Rossetti in the ribs. "Turn it up for the gentleman."

Gerontian-ffylde realised the marchioness's voice was coming from the tiny receiver.

"*Mmmm, what a powerful man you are. What a perfect chest. I do so like strong men. I always feel faint when I stand close to a strong man, as though I'm being overcome.*"

"*Yes, there is something about us, I suppose.*"

"He's our entertainments officer, you know. I gave him the job because he amuses us so. He holds the battalion together in his way. All the Jocks laugh at him."

"*I can actually feel the strength radiating from you.*"

"*My mother always said I had the power of attracting women.*"

"*O, Lieutenant Smith. Not your mother, too?*"

"Leads from behind, actually. When they aren't laughing at him, they're busy hating him. Good for morale, and all that."

"*My mother is the first woman in my life, apart from my wife.*"

"*Is your wife as attractive as I?*"

"*I love her deeply.*"

"Who did he marry again, Colonel Bob?"

"Some oiky little grocer's daughter from Glasgow. A semi-parvenue."

"*Can I stand a little closer? Am I being amnesic, darling?*"

"You know, only half newly made it. She's more snobbish

than we are. Absolutely stupid into the bargain. So stupid, in fact, even a cavalryman would notice."

Heavy breathing filtered through the loudspeaker. "*Aaah*," said the masculine voice.

"*What a radiant sporran you have.*"

"I'll say," shouted Jamie Rossetti, dancing a little jig of delight. "I'll say it is." Col. Strachan again roared with laughter, his whisky slopping over the rim of his goblet.

"*You don't keep your batteries in it? Let me look.*"

"*Lady Jayne . . .*"

"*Do you like that?*"

Faintly: "*Well, yes. I must admit I do.*"

"*What do you keep inside it, then? Or is it a secret, like what a Highlander wears under his kilt?*"

"I'll say," Rossetti shouted again. He threw his goblet at the tent wall and it bounced harmlessly back. "I'll say—I've bugged the bloody thing."

"*I never did find out. Bodkin's so old it's hardly worth looking.*"

"*In the regiment . . .*" (the masculine voice had become dreamy) "*. . . the men have to parade over a mirror set in the guardroom floor before they can pass out.*"

"*What lovely sights there must be. I think I'd pass out, too. Let's play at passing out. There, stand on my handbag mirror.*"

There was a scuffling sound.

"*O, Lieutenant Smith, I think I'm going to faint. I think it's the biggest I've ever seen.*"

"He wrestles for the regiment, you know."

"*Yes, Lady Jayne.*"

Col. Strachan had his head helplessly bowed on Rossetti's shoulder, and was shaking.

"*Call me Jayne.*"

"*Jayne.*"

"*Me Jayne. You Tarzan.*" There was the sound of a falling body.

"*Aaah, let go, Jayne, for God's sake.*" His cries became softer. "*. . . aaah.*" His voice became so muted the transmitter in his sporran could no longer pick up the vibrations.

"The oaf must have pushed his sporran to one side." Rossetti wrung his hands. "It must be round his behind."

The marchioness's voice suddenly boomed, "*Darling, I*

think I'll take . . ." A stream of static crackled through the receiver, which went dead.

"The stupid brute. He'll ruin it if he rolls over. He'll crush it to bits."

The idea that was idling through Gerontian-ffylde's subconscious mind came to the surface and crystallised. "Is she like that with all the officers?"

"God bless me, Puff, as restrained as ever. She tries to lay the lot of them."

He was intrigued. "Do you think she'd help us recruit a few more victims?"

"Help . . . ? She'd be ravished in the most literal sense. She's running out of material. I even found her stuck around Rossetti like a limpet one night. It took three men to prise him free." Rossetti blushed, the colour rising to his straight black hair. "We've had to peel her off every man in the regiment . . ." The pipe major snorted. "Except for McGurk, that is. Pipies are usually too boozed up to worry about women." Col. Strachan poured the pipe major a solicitous dram.

"I've had rather a whizz of an idea," Gerontian-ffylde said. "At least, I hope it's a good idea. Why shouldn't we ask her to do a Duchess Jean for us?"

"Duchess Jean? Who's she?"

"Who was she, you possibly mean. She was Jean Gordon. She was Duchess of Gordon in the 1790s when she helped to raise the Gordon Highlanders. A right randy old cow she was, too, by all accounts. She was laid by everyone who made anyone in the eighteenth century. Even Robert Burns laid her in one of his off-moments, although he wasn't a choosy sort of bloke. Or she fancied him and insisted on having it off with him by ducaless command, if that's the word for it. It may have given her the idea, for the next thing that happened was that she was helping to raise recruits for the family regiment, and giving a kiss and a shilling to every man who joined the colours. God knows what happened behind the recruiting tent."

"What a fascinating prospect," Col. Strachan said.

"Didn't some titled woman offer recruits a kiss back in the sixties?" Rossetti's bright black eyes inspected Gerontian-ffylde.

"That was strictly on the up-and-up though . . . not at all what I have in mind for Lady Jayne . . . I suppose the Glasgow thugs would fall for a bit of slap and tickle."

"Depends where they were tickled, dear boy."

"Don't be lewd, Rossetti. You're speaking about the lady who has swooned under a brother officer."

"What do you think, Colonel Bob?"

"You won't get the local men."

"We could adopt her as regimental mascot. Think of the publicity we'd get."

"I suppose you know the publicity side best, Puff, with a nickname like that. But none of them will touch her now."

"Who won't?"

"The local men," Col. Strachan said finally. "They've all been through her."

4

Gerontian-ffylde sat in the raised black marble bath at Breacogle and squeezed a lime on to his tongue. He took a pinch of sea-salt from the saucer beside the bath and dabbed it over the lime juice. Then he drank off a glass of tequila. Angela Proof, kneeling behind him in the scented peat-brown water, went on scrubbing his back.

"You mean you actually had a transmitter in his sporran? And he didn't know about it? How utterly scrumptious."

"It was marginally amusing, I suppose. A fraction higher on the left, darling." Gerontian-ffylde was not sure if he wanted to talk about the seduction.

"What happened when, you know . . ." She tweaked him hopefully.

"It fused, I suppose. It all went dead."

"Just like poor Smithy's luck, from what you say of him. He must be an awful slob."

"He is," admitted Gerontian-ffylde. "In a democracy, he'd be taken out and shot. He's as odious and as stupid and as appalling as that. All the same I don't know if it gives us the right to gloat over his private life."

Angela Proof began to laugh. "Why, you're going all moral. What happened next?"

"Aren't you being a little prurient?"

"Should I know that word, lambchops?"

"It means dirty; taking an unhealthy interest in

obscenity." His voice was cold.

"Don't try to tell me you weren't laughing." She realised the conversation had suddenly gone sour. She felt uneasy, as if she had been caught peeping through a lavatory window.

"Isn't it all a little sleazy? All of you salivating over a tawdry piece of copulation. I don't want to become an auditory voyeur, if that's how to put it, no matter how you lot want to take your bizarre pleasures."

"I think you're being rather nasty. To us and to them. You make them sound like a pack of ravening beasts."

"A stupid regimental wrestler coupled with a titled nymphomaniac . . ."

"But it's funny, darling. It really is." Her voice was slightly desperate. To cover her nervousness, she squeezed the bath sponge gently over Gerontian-ffylde's back and began to soap him with the other hand.

"Is it? I'm none too sure of that, or of our motives for finding amusement in it."

"O, darling, now you're making me feel guilty."

"Not you, too, Angela? I thought we left that for the lower middle classes?"

"Don't be beastly, Puff."

"I'm not being beastly: merely making a factual observation."

"You should have been a doctor or a scientist then." Her voice began to curdle.

"What?" Gerontian-ffylde realised he was losing his temper, as his own conscience refused to stand up to scrutiny. "Don't be so bloody disgusting."

"But you're very clever, aren't you?" She became scathing. "You're clever enough to become a doctor."

He flicked the bath sponge out of her hand, and reached for his black towelling bath robe. He got out of the bath. "What's being clever got to do with being a doctor?"

"I thought all doctors were very clever."

"I never knew rugby was a haven for intellectuals."

"Don't be enigmatic." Angela thought what a ridiculous situation she was in. Sitting naked in a bath and talking to a man about morals and intelligence. What on earth had gone wrong?

With stilted and contrived patience Gerontian-ffylde exclaimed, "Doctors play rugby when they've killed off another patient or two. It's a sort of ritual. It's all they're fit for upstairs. They're dumb. Rugby is the summit of their intellectual achievement." He was suddenly infuriated and threw a rubber duck into the lavatory. "Most of them are dumb, darling. They're thick. It's all a big hoax. Like EVERYTHING is a big hoax."

"I suppose research workers aren't brilliant either?"

Gerontian-ffylde lifted the bottle of tequila from the bunk-seat and refilled his glass. He looked around for the limes, and began to pace up and down the warm bathroom, his white hairy legs spiky and ridiculous under the black bath robe. He was already slightly drunk and garrulous. "You don't honestly think backroom boys are brilliant, do you?" He gave an interrogative grunt. "Backroom boys stay in the backroom more often than not because they belong there. They plod, dear girl, plod along well-trodden scientific pathways that would drive any of the ancient scientific philosophers to the hemlock bowl."

"I'm sure," she said, soaping herself with the sponge and staring in pretended astonishment at the vaulted ceiling.

He ignored her. "Most of us, for example, think intuitively and correctly." He squashed another lime on to his tongue and went through the ritual of the salt again. He swallowed another glass of tequila, his face screwed up. "We realise something is true and find the proof afterwards, like knowing which loaf of bread is good, or which person you can trust. People like Archimedes are the essence of it. There he was lying in his bath and he realised he was on to something when his weight, or whatever he was doing, made the water spill over the top . . . But he worked out the formula later, knowing he had already instinctively discovered a scientific truth."

"Like this, darling?" Angela's hand playfully beat on the surface of the water, which lapped and splashed against the rim of the bath.

He paid no attention, his voice slurring, but inexorable. "Nowadays scientists work in reverse. They take a fact and demolish it into unworkable components, then proudly say it can't work when it obviously can't work because it's been ripped to bits. They've become intellectual knockers. It's probably why the Scots are so good at research work."

"I thought you liked the Scots."

"I do. I love them, except they've become a nation of knockers. They hate original thought nowadays because it frightens them." His fingers were sticky with salt. He drank another glassful. The bottle tilted again. "The result is that everyone is afraid to think forward any more in case the knockers, who outnumber them a thousand to one, make the creative thinkers look ridiculous."

"Oh, darling, they did make penicillin or something. And what about inventing TV?"

His eyes were shiny. His words were beginning to adhere to each other. He was incapable of stopping. "Digby claims all the trouble comes from people with a Scottish arse degree." He gave up the ritual of the salt and limes and gulped from the bottle. He shuddered and involuntarily thrust his fingers into the saucer of sea-salt, sodden in the steamy air.

"An arts degree, do you mean?"

"An arse degree," he shouted at her. "An arse degree. An arse degree is what I said and what I mean. All struggling with outmoded and useless concepts packed between their ears like so many cerebral sardines.

"Digby's the perfect example. You know as well as me he was regarded as one of the country's most promising writers as a lad, but he became obsessed with being flippant to show he was amusing and eventually thought his thoughts weren't worth recording. That's why he dried up and went to work for Lord Acarid."

Gerontian-ffylde staggered against the bath and almost fell in. Angela Proof stood up and took his arm. "Digby's much too bright to be a reporter, darling."

"Don't you believe it," snarled Gerontian-ffylde, shaking off her arm. He realised at last what was troubling him. He wondered why the photographer had vanished so suddenly after taking the picture at the Games. Surely he couldn't work for Lord Acarid, too? "It wouldn't surprise me to find Digby down there tomorrow." He slid to the floor and fell asleep.

Angela Proof looked like a typical Ministry of Aggression

secretary, all worry beads and Chelsea, week-end parties on the river, the occasional and boring attempt to enjoy marihuana, and meals in squalid and highly expensive restaurants where the ambience had to be "loving" and the service repulsive. The resemblance, however, was superficial.

Her only concession to a traditional background was that she was from an Army family, with the rare exception that she hated her mother, who had eventually deserted Angela's father and run off with the naval captain who had been best man at their wedding, leaving two emotionally-devastated families behind them. Angela had been ten at the time, and the traumatic experience had left her with a deadly antipathy towards her mother and also to the prospect of entering matrimony with anyone whom she had not investigated for loyalty over several years. Marriage, she believed, was more than a sacrament: it was a life-permanency, and certainly a stable base on which children should be able to build their lives. For this reason alone, she developed fanatical loyalties to people she loved. She had also been in love with Gerontian-ffylde since the days of the travelling sculpture exhibition.

When she learned that he had joined the Ministry of Aggression, she had no hesitation in using her father's influence to be given a secretarial post in the Ministry. She had made sure she was "available" in the secretarial pool when Gerontian-ffylde had been upgraded to the status where he was allowed his own secretary, and had been with him ever since.

When she was very sure of him, she eventually permitted him to sleep with her at her small flat in Knightsbridge on Saturday nights, but she still would not marry him. "I know it sounds crazy and freaky," she told him, "but to me it actually feels more moral, knowing that we don't belong to each other, before we've achieved the harmony I'd like to reach before we do marry." Sundays were spent with Gerontian-ffylde's bizarre collection of friends: a group of artists and film-makers who had formed a colony in Wapping, and lived in a riverside tenement, which had been badly reconstructed from a fish-merchant's stores and office.

She had been paying one of her unpleasant and irregular

visits to her mother to help sober up her second husband (technically Angela's step-father and to whom she still referred as the Boy Friend) when Gerontian-ffylde had been summoned to Scotland. After she read his note, she hurried round to Euston and booked herself on to the late afternoon sleeper to Inverness. Emilio had met her in the gloomy plastic station in the Highlands and had roared south and east in the jeep, scattering tourists on the wayside. They arrived at Breacogle in the morning at eleven. At seven in the evening, Gerontian-ffylde arrived and started drinking from the bottle of tequila which he found in the sideboard. A ticket round its neck read, "With the compliments of the Mexican Tourist Board, Olympics '68." He had shaken it and said, "They distil it from cactus, darling. And they also call it mescal, which I'm sure must be short for mescalin. It makes me hallucinate, anyway."

They woke at midnight and went down to the kitchen for supper. "What was all that curious Wapping-type talk about?" enquired Angela, heating lobster bisque.

"I don't really know," replied Gerontian-ffylde. He was nervous, and his hands shook slightly. "I think I'm worried about that silly recruiting campaign I'm supposed to organise. I'm sure Basil Makebelieve is having some sort of affair with old Strummet, and the only reason we went up there was so that Basil could see his playmate." He accepted the lobster soup and she slid a bottle of tabasco sauce across the plain wooden table towards him. "I'm also sure a photographer has a picture of half the Cabinet walking around like tartan zombies, giving the whole sordid game away . . . It's all supposed to be hush."

*   *   *

In Strummet Castle, the valet, Cinnamon, was ironing the Sunday newspapers flat and creaseless before carrying them through to the Sheraton occasional table in the turret room where the marquis liked to examine them in the hope of finding references to himself or, at best, his family. Cinnamon tittered. "The old pervert won't have far to look today," he said to Griselda, the head sauna girl, who was lying on the dressing-room floor, experimenting on herself with a small pot of silver-frost paint. He examined the front page of the *Sunday Tentacle* again. "It looks as if he's got his hand right up her crutch. I'll bet this drags him away from his timetables."

A blown-up photograph showed Basil Makebelieve leering satyr-like, half at the camera and half at the marquis's back. Inadvertently two fingers of his left hand were extended towards the tartan-swathed clan chief's back, while his right hand had vanished inside the marchioness's low-slung stole. She herself was smiling. The implication was instantly apparent, and obscene. The picture editor, on the instructions of Lord Acarid, had cropped the faces of everyone else from the photograph, on the grounds that little would be served by alerting other newspapers to what looked like a superb political exclusive. The picture carried the simple headline in a mixture of types to accentuate the meaning:

Highland Games (and fun)

The marquis was idly flicking through a timetable listing the days on which trains ran through Sennar, Jebel Qren, Khashm el Girba, Wad el Huri, Gedaref and Kassala, in the Sudan. He put down the screwdriver with which he had been turning the pages, and gave a little squeal of pleasure when he saw the photograph. Then he realised the impression it gave. He shouted at the marchioness, who was gazing from the turret window, "You bloody slut. I suppose you've been fainting again."

The marchioness looked round, wondering where he had obtained his information. She crossed the room and looked at the photograph. "How positively ducky," she said. "I look absolutely gorgeous in tartan." She ignored his outburst.

He hit her across the jaw. "You bloody bitch—look at me when you speak. I know you and your lustful habits. Whenever you see a naked man you force yourself to pass out from shame, don't you? So you need never reproach yourself for starting a fresh affair." His eyes were tormented with rage. "You always claim you were laid when you were out cold, and didn't know what you were doing."

Her mouth began to quiver as she realised that he had seen directly into her mind.

"Then it's too late to stop," he jeered.

"How dare you." She fought to regain control.

"You've been screwing that little guttersnipe, haven't you?"

"What if I have?" She purposely tried to put him on to the wrong scent, out of perverseness.

The marquis picked up the screwdriver. "I don't mind you screwing people of your own class." His voice was repellent. "I don't mind at all." The point of the screwdriver was directed towards her throat. He had begun to glare. "But keep your hands off guttersnipes, and keep your hands off my property . . . you understand?" He took a swift pace forwards. The blunt blade was jammed into her milky skin. "Or I'll butcher you, and I'll divorce the remains. I'll fix both of you."

She pushed the point of the screwdriver disdainfully away from her. "Don't be theatrical, Bodkin," she said.

Her disinterest made him scream with rage and he almost stabbed her. "You whore: you worthless throb." he tried feverishly to think of an insult, chilling in its horror. He shouted, conscious of its awful defects, "Anyway, I screwed you before we were married."

"Darling," she faintly replied from the door, before she slammed it in his face. "So did your regiment."

*　　*　　*

Angela was still asleep when Gerontian-ffylde awoke. He scribbled a single-word goodbye note and left it on her pillow, then he showered and ate. Forty minutes later he was driving north-west across the Highlands, avoiding the skeins of Sunday tourist traffic, and through the granite passes, gouged between the shattered vertebrae of the mountains. He drove fast and forcefully, pushing the Maserati until the engine moaned on the hairpin bends and vicious gradients. At five to three he was crunching up the gravel driveway of Strummet Castle and drew up at the bleached oaken doors.

It was Cinnamon, in a short white surgical coat, who

answered his knock. "Ah, Mr Gerontian-ffylde," he said. "His lordship asked if you would join him in the sunken garden. He especially enquired if you would, uh, bring your own equipment." Cinnamon's face was impassive. "To save you the trouble of going back to your room, sir, I took the liberty . . ." He revealed a birch switch in his right hand. "For you, sir."

A blare of brass-band music flooded the sunken garden, secluded in the central courtyard of the ancient castle. The music, from a loud-hailer rigged up in a turret slit, changed to "Colonel Bogey", and Gerontian-ffylde wonderingly took in the row of straw-roofed pinewood cubicles, fronted with red and white curtains, which stretched down the east wall. Beside the lily-pond, amidst a white, starry canopy of Tibetan rhododendrons, was a long log hut, with a shingle roof and small, green-glass windows. At one end, a curious half-storey box had been built on to the roof, giving the building the appearance of a large boot. Again the music changed, this time to "O But Ye've Been Long a' Coming" and above the crescendo of tympani and hoarse roaring of the brass, Gerontian-ffylde could hear the delighted shrieks of people inside.

A billow of steam escaped from the log cabin as the door opened, revealing the marquis in a white bathing slip, his birch broom loosely hanging by his side. "So glad you could come, dear boy," he called. "Do hurry up. Don't keep the party waiting." He behaved at last as if Gerontian-ffylde was socially acceptable. At the meeting on the previous Friday, he had ignored him. "It turns out I knew your second cousin, Bertie. I must tell you about him and me in Tobruk . . ." Unbelievably Basil Makebelieve rushed half-naked from the steam and hurtled into the lily-pond. He clawed his way out like a dog and ran back past Gerontian-ffylde and disappeared into the shrilling interior of the cabin. "Undress over there." The marquis waved at the cubicle. "Pick any of the empty ones. You'll find a bathing slip inside. We have to wear them for the sake of propriety, you know." He went back into the cabin. The shrieking attained a new pitch of pleasure.

With increasing disbelief and embarrassment Gerontian-ffylde stripped off his clothes and picked up the bathing slip, which seemed to be a puzzle of whipcord and smooth white opaque nylon. After a few minutes he worked out how to achieve a semblance of modesty and tied it on. But how on earth was he to carry his small clipboard? Should he hold it in his hand, or tuck it in the waistband of the skimpy *cache-sex?* He tried the board under his arm, but it looked so odd that he decided to leave it in the cubicle. Beneath the plain wooden bench he discovered a pair of rope-soled sandals. He pulled them on and, switch in hand, began walking across the paved courtyard to the log cabin. He was blushing. He felt exactly as he did when he went to take his first shower at school.

He stepped into the dimness. Screaming white and black particles of flesh spun past him, now dark, now shining redly molten. Demented gouts of steam tossed and worried through the dense air. A face met his. A hand was on his nipples. His vision shattered and blacked out. Other hands tormented him, acutely pleasuring yet vilifying him. He was falling backwards. A glitter of sound assaulted his head. He writhed on the screaming heat of arid pine boards.

Needles of white-hot power irradiated his skin and ran wetly over him as the ice-cold water broke in a turmoil. A shrill ecstatic laugh pierced him. Tongues licked him. Twigs swishing flashed across his skin, over his unprotected buttocks. The glow started somewhere in his abdomen, he thought, and spread downwards to his groin and thighs. The darkness was easing as his pupils expanded and adjusted. His body was alight now, blazing with power, his finger-tips tingling with pleasure. His hand touched black and white flesh, his fingers slipping inadvertently under dark warm fabric into moist pleasure. White pain blinded him and twigs again shrieked into his buttocks. *"Ei, ei, ei."* He discovered his hands which had gone involuntarily to protect his buttocks had fallen away. He was alone again in the tumult of music and cascading steam and water.

He found that he was lying on the lowest tier of a three-layer set of bare pine boards. In the rosy light of enormous canisters of red-hot stones, ash-blonde girls in black bikini bottoms were alternately hurling water on to the stones and emerging from the giant-whistling steam to lash out with their birch brooms, apparently wildly, at the guests. He made out Professor Knapbone, his scrawny body writhing in a tormented arabesque, shouting something like "Group activity", as twigs cut into his buttocks. Lorimer, the Minister for Internal Security, Scotland, his glasses fogged over with steam, was leaping blindly in the air and attempting to close on an almost-naked girl, slippery with sweat.

Above him, Gerontian-ffylde heard a body rolling and groaning. It gradually came to him that it was Tony Pleasance. He coughed and loudly said, "Excuse me."

"Is that you, Gerontian-ffylde?"

"Yes, sir."

"How in God's name are we going to explain this away?"

"I don't think we need to, sir. No one could take a photograph in here. The steam would refract the light; the lens would mist over too. Our real safety is that everyone's compromised."

"Hopelessly."

Cinnamon smiled as the remark came over the multi-phase control panel on the mezzanine floor of the bath-house. He depressed switch seven and flipped up switch eight and listened in to the conversation between Professor Knapbone and the *au pair* girl. The sociologist seemed quite oblivious to the fact that she could not speak English. "The formal requirements of the organisation . . .", he was saying.

"*Yksi.*"

"aah . . . may be deflected by interests and status-anxieties outwith the group . . ."

"*Kaksi.*"

"aah . . . and also by ego-oriented needs and task structures . . ."

"*Kolme.*"

"aaah . . . the latent differences between background status and ethnicity . . ."

"*Helja.*"

"aaah . . . must be surrendered otherwise the organisation may become . . ."

"*Viisi.*"

"aaah . . . unrealistic in a variety of ways, say, in the formation of behaviour codes . . ."

61

"*Kuusi.*"

"aaah . . . Individuals bring with them to institutions such as the army their own commitments, statuses, outside . . ."

"*Seitseman.*"

"aaah . . . interests and a strong and resilient tendency to protect their private . . ."

"*KAHDEKSAN.*"

"O, my god . . . concerns against encroachment of the institution . . ."

"*Yhdeksan.*"

"aaah . . ."

Cinnamon shook his head, wondering if it was the sexual ambience of sauna bathing that had made Knapbone so incoherent. He closed the key. The marquis was almost in position and had manoeuvred Makebelieve into the corner beneath the infra-red camera and was exchanging swift cuts with him. Both men were naked and had a look of indescribable pleasure on their faces. Suddenly the marquis stepped forward so that Makebelieve appeared to touch him. The valet raised the powerful compressed hot-air jet and blew down over the camera body and lens and on to the bodies beneath him, dispelling the steam for a radius of twenty inches. He exposed at least eight frames before Basil Makebelieve moved out of focus. The steam swept instantly back.

Gerontian-ffylde raised himself on one elbow. "Could I make my report and suggestions to you, sir?"

"In a sauna bath? O, well, I suppose so. They say that important news always flashes fastest through ministerial lavatories. Or was that flushes? I can't quite seem to collect my wits in this heat."

Gerontian-ffylde slowly told him about the Duchess of Gordon and how she had recruited men for the Gordon Highlanders. "Provided the marchioness plays her part," he added, "I can see no reason why we can't combine tradition with something so basic they will all be interested in joining the Strummet Foot." His hidden smile was acidic. "What you might call bending over backwards for the cause."

"What a brilliant idea," said Pleasance. He rolled over.

"Basil," he shouted, above the screaming. "Basil, I think we've got the answer to it all. Bring Bodkin across, will you?"

More steam pierced and shocked the air, and Basil Makebelieve emerged from the gloom, his switch in one hand. The marquis was firmly gripping his other wrist. No sooner had Gerontian-ffylde been made to repeat his recruiting plan than the marquis unaccountably vanished into the wraith of steam at the far end of the cabin.

An arm curled over Gerontian-ffylde as he lay back on the pine board, and the marchioness was beside him, her dark mound showing clearly through the drenched nylon monokini, and almost level with his eyes. "I hear you've the duckiest scheme for me, darling." She bent forward, her wet breasts slithering over him. "Let me make you the first recruit." She kissed him, her body hot and mucoid and, he remembered later, scented with lemon and aniseed. At first he struggled, then, to his absolute and manifold horror, he felt himself engorging. He heard Pleasance demanding, "What the hell has happened?"

"Worried, dear boy?" It was Makebelieve's voice. A hand traced a path through the sheen of sweat on his chest. He heard the Minister of Redeployment continue, "I dare say you are. We didn't know it would have this effect."

"What in God's name are you talking about? What have you done to us?"

"It was Bodkin's idea, actually. He dropped a few grains of cantharides into the steam jet. It must have sublimated and percolated everywhere."

"Cantharides, you bloody fool? It's supposed to be poisonous."

"I suppose Spanish fly is deadly in its way." Makebelieve giggled. "It's certainly a beautiful way to die, though, darling, isn't it?" The shrieking rose again.

Only the faintest tremor of shame remained three hours later when Gerontian-ffylde dressed in the red and white fronted cubicle. Elevated, yet strangely enervated, he let himself out of a wicket gate in the castle wall and found himself in the field where the games had been held. Had it been only the day before? One of the mysterious poles confronted him, but he felt so emotionally drained that he had no interest in discovering its purpose. Without ostentation, he walked around the castle wall and through an archway and found his Maserati. He decided to call in at one of the hotels for a quick drink before driving to Glasgow. He avoided the Strummet Arms and went into the Strummet Cave.

A voice said, "I thought you'd have been here hours ago, dear boy. Give this gentleman a drink, landlord; a large vodka, I think . . . You do look careworn." Two glasses, one with a trace of lipstick, were in front of Digby, the reporter, and a cigarette, with a faint crimson smudge, was still burning in the ashtray.

"Oh, Christ. I had a premonition you would be here. You aren't on holiday by any chance?" Gerontian-ffylde's voice was distant. No matter how friendly he was with Digby, he knew he had to stay aloof. He could possibly explain away the recruiting campaign, but if the sauna bath episode leaked out, it could topple the Government. He remembered how the Macmillan government had creaked after an innocent bathing party.

"Don't tell me *you* are?" Digby had immediately assimilated the coolness and his voice was reciprocally cool.

"What else? I'm motoring south . . . I couldn't give you a lift anywhere?"

"You aren't trying to get me out of here by any chance?"

"Why on earth should I do that?"

"I wonder."

"You aren't being very friendly."

"Come to that, neither are you."

Gerontian-ffylde hesitated, knowing the question had to be asked. He enquired, "What are you doing here?" He indicated the other glass. "Who's your girl friend?"

"The lord sent me on a pilgrimage back to Scotland. A reverent journey into the past. I thought I couldn't do better than step back a couple of centuries and see Strummet country again." He pushed away the ashtray. "I don't know who that was. One of the local girls, probably."

"Are you writing anything?" Both men were fencing and knew it.

"He thought I should do a couple of pieces on the breakdown of feudalism in Scotland. The owner here claims it's worse than ever. He says he can't sell horse-dung or ice-cream because of his feu charter. That's his sort of ground lease."

"Trying for an interview with the marquis?"

"He's not supposed to sell drink either. The feu superior—that's old Strummet himself—has told him not to, although the magistrates have given him a licence. He says he might go to jail for contempt of court. It's an old Scottish custom."

"I could possibly fix up an interview for next week sometime."

"O, come off it, Puff." Digby tired of the interchange. "With that old ratbag? What possible interest could his views have to the Press? He's almost as incoherent as the rest of the Scottish aristocracy."

"Where else are you moving to?"

Digby ordered two more drinks. He said, "If I didn't know we were friends, I'd detect a certain shame in your behaviour. A shame at trying to obscure certain facts and trying to entice me away from them."

"Nothing was further from my mind."

"Stop moving about on that stool. You look positively shifty."

"My leg has cramp, that's all."

"You haven't got a boil by any chance?"

Gerontian-ffylde flushed. Digby couldn't possibly know. "Certainly not."

"How're the weals, Puff?" Digby reflected that the essence of journalistic enquiry was the question completely out of sequence.

Gerontian-ffylde had turned bright red. "Who in God's name told you about that? Keep your voice down, will you?"

"If I didn't know you, I'd say you'd gone bent, too."

"I'll do a deal with you," said Gerontian-ffylde. He was desperate. "I'll give you an exclusive about the Cabinet visit."

"Bribery, Puff, ill becomes a gentleman."

"You horrid little inky beast. Two hundred years ago, I'd have run a sword through you."

"Two hundred years ago, I wouldn't have spoken to you, far less allowed you to contemplate duelling with your betters."

"Are you daring to speak to me?"

Digby allowed only the faintest affection to colour the neutrality of his voice. "I thought the situation was reversed."

To mask his feelings, Gerontian-ffylde ordered two more vodkas. "I'm sorry," he said. "I keep forgetting." When the landlord went away, he said, "You wouldn't like to come to Glasgow with me?" His voice was slightly pleading. "Keep me company while I go round the bloody place. How about it, for old times' sake?"

"I don't mind," said Digby. He knew that nothing was scheduled to happen at Dunstrummet for ten days, when the marchioness was due to drive to Glasgow for the opening of the recruiting campaign. Digby went to pay his bill.

He came back into the bar to collect Gerontian-ffylde and found him staring at an insubstantial man, who was completely grey. Even his shoes were grey.

"I'm sorry, I don't understand you," Gerontian-ffylde was saying.

"Hello, professor," said Digby. He added, "This is Professor Pry who is doing important research on the Celtic influence on Norse bone fish-hooks in the Castle library."

The professor said, "How delightful to meet you; I am sad that you are leaving."

Gerontian-ffylde stared at him, still baffled.

The professor said, "When the fish are still there's no froth on the hook; white froth shows the fish are moving."

Digby refused to say anything.

The professor tried again. "The marquis is in fine spirits; fine as these spirits are, they are no finer than yesterday."

Gerontian-ffylde said, "I'm terribly sorry. I must be going now,"

The professor said, "Wise men treat parting as a reward; fools treat parting as a sorrow; we must treat parting as goodbye."

Digby politely repeated goodbye and followed Gerontian-ffylde through the door. He was smirking.

"What on earth was all that about? What are you laughing about?"

"I thought he'd fool you. He's a Scots academic."

"But what on earth was he saying?"

"It's the way they communicate that's throwing you. They use these academic sentences: two antitheses separated by a semi-colon. They can go on for days like that."

"But what happens if someone wants to understand them?"

"There isn't much fear of that. They all opted out of the community years ago. They don't care if they're understood or not."

Gerontian-ffylde decided to try Digby's technique. As they got into the Maserati, he suddenly asked, "Who's your source?"

"He . . ." Digby almost added something. He said idly, "What you might call a whipping boy."

Gerontian-ffylde's voice rose over the thunder of the engine as he revved it. "Don't tell me that Basil Makebelieve has leaked already?"

"It wasn't Basil's turn. Nor Tony Pleasance's. Nor that phoney professor what's his name."

"Knapbone."

"And nobody would bother asking that creepy little Scottish minister anything."

"Who else could it have been?"

"What, and let you lot persecute him for doing a public service? We may be friends, but that doesn't entitle you to ask me to break a confidence."

"I'm sorry. I shouldn't have asked that. You've rather floored me." He changed down and cornered under a railway bridge. "Are you going to do the recruiting story tonight?"

"It depends what you offer in exchange. If it's going to embarrass you personally, I'll bend it a little. I suppose you and your masters are worried about the suicide angle?"

"Christ on a crutch. How did you get hold of that?"

"If it wasn't that I had a vested interest in getting Glasgow cleaned up, I'd make sure it was our splash tonight, D-notice or no D-notice."

"But you won't, will you?"

"No, I don't suppose I will. Not if you're going to clean up that blot on civilisation."

A hotel noticeboard, garish and large, reared from the banks of green heather. "No bus parties. Visitors welcome." Gerontian-ffylde asked: "Another drink?"

"I don't think their manners appeal to me. They're probably escaped Glaswegians, gone snobbish. It often happens to people who get out."

"You're joking."

Digby adopted a whining, suburban Glasgow accent. "It used to be the second city in the Empire. It's very proper in the Victorian fashion. More little fingers straightened over teacups there than any other city in the Commonwealth. And if you swear in front of a lady, we'll rip your face open with a razor to teach you some manners."

"They should be glad to get out of it."

Digby resumed his normal accentless voice. "Recruiting won't present any problem, if that's what you mean. These two battalions you've to recruit." Gerontian-ffylde stared at him. "What a perfect way to continue the phoney war. Fix up a Protestant battalion and a Catholic one, and they'll flock to join."

"Doesn't religion forbid violence?"

"What's religion got to do with it?"

"But you said Protestant and R.C."

"You don't think they go to church, do you? Don't be so naive, Puff—and play down the danger angle."

"Danger? Why should toughs be afraid of danger?"

"Most of them are psychopaths."

"But I thought a psychopath could commit any crime and not feel remorse. Surely they would have to be pretty brutal to do that?"

"Didn't you know? The latest scientific find is that psychopaths are all physical cowards. It's probably the key to the entire outbreak of violence in Glasgow."

"What, fear? Don't be ridiculous."

"Yes, of course, fear," mimicked Digby. "Violence is probably the most contagious form of fear there is and violence is endemic in Glasgow. Most of these hooligans only began to carry weapons because they were afraid of being done, as they put it. They imagine all the other neds are lying in wait for them, so they are automatically violent in return, or even beforehand. It's a sort of group paranoia, as though they all suffered from feelings of persecution."

"Are you trying to say that violence is inspired by fear?" Gerontian-ffylde had never previously heard the concept put forward. "What a bizarre idea."

Digby was expansive, even airy. "Indeed, bizarre, but that's how it basically started in Glasgow. The trouble is they find how simple and satisfying violence is, once they get over the first repugnant hurdle of actually sticking a knife into somebody. They like it after that. I've actually spoken to neds, scarcely more than kids, in fact; just out of court and joyfully talking about putting the chiv in up under the rib cage and feeling for the heart with the point so they could penetrate it. You'd have thought they were talking about their first women."

"Out of court?" Gerontian-ffylde was incredulous. "You mean after release, don't you?"

"Released, my bottom." Digby was purposely coarse. "They also discovered in Glasgow how easy it was to break down the forces of law and order. It does depend on everyone playing his part in society, you know. When one faction refuses to accept this concept, everything topples. So the thugs broke it down especially when they realised that in the unlikely event of being caught, they met up with the do-gooders who gave them easier and lighter sentences or none at all. That's what really encouraged them to try mob rule. That's what really made them split their sides laughing."

"If you really believe in this fantastic theory why don't you stay and do something about it?"

"Who, me?" Digby laughed. "Why me? I got out of this bloody country for several reasons. It's got nothing to do with me any more. I'll tell you something, though. Even the London criminals claim the Glasgow thugs are brutal. They claim they civilise them, you know, after they've been south for a year or so. The London hoods say they move them one step up the criminal ladder by stopping them from using violence all the time, and making them use it instead for a purpose. It could well be of use to you."

"Don't speak in riddles." Gerontian-ffylde took the narrow tarmac track past Ballachulish Bridge.

"In Glasgow, they attack you from behind to rob you, then they give you a kicking in the face and guts for their own satisfaction after they've taken your money. I've even heard of one of them putting hydrochloric acid into a girlfriend's eye drops when he broke into a house and found the bottle. Violence feels good to them, I suppose. The London mobs train them to use violence to take over other people's property, then get to hell out of it before they're caught. They despise the Glasgow hoodlums for being unsophisticated."

"How on earth could this help me?"

"It's this move up the ladder. Criminals are all snobs at heart. They all want to be accepted, wear smart clothes, have good table manners. If you ever have lunch with a hood, he'll watch you like a hawk, in case he's picking up the wrong knife . . . Just you tell them they're moving up in the world by having a go at Lady Jayne. Tell them they're joining a League of Gentlemen: they'll lap it up. They all went to the cinema to see the picture, and I'm not kidding."

"I wish you wouldn't use expressions like have a go at."

"It's true, isn't it? If she fancies them, she'll see them all right." Digby laughed, a shade cruelly, at Gerontian-ffylde's embarrassment. "And if you still have trouble getting recruits, I'll bring them flocking in."

"Yes?" Gerontian-ffylde displayed only the faintest interest.

Digby was still smiling. "I'll go round some of my old criminal contacts. I'll tell the Protestant thugs she's a Catholic, and they'll be there like a rat up a rhone-pipe, as they charmingly put it . . . and I'll tell the Catholics she's turned Protestant and they'll be after her even harder—to revenge themselves on her. You'll be flooded out."

5

"Lady Jayne will be at the lunch," said Gerontian-ffylde.

"How did Digby get an exclusive on the recruiting drive? He's a friend of yours, isn't he." The newsdesk man made a statement of the question.

"He must have flown up from London after a tip-off there. It had nothing to do with me."

"It's a Scottish story. It should have been ours for a change. Why didn't you tell the *Daily Flute* first? Why should the *Tentacle* get all the exclusives?"

"I have to be fair to all the papers. You know I can't go giving exclusives to one paper and not the others."

"The bloody *Tentacle*'s always getting away with murder."

"The marchioness would be delighted to see you." To close the matter Gerontian-ffylde said, "Why don't you bring your lady wife?" He felt slightly degraded.

The newsdesk man gushed, "My wife . . . I'd love to . . . I'll check to see if she's anything . . . I think she might squeeze in lunch with the marchioness."

A battery of phones started ringing. "There *is* one thing." The accent was fake, precious. "What do you call a marchioness? I mean, how do you addr . . ." The newsdesk man picked up a receiver from the tangle of telephonic equipment and began talking rapidly into it. "I've got this man lying on a chimney stack near the docks. I want to exploit the human angle in this and make it tug at the heart strings of our readers."—he waved a peremptory goodbye— "He's trapped you see. The ladder has collapsed. That may mean nothing to the average reader: just another person trapped on a disused factory chimney in a slum area. So I want to make them care. I want to make every woman care. I want you to bring his wife down from her house and get her to the base of the chimney. What no one knows is that the chimney is due to collapse." His voice hoarsened. "We've got twenty minutes to get her there. Just as it comes down, I want pictures of the wife staring up, terrified, and the tears runni . . . Don't you dare speak to me like that . . . how dare you threaten to put the phone down on me . . . I'll suspend you." His voice had risen to a shout. "I'll fire you . . . hello . . ." He looked round wildly and saw that the new editor, attracted by the shouting, had come out of his room and was standing beside Gerontian-ffylde. Both men were staring at him, their faces incredulous.

The editor said, "I think you'd better come into my office, Lawson." He turned to Gerontian-ffylde. "It was so nice to see you so soon after arriving here. I'd love to come to the lunch." He looked despairingly at Gerontian-ffylde behind the newsdesk man's back and added, "I've still got a lot to clear up, of course." He took Lawson into his room. He, too, began to shout.

Gerontian-ffylde had acceptances from every newspaper in the country for the lunch invitation, mainly because of the article which Digby had phoned over to the *Tentacle* office in Fleet Street. The Cabinet had been infuriated by the article which had been made the splash under Digby's by-line and datelined, "Strummet Castle". In retaliation, or so they thought, they had refused permission to all Press officers even to confirm or deny the contents to any other newspaper. It read:

A new atomic strike force for the British Army is to be recruited in Scotland where two extra battalions, each of 300 men, are to be added to the centuries-old Strummet Foot.

A top-secret Cabinet meeting decided this tonight at

the Castle here, home of the Marquis of Strummet, who is honorary colonel-in-chief of the regiment.

The new streamlined force is to be equipped with the latest nuclear weapons, still on the secret list, but capable of containing any opposing army in the world today.

The new force will be called the Atomic (S) Brigade. The (S) is said to stand for "Scottish".

Members of the Cabinet made a hush-hush flight north in the Minister of Aggression's personal heliplane, which touched down in the Castle grounds at 3.46 p.m. on Friday.

After two days of meetings and discussions, it was decided to increase the Strummet Foot to brigade strength. Normally three battalions from different regiments make up a British Army brigade.

The Strummet Foot, raised in 1688, has lost its tag of private regiment to the Marquis and is now part of the Regular Army. Although it was financed by the Treasury, the Marquis had disciplinary powers over the regiment and, in theory, retained the right to order promotions.

The only other "private" regiment in Britain is the Atholl Highlanders, owned by the Duke of Atholl, but it is not part of the Army and never has been.

Digby's only reference to the sauna party came near the end. "The 58-year-old marquis, who is keen to promote tourism in his clan territory, hopes to whip up interest in certain projects which he has started to attract wealthy visitors, both from the south and abroad."

"You never could resist a nasty crack," Gerontian-ffylde said as they breakfasted in a small hotel on a moor near Stirling. They had stayed the night there after driving south from Perth Prison where Digby had interviewed a safe-blower, trying to ascertain how Scottish criminals would react to being asked to join the Army in return for their freedom.

"As for your 'S' for 'Scotland' gibe, I almost threw up."

"I've often thought of producing a booklet for readers called, 'Newspaper codes and how to crack them.' Our best work might not go to waste then."

They finished off breakfast and went for a sharp walk along the moor road. They came to a monument. "I suppose more of your revolting ancestors fought here, Digby?"

"Commanded the cavalry again, as far as I know. But it wasn't much of a battle. The only casualty of note was an elderly piper who got stripped and thrown into a bed of nettles one November morning."

"Rather stinging rebuke, wasn't it?" said Gerontian-ffylde, staring blandly at the monument. It was railed in with sharp spikes in case anyone tried to get close enough to read the fading inscription.

"Poor old man." Digby avoided the invitation to begin punning. "He wrote a pibroch to sum up his feelings and called it, 'Too long in this condition.' "

"Come out of the past, Digby. You're being Celtic and morbid again."

Digby quoted. " 'The fate of the Gael is to lose all.' I don't know who said it, but it's so symptomatic. Most of the traditional Highland tunes are laments. I often wonder if the Scots aren't all depressed by inheritance." He shivered suddenly. "Let's get back to the hotel."

They paid their bills at the secluded hotel and drove to the lunch party, which was held in a restaurant in Stirling, almost equidistant from Glasgow and Edinburgh.

On the seating plan, Col. Strachan and Lady Jayne were at the head of the table, with the editor of the *Tentacle* on her right. An assortment of newspaper executives, with the brilliant red tunics of the Strummet Foot officers scattered among them, encircled the guests of honour. At the far end sat a woman with acne. "Ai thought Ai was to sit next to the Marchioness of Strummet," she complained, as she slit her roll and made it into a buttery sandwich. "That's what mai husband told the neighbours last night. Ai just hope there are no photographers hereabouts." Lieut. Smith, the entertainments officer, who was on her left, consoled her. "I married a Glasgow girl. I'm certain Glasgow girls are better than anything else . . ." He halted, but she had not noticed his solecism.

"You're very nice," the woman said. "Ai like you . . . there's no need to shrink away. Ai think Ai'll tell you something. If you want a hint on how to succeed in Glasgow, have a spectacle. We always have one with the Hutchesontown Tories. We always have a motorcade and they're a great success, Ai can tell you, and very popular, too."

Lieut. Smith noted down her remark. After lunch he told Col. Strachan, who, replete with port, inadvertently agreed and mentioned it to the marchioness. She threw her arms around his neck and kissed him. "Gorgeous," she breathed. She attempted to put her tongue into his ear, but he pulled away.

The suggestion did not percolate to Gerontian-ffylde, nor Digby, who had been ordered by Lord Acarid to accompany the recruiting entourage on its passage through the West of Scotland, to collect feature material for a series of articles provisionally entitled, "Escape from the Slums to Glory".

The next morning, they ate instant-dip kippers in a Lanarkshire hotel, the dark stain running out of the soggy flesh and rivuletting brownly on to their chill plates, while they waited for the marchioness to descend from her room. Tents had been erected in a local park, where the foliage was dying in the sulphurous fumes from surrounding steel works. Lieut. Smith was somewhere in the outback of the county, arranging transport for volunteers.

A pile of morning newspapers lay on the floor beside Digby, where he was dropping them after reading the differing accounts of the lunch. He threw down the *Daily Flute*. Gerontian-ffylde saw it fall. "Don't some journalists stink," he said. He was thinking of the newsdesk man again.

Digby took instant offence. "That's a disgustingly rude thing to say."

"I'm sorry. I don't mean you. You're different, Digby. You're not like other journalists."

"How do you know that?" Digby's eyes had half-closed and had become malevolent. "Have you ever really known another journalist?"

"No, I haven't. But we all know what national daily journalists are like, corrupt and hard-bitten, rather nasty personal habits and untruthful. Like that newsdesk man."

Digby laughed at him. "He isn't typical and you know it.

You're only revealing your lack of acuity. It's an index of how addicted you are to cheap TV shows which seem to be put out only to discredit the National Press."

"You really can be the most malicious person I know." Gerontian-ffylde coloured slightly. "There's no need to look at me like that. Other people say it, too. Some people claim you're the biggest swine they know."

Digby appeared to be unconcerned. "That's their misfortune."

"Don't be so pompous."

"It's strange that I get on well with intelligent people. I've never heard of one of them calling me a swine. Only the cruds do."

"There you go again, being your normal appalling self, quite incapable of seeing, far less admitting, that you're wrong."

"Why should I apologise for getting on well with geniuses? Because the converse is so hard to palate?"

"Are you trying to say the people you're rude to aren't very clever?"

"All I'm saying is that I'm only rude to people who are rude to me first. If you examine the situation, you find that I rarely initiate a hostile series of remarks, or actually begin an angry discussion. I didn't begin this—you did."

"But you seem to hand so much out to people."

"I don't. I resent that. I only hand things back in self-defence in equal measure. I'm only a bastard to bastards. If you think I'm one, you merely identify yourself as a considerable bastard."

He demanded suddenly, "Have you been given a kiss yet?"

"That's exactly what I mean," snapped Gerontian-ffylde. The corner of his mouth lifted slightly in distaste. "You really are a bastard, Digby, sliding in smart questions under cover of another conversation. You can never let up. You always must get in that extra loaded question."

"Supposing I said that I asked out of friendly curiosity?"

"I wouldn't believe . . ." Gerontian-ffylde looked closely at Digby, trying to penetrate the expressionless face. ". . . I don't know."

"You've known me for years, ever since you dumped

your obscene sculpture exhibition in that Welsh quarry. Have I ever done anything discreditable that you know of? Professionally, I mean? Did I write up that disgusting exhibition in the sauna bath? A lot of people would rightly claim that I shirked my moral duty; that I should have recorded it and informed the country of the habits and calibre of its leaders."

"No, I must say you haven't. But you look as if you would, all implacable and stone-faced. I just have the impression that journalists can't be trusted even after working with them for years and knowing they really can. Possibly it's become customary . . . it could even be because I've got things to hide."

"Don't you think it really is an index of how addicted you are to cheap TV shows? Aren't you being rather impertinent in the final analysis?"

Gerontian-ffylde looked away to begin with, then forced his eyes back to Digby. "I don't know what it is about you, Digby, but you have the most dreadful power to make me feel ashamed of myself. It's probably the basis of my ambivalence towards you. Most of the time I like you. For the rest of the time, I could cut your guts out because you know so much about me and have this ability to make me see things which I don't really want to see at all, especially about myself."

Digby laughed. "If you must know, it was only because no one could see that I asked the question in the first place."

"See? Who couldn't see what?"

"Couldn't see if you were kissed or not. The steam was too dense."

"Look here, Digby. Who told you about that? If you must know, seeing you would probably crawl back and examine the boards with a magnifying glass, I did get a kiss, but that's all. You know me better than that, damn you. She's too old for me. She's very amusing and great fun, but she's not my age or type. I just don't fancy her."

Three weeks later, Gerontian-ffylde stood in the shadow of a huddle of recruiting tents, erected on the grass beside a large, dingy church in Paisley. He looked worriedly at Col. Strachan.

"Do you think we should call a doctor?"

"I know I'm only here for the day, but personally I don't see anything the matter with her." Col. Strachan and Professor Knapbone had arrived for an inspection of what the sociologist called the national recruit-impetus.

"These fainting fits look pretty ominous to me."

"I suppose they do. How many has she had now?"

"She seems to be fainting in relays; more when we're busier, naturally. Since we started she's flaked out about 150 times."

"What an odd coincidence," said Col. Strachan. He examined a list secured to a clip-board.

"What's that?"

"We've raised exactly 148 recruits." Col. Strachan looked over his shoulder as the entertainments officer crunched across the grass behind him, rendering the acid-mottled blades into pulp. "Don't slink up like that, Smith. What do you want? You look as if you've been gobbling the mess port and forgetting to put your name into the book again. You're going purple in the face."

"Nothing, sir." Smith, possibly the only man there capable of giving a rational explanation, felt frustrated and jealous. One hundred and forty-eight now . . . He walked away, his brogues still mutilating the Christ-exhausted grass. He could tell them the real figure, he thought. And why. But he wouldn't.

Col. Strachan stared suspiciously after him. "Perhaps her tent needs better ventilation. God knows why she insists on keeping the flap down. It looks like a fortune teller's booth in a fun fair. Who's in there now?"

"Man by the name of Doolan." There was a thud within the tent and, eventually, Anthony Doolan, his face as stiff and shiny as a red-hot poker, appeared at the tent door. "Lady Jayne has fainted, sir," he reported.

"That makes it 149," Col. Strachan observed erroneously. The thought suddenly struck him. "Good heavens, you don't think . . .?"

"I think we should change the subject, colonel," said Gerontian-ffylde swiftly. "And I don't think you should mention this to Knapbone . . . we're having the week-end off." He was spiteful. "It should save her from going into a permanent coma."

"You can't have this week-end off, old boy. We're having the motorcade tomorrow."

"Motorcade? What motorcade?"

Digby walked around the corner of the tent with Professor Knapbone. "Coming to the motorcade tomorrow, Mr Digby?" called Col. Strachan.

Digby was incredulous. "You aren't having a motorcade in Glasgow tomorrow?"

"Why ever not? Glasgow people love spectacle. Think of the last tram procession. There were a quarter of a million people in the streets."

"It should be quite exquisite." Digby decided to live up to his image of being a swine. "In that case I think I will."

"Are we lunching together?" asked Gerontian-ffylde. They drove through Paisley and found a roadside hotel. He ordered for everyone, while Professor Knapbone went to the men's room to scrub his hands for the regulation four-and-a-half minutes. The waiter served the others, and, as Professor Knapbone returned and sat down, slipped a plate of smoked salmon before him.

"Smoked salmon?" Knapbone recoiled from his plate. "Halt immediately!" He started to pull away the plates from Colonel Strachan and Gerontian-ffylde and collected them in front of him. He took out a double-lensed magnifying glass and began to examine the scales of the fish. "It's a damned good job I did some ichthyology," he grunted. "Just as I thought. Imported frozen and smoked here."

"Look here," snapped Col. Strachan. "I happen to like smoked salmon. Give me it back."

Professor Knapbone rapped on the table with a fish fork. "You don't appear to understand," he said. "There has been an outbreak of botulism in certain of the lakes where salmon for smoking is caught. All fish coming from there may carry the germ, which is highly toxic, even if the fish is cooked at a high temperature immediately after catching. This has merely been smoked."

"But it may not have come from an infected lake." Col. Strachan was earnest and pleading. "I love smoked salmon."

"I know it mayn't, and so do I. Mr Digby appears to be the only person who doesn't. But better safe than sorry . . ."

He scraped all the smoked salmon on to a single plate. "Waiter," he called. "Remove this offensive material and burn it."

In a hotel in the centre of Glasgow the next day, Gerontian-ffylde drank a final glass of tawny port after lunch and said, "I thought Bob Strachan was going to have a heart attack when Knapbone stole his smoked salmon . . . Good heavens, what's this coming?"

Lieut. Smith was picking his way between the tables, his enormous feet moving as nervously as if he was crossing a minefield. A brogue scuffed the vacant chair. He sat down, reflexively grinning.

"What do you want?"

"Colonel Bob sent me, Puff."

"Puff? I don't think I like your familiarity, Smith. I do outrank you, you know."

Lieut. Smith's oblong face became crimson. "I thought you were only a P.R.O."

"I rank as a colonel, Smith. Stand up when you speak to me."

"I'm awfully sorry, sir. I do apologise. Colonel Strachan sent me to ask when the motorcade should start."

"When we get the marchioness out of bed. She never gets up until two, unless she's lunching, which she isn't . . ."

"Would three be all right, sir?"

"If you like." In the same breath, Gerontian-ffylde turned to Digby, as if Lieut. Smith no longer existed. "So we could take a salmon tonight if we can get rid of all this scrofulous soldiery. If we leave at six, we could be on the water at Breacogle by eleven . . ." He swung round at Lieut. Smith. "Are you still here?" The entertainments officer stumbled to his feet and hurried out.

"Why on earth did you do that? And you have the cheek to call me a swine."

"Bloody ox . . . only a P.R.O., indeed. I've discovered he's the fool who consorted with that spotty newsdesk woman and came up with the motorcade idea. It's all his fault. I hate buffoons like that: they make me nervous."

"You leaned on him a little, didn't you?"

"He needs a lesson." There was screaming in the street.

"I caught him taking it out on one of the men. I dislike people like that. If you must know, and you can jeer if you want to, he isn't a gentleman. It still means something to some of us . . ." The screaming rose higher. Gerontian-ffylde affected to notice it. "What on earth is all that noise?"

The screaming was pervading, throbbing with fear. Digby hardly needed to look to identify its source. Outside the streets had filled with a morass of men and boys, shouting, chanting hoarse slogans, and wearing a mixture of green and white cheap scarves with matching machine-knitted tammies. Others were decked in long blue scarves, slashed with thin white and red stripes. The Saturday-afternoon shoppers had vanished. Pavements heaved as a mob of thirty youths forced the remnants of the pedestrians into the gutters, and as they ran, brandished their scarves above their heads in long ribbons, shouting, "Rangers . . . Rangers, fugra Pope. Rangers, cha, cha, cha." On the far side, slamming in the other direction, a violently antagonistic group was screaming, "Celtic eas-y, Cel-tic eas-y . . . fugra Huns." Sporadically they stopped to swill down cheap dessert wine from the necks of their bottles. One youth vomited down a shop window and on to the pavement. A fleet of buses, scarves fluttering like obscene pennants from the windows, roared past with oaths spilling from the passengers. The two groups clashed, and there was the dull clang of a shop window going in, and Gerontian-ffylde saw, white-faced, that a youth had been thrown bodily into a baker's shop and lay bleeding among the trays of bread.

"What in God's name's going on?" Gerontian-ffylde demanded. "Has this city gone mad?"

Digby began to feel ashamed of himself, perversely and secretly revelling in the experience. "I'm afraid I didn't tell you. There's a Rangers-Celtic cup final on today . . ." He gestured in helpless confusion outside.

Men scattered away from the pavement as the rioting football supporters fanned out. Bayonets and meat cleavers appeared. Blood erupted on a youth's face, his cheek falling open in a bright red spray, as a jagged tumbler whipped into the flesh. He went down, the blood pouring into his mouth. A boot crunched into his other cheek, laying it open along the maxillary bone. A skinny youth with glaring eyes ran about on the cleared pavement, his scarf brandished above his head, chanting, "Ea-sy . . . Ea-sy." The mob was separating now, spitting great streams of viscid saliva over the green sections of Corporation buses, others kicking at the orange panels.

Gerontian-ffylde was scarcely capable of accepting that the scene he saw had been enacted. He was in a trance of disbelief. "What happened?" he repeated over and over again. "What started it?"

"He waved a Union Jack at the Celtic supporters."

"Don't be repulsive." Gerontian-ffylde's mouth was a thin ribbon of dislike. "That's what I mean about you bloody journalists. You're all the same at heart: cynical and disbelieving and always ready with snide cracks." His eyes were horrified. "It's our national flag. Don't make that shoddy with your cheap utterances."

"Godinheaven—look out the window. Look out, I tell you." Digby forced him against the metal window frame and compelled him to watch the rest of the riot.

Six more youths danced in a poisonous mime around the youth lying on the pavement, the blood darkening and clotting as it made contact with the air. They were brandishing Union Jacks and thrusting them into the face of the youth on the pavement. "Die, you papish bastard, die," they chanted. "Die you papish rat."

A furniture van came from nowhere and rammed on to the pavement, cutting off their escape. From the doors spilled long-haired roughs. There was a single shriek of "Ness" and the thugs swept away. All that was left was the youth, apparently dying, and a litter of axes, bludgeons, swords, razor-edged chisels, stiletto-pointed packing needles, abandoned in a confusion of violence on the pavement and in the gutter.

"It's the 'Untouchables'," said Digby. "They're under-cover police nicknamed after an American TV serial. Ness was their leader." A youth, squealing in terror, was flung into the van, which shook as his body banged against the metal sides. Two more youths, their arms pinioned high up their backs and seeming to walk on tiptoe, were thrust into the van. An ambulance, its siren baying in two-tone doom, sped to the kerb.

Digby said, "Let's go down and see what's left." They almost fell over a youth huddled into the doorway, trying to evade the police. He straightened up as Digby asked him what had happened.

"You Glesca, mac?" Digby said he wasn't. "They were wavin' these Irish flags to annoy us, an' shoutin' Huns at us. These papish rats are all troublemakers. It's thae fuggin' rodents." Unable to contain himself he screamed, "Rodents . . . We waved the Union Jack back at them. Christ, it needles them. You canny wear a Rangers scarf by yersel or they'll chiv or hatchet you. That's why I'm armed." Digby could see the outline of what seemed a hatchet head under his tinsel-specked sweater, the haft presumably thrust into his waistband. "You want to see the rest o' my gear, mac?" The youth flicked back the cuff of his left sleeve, revealing a honed butcher's knife, loosely taped to his forearm. A flaccid smile of bravado, lips loose and wet, shimmied over his face as he leaned forward. "This is the gear, mac. This is for when I'm out with the heavy mob." To his speculative horror, Gerontian-ffylde could see a bayonet hilt slung between his prominent shoulder blades. "A beer can opener's good an' all an' the coppers canny get ye for carryin' a weapon."

His accent was disintegrating as he manoeuvred further into the doorway. "Just stand in front of me will ye, mac, till that fuggen fuzz gets out of the way. We sing the National Anthem like. You know, 'God Save the Queen'. It really gets them, the dirty rats, an' we go into Hail, hail the Pope's in jail . . . let the bastard rot there . . . what the fugg do we care . . .

"We got it ontae the network once. We were chantin' 'Rangers, fugra pope,' . . . It was on the network . . . You could hear it all over Britain, all over the world. All the way from Glesca. That's us." He shouted, "We are the people."

Gerontian-ffylde said awe-stricken, "I wonder what a sociologist would make of all this?"

"Thae fuggen sociologists." His accent thickened. "What dae they ken? They ken what we tell them tae ken . . . and what dae ye mean, mac? You tryin' tae be funny? You want tae see the world in action mister? Dae ye? Dae ye want to see it?" His fingers were darting like scorpions into the cuff of his left sleeve.

He was losing control of his face, his mouth slackening and white-flecking. He was edging round so that his back faced the street and a potential escape route. "I'll get ye, ye English bastard."

In a blaze of movement Digby's right foot swept up and ravagingly tore into the youth's testicles. He bucked and shrilly screamed like a rabbit, his spine arching into an ellipse of agony. As he began to fall, Digby smashed his other foot across the hoodlum's ankles, lifting and sprawling him sideways. Down, down he went, his lips stiffened and curling back from his teeth. The reporter pounced forward, crushing his knees with sledgehammer force into his ribs and hit him again against the roadway, exploding and whooshing the breath out of him, the ribs buckling and cracking into the chest cavity. As suddenly Digby was back on his feet, kicking a hand, any hand, free from the twitching body. Bloodily he stamped his heel across the metatarsals, pinning the palm in a new and violent stigmata to the pavement. He let out an exhalation of breath which quivered foolishly between bravery and reactive cowardice. He could have bellowed, but did not know how strong or weak his voice might be.

The furniture van had backed up behind him, its cavernous interior looming like a dungeon. Three men pushed past him and threw the body inside. "Thanks, mate," one said. "Phone in some time, will you?"

Gerontian-ffylde was still dazed and asking pointless questions. "Do they think you're in the police . . . ? We aren't taking the marchioness into that screaming mob . . . ? What will they do with . . . ? Where did you learn this violence?"

"Let's forget it, shall we?" Digby's face was white with shock. "I had to live in this city for a couple of years, remember? I had to learn to protect myself like the others . . . Anyway, she'll be all right. They'll be off the streets in less than ten minutes when the game starts . . . I thought you were putting her into a scout car anyway."

When Lady Jayne emerged from her room the streets had cleared, although it was a sunny Saturday afternoon, and the pavements were empty. It was almost four o'clock. Three scout cars were drawn up at the hotel door, and Col. Strachan, in denims and a leather-patched khaki pullover, helped Lady Jayne into the turret of the leading car. Beneath her, Lieut. Smith crouched at the wheel. "I know Glasgow like the back of my hand," he had assured Col. Strachan. "Our best route is over the river through the Gorbals to the Victoria Infirmary, returning via Queen's Park, then we can do the west end of the city."

Chattily he added to Lady Jayne as he tore down Renfield Street, "There seems to be some football match on today. We should see a lot of crowds and they should see us, I hope, eh?" He ignored a police signal and forced his way on to the bridge over the Clyde, odorous and brown, then swerved and made for Crown Street in the Gorbals. A thin stream of unhappy, angry men in green and white scarves and tammies met them, returning from Hampden Park where Rangers had beaten Celtic 3–1 in the final of the newly resurrected Scottish Summer Cup.

Lieut. Smith pressed on into the seething crowds, mainly Celtic supporters who, unable to bear the humiliation of seeing their team beaten, had sportingly left Hampden early. The crowds grew even thicker. The scout car was forced to halt. At the far end of the street a low howling began. The scout car was rocking. Lady Jayne fished in her handbag and pulled out a toy Union Jack which she waved at them. "Fight for your country," she called, smiling and waggling the insignificant flag. Rage engulfed her. A forest of scrabbling hands reached up for her. "Kill the whore," they screamed. The aerial was being dragged off. The wheels were being bounced higher in the air. Lieut. Smith's eager voice came over the wireless: "Can I open fire, sir . . . ? Permission to open fire . . ."

Truncheons flailed in the air as mounted police gouged into the crowds. They separated in a hail of bottles. The howling grew to a constant high-pitched moan. At the far end of Crown Street, the bus carrying the victorious Rangers team nosed its way into sight. Bottles and slates ripped off the buildings were falling on to the bus roof. Shrieks and screams echoed off the soot-smeared walls. Even women and children were jeering. Excrement,

85

pails of urine, were being flung across the street and on to the bus.

The police manoeuvred the bus alongside the scout car, and Lady Jayne was dragged from the turret, her clothes shredding as the frenetic hands reached and scrabbled at her Dior suit, ripping her sky-blue cashmere sweater and her flimsy black lace brassiere. Her pointed breasts were exposed, the aureoles darkening in response to the violent handling. As Digby scrambled into the bus behind her, he saw her eyes were closed and her face was set into a rigid, hallucinated smile, then she was carried away to the rear seats. He looked round and saw that a footballer had lost his shorts, and sat with only his jock-strap covering him. The marchioness half came round, thrilled in a spasm which shook her from head to toe, and fainted away again. The footballer said, "Christ she only looked at me. I didn't touch her, honest. I swear I didn't touch her. You'd think I was a bloody vampire or something."

In Strummet Castle, Cinnamon was ironing the Sunday newspapers before carrying them into the turret room. He tittered. "The old queer won't have far to look today either," he said to Griselda, who was lying on the dressing-room floor. She had abandoned silver paint and was trying out the effect of gold leaf. He examined the front page of the *Sunday Tentacle* again. "A right pair of knockers she's got, too," he said.

The photograph, which was printed across five columns, showed Lady Jayne being dragged into the bus, her torn brassiere hanging from her waist, and her sweater in shreds. The artist, who had prepared the photograph for block-making, had, under a standing house rule, painted out the erect nipples and expanding aureoles, but the magnificent breasts remained quite exposed.

A two-deck headline in 42-point Sans upper and lower case was set in a hood above the photograph and read:

Out with her recruits
in football riot

Under the photograph, an enterprising sub-editor had

added a smaller headline, "Lady Jayne's two points for better privates".

The article beneath the block mentioned that Lady Jayne had fainted, and that her recruiting tour had been marred by fainting fits "of varying severity and unknown cause".

The marquis laid aside the timetable of the mammy-waggon service between Ibadan, Egbeda and Asegire in the Western Region of Nigeria. "What pretty breasts," he exclaimed. "It makes me feel quite proud to be the overlord, the feudal superior in perpetuity, as it were, of a pair like that. Demned better than the photograph of that little poof Basil trying to goose my wife. What do you say, Cinnamon?"

The valet made a non-committal sound.

"Fainting," shouted the marquis. "What's this? What has that harlot been up to? Fainting fits, by Christ." He hobbled about the room, trumpeting in purple apoplexy and throwing masses of timetables in the air. "Fainting fits? The bitch; the nymphomaniac bitch. We all know what she's been up to. I'll sue her. I'll sue the bitch for divorce. I've had enough of her cheap vulgarity."

He seized a walking stick and started smashing the furniture in his fury. "I don't mind her fainting with someone of her own class," he was shouting. "It was touch and go when I discovered she'd fainted with that ageing TV writer. But this . . . She's maligning the family name." In a final stroke he splintered the walking stick. "She's maligned it once too often."

He whirled on the valet. "Bring round the Rolls . . . the season might not have opened yet, but we're going to Edinburgh." He threw the splintered walking stick against the wall in a show of triumph. "We're going to litigate. We're going to law."

By mid-afternoon, Cinnamon, in his chocolate and beige uniform, was waiting beside the silver Rolls-Royce at the castle front door. He helped the marquis, still shaking with anger, into the rear seat and drove him calmly to Edinburgh, where they spent the night in separate hotels. In the morning, Cinnamon propelled Lord Strummet to the office of the old-established legal firm of Wort, Odhar and

Meiklem, whom he retained. The senior partner, Mr Duncan Odhar, a sharp, acaritic figure in gold pince-nez, sensed the financial lustre attached to the case and not unnaturally dealt with it in person.

"You appreciate, my lord, that divorce hearings have changed since you last . . . since your previous . . . excuse me, my lord. Divorces have been held in territorial courts since last year. Your court is in Glasgow where these actions are now heard before the new divorce judge. It's rather a bad system in a way. We much preferred to have everything in Edinburgh where young advocates could get their training with undefended cases on a Saturday morning."

"At thirty quid for ten measly minutes, I should bloody well think you would," grunted the marquis.

Odhar flustered. "You must agree these litigants were given value for their money."

"I couldn't give a monkey's how much they paid. It's me I'm worried about. How much less will this new scheme cost? I suppose the idea *is* to cut down costs."

"O no, my lord." Odhar seemed horrified. "It works out at slightly more in your case. I'll have to engage solicitors in Glasgow for you, and brief counsel here. The advocates still live in Edinburgh, of course. If you wish, in fact, we could have a preliminary meeting with counsel today." He pinged his bell. His fawning manner had vanished. "Get me McPhuig's clerk on the phone," he snarled at the office girl who entered. "And hurry up. Don't keep his lordship waiting . . . On second thoughts get him yourself and tell him I'm bringing the Marquis of Strummet round for a consultation . . . Stir yourself," he hissed.

His toothy smile returned. "More tea, my lord?" He walked across to the tray. "I do feel McPhuig is your man. He's taken silk, Queen's Counsel, you know, and I think young Lorimer would make an admirable junior. He's shaping quite well. He was successfully proposed at Muirfield last week." He noticed the marquis's blank stare and added, "It's a golf club."

His smile was more ingratiating than ever. "There is one thing, my lord." Now the smile seemed edged with fear. "I do hope you understand. You appreciate that advocates are special people . . . ?"

"Special? What do you mean, special? Have they developed twin penes, or something interesting like that? I'd like to think so. Most of them look under-sexed to me."

"Nothing like that." Odhar, attempting to equate the grandeur of the marquis with the hauteur of the Faculty of Advocates, was in a quandary. "They won't shake hands with you, you know. Advocates never shake hands."

"Good god, Odhar. You don't think I want to touch one of you legal fellows, do you? I'd rather touch a mad dog." He rose. "Hurry up, man. I haven't all day to waste."

The marquis led the way down the steps of the office and Cinnamon opened the rear door of the Rolls for him. Almost as an afterthought, the valet raised the jump seats for Mr Odhar to sit on, alongside a junior partner, Hamish Patron, whom the lawyer had summoned to take notes.

Like a swan the car moved through the mid-morning traffic, curving up to Queen Street, and arrived at the advocate's chambers in the New Town. "It was built in the 1800s," said Mr Odhar, "but by tradition we still call it the New Town. We're very fond of tradition here."

"Pity you didn't get a real one then," muttered the marquis, determined to revenge himself for Odhar's presumption about the social position of advocates. He strode past McPhuig into the chambers, which were, in fact, merely a room in his house. The marquis did not offer to shake hands.

"What's all this, then?" he barked at McPhuig. "When can I get my divorce through, then, eh?"

McPhuig ignored him and said to Odhar, "I believe your client wishes to obtain decree of divorce."

"He feels he has endured sufficient of his wife's behaviour."

"What do you think would provide the best grounds for your client to proceed on?"

"I have the feeling that adultery would provide a suitable ground."

"Has he sufficient evidence?"

Mantling with fury, the marquis realised they were daring to talk about him in the third person, as if he was no longer present, or even existed. The strange half-gibberish conversation went on. Odhar was saying, "I understand the . . ."

"I most certainly have," snapped the marquis, in an effort to be recognised.

McPhuig frowned, attempting to make his soft golden moustache bristle with disapproval. His slightly florid face suffused with the effort. He pointedly addressed his questions to Odhar. "What sort of corroboration has your client?"

The marquis realised he was being totally ignored. "Look here," he thundered. "Mind your manners when you're in the presence of a marquis. It's me: the Marquis of Strummet who wants a divorce, not some mythical *parvenu* from this snob-crippled city. Pay attention to what I'm saying."

McPhuig's lower lip perceptibly quivered. It was the first time a client had dared to address him like that in his professional life. He whispered, "We do not normally address ourselves to clients. We find them too excitable or incapable of telling us what actually transpired."

The marquis was beside himself with anger. He shouted, "How do you know what actually happened then? Are you a pack of clairvoyants? You mark my words: I'm the man that's paying you lot. You'll do exactly as I tell you, do you hear me?"

McPhuig was breathing heavily. Not merely had the marquis walked past him without giving him the opportunity of refusing to shake hands, which always put people in their places. He was actually ordering them about. It was almost too much to tolerate. He emanated what he hoped was a forbidding silence.

The marquis said, "My plan is to name every recruit in both my new battalions."

Odhar exchanged a glance of instant complicity with McPhuig. "Do you mean them all?"

"I do."

"But some of them might not actually have committed adultery with her."

"What does that matter to you? You don't mean to say you worry about them! Can they prove they haven't?"

McPhuig's face became more florid. "It would mean a great deal of preliminary work for Mr Odhar. Perhaps

90

some of the men are married and have homes apart from the barracks. It might be difficult to trace them."

"What do I care about that? As far as I'm concerned, the dirty cow could have committed adultery with all of them. I want my name cleared up and the name of my clan untarnished. I don't care who gets hurt in the process."

He added, "And I want that little poof Makebelieve involved. If Basil's been groping my wife in public, god knows what he's been doing in private."

McPhuig's face was tortured as he attempted to hide his emotions. This was fantastic. This was a goldmine. A cabinet minister. A marquis and his wife . . . The free publicity from the newspapers alone would be worth thousands from the Legal Aid Scheme, when the criminals read about it.

The marquis was still nodding vigorously into the silver silence which had risen in the room, as McPhuig's junior, Lorimer, came in. He was an even more hygienic version of his brother, the Minister for Internal Security (Scotland).

The silence became omnipresent, manifold, paramount. Odhar intruded, almost hesitantly, as if breaking the precious spell was sacreligious: "There is a major point which must not be overlooked. The marquis has been married for only two years and ten months."

"My poor fellow," said someone. An excited gabbling arose. McPhuig smoothed his moustache, his forefinger and thumb stealing across his face in opposing directions, then he decided to clear his throat. Somehow he resembled a teutonic seal lolling on the sea surface, his round golden head and sprawling moustache rising sleekly above his sloping shoulders, suitably encased in his black, legal pelt. In his hand was a copy of the *Law Times*. He said portentously, "I know it's an English journal, but it contains quite a good definition of the old law." He began to quote: "Marriage is a contract entered into willingly by two parties for three years certain and terminable thereafter at the option of the parties . . ."

"Do you fools mean you can't get her out of my house for another two months?" McPhuig turned away scarlet, the fine network of broken veins on his nose standing out. (Odhar explained later, "If you had not been titled, he would have refused the brief because you called him a fool.

Members of the Faculty are very conscious of their important position. You mustn't call them fools." The marquis retorted, "But he did, didn't he? That's why we encourage *snobismo.*" His voice was scornful. "They always come crawling back for more, no matter how hard we kick them." Odhar could only look at him and was incapable of speech.)

"You mean she can go around the country, maligning my family name and I can't discipline her? That I can't rid myself of her disgusting presence? By god, what a mess of the law you oafs have made. This is law at its most preposterous."

"Not necessarily," said Odhar. He was swiftly adding figures in his head. "We don't mean that at all. You can prevent her from doing anything you feel like. It's relatively simple to prevent anyone from doing anything in Scotland."

McPhuig had also been doing sums in his head. At first count, it seemed to be about £60,000. His pique vanished, and he cleared his throat resonantly again. "We would advise you to take out interdict." It was as if he was pronouncing a sentence of death.

"Interdick? What the devil does that mean? It sounds like a perversion."

"O, very witty, Lord Strummet," said Odhar, his little eyes glittering behind his gold pince-nez. "If you feel she is maligning the family name, there is no reason why you should not reciprocate." He leaned forward. "But please do not discuss this with anyone outside this room."

Lorimer said, "We would advise you to put your allegations into writing. You could, for example, say that her habits were grieving you because she was corrupting the children's minds. I take it there are children? My brother . . ."

"Your brother?" The marquis was startled, then realised how familiar the name sounded. "Lorimer," he said. "Of course. It used to mean the chap who made horses' bits when lorimers indulged in honest work . . . Is your brother one of those politician fellows?"

"He is, your lordship." The intimate quality of his smile indicated that his brother had told him about his stay. "You could say that her immoral behaviour was causing you concern because she is stepmother of your children and you wanted to deny her access to them and forbid her entry to your house."

"Give a few examples of what she's been doing," added Odhar. "Indicate your belief that she is having carnal relations with your privates . . ." He flushed. "With your regiment would be better, perhaps."

The marquis burst out, "That's just what she is doing. She's insatiable. She seems to do it for the number of scalps. Even you lot could make her . . . Between ourselves, I wouldn't bother: she's appalling in bed."

McPhuig had begun to frown again. Before another tiff could occur, Odhar continued, "An interdict is then sought. It is a superior form of the English injunction. An intimation is hung on the walls of the court for seven days so that the defender can lodge answers, as we describe it, and arrange to defend the action, if they wish."

His pince-nez could barely obscure the bright malevolence in his eyes. "This is where someone invariably tells the newspapers . . . Somehow, somewhere"—he acted as if it was all part of a great mystery—"a copy of the petition falls into the hands of the Press and they're stupid enough to publish it: or at least some of them are."

"Where do they get it from?"

Odhar put his finger on the side of his nose. "Our next move is perhaps to change our minds and withdraw the petition. Unhappily this might occur before she had time to answer the allegations. She assuredly can not answer allegations which no longer exist, and we have her, like this." He made a pinching movement with his thumb and forefinger. ". . . We also have the opportunity of dealing with the Press again."

"Dealing with them?" The marquis was disbelieving. "After what they did to our secret Cabinet meeting? I hardly think you can deal with them. Do a deal with them, more like it."

"You're referring to an English paper, Lord Strummet. We've had the Press muzzled for years in Scotland . . . although that fellow Gordon used to be quite infuriating at times. I fear he must have seen through us."

The marquis sniffed. "Go on," he said. "Tell me more."

"Someone brings the publication to the attention of the court, and the newspaper is hailed to the bar of the court for sentence. There's no trial, of course. They're guilty of contempt before they start . . . It also means that nothing gets printed in rebuttal again." His voice was hissing. "The statement can never be refuted by her. *Ever.* No matter what she does."

"It all sounds rather expensive, what?"

"A few pounds, my lord, and she's blackened for life . . . Meanwhile we shall begin to collect evidence for the divorce."

McPhuig's back was turning. The interview was apparently over. This time the marquis scarcely cared. What an excellent system it was, after all, he thought. Scots law most certainly had things to commend it. No wonder they wanted so desperately to keep it intact.

As he drove off in the Rolls, the legal conference went unhesitatingly on. Odhar said, "What a money-spinner. I think we should precognose both battalions of course."

Lorimer said, "I heard she's screwing the entire brigade. My brother told me he's sure she's got the clap." Patron turned away white-faced, and put his hands in his pockets.

No one noticed. McPhuig said, "In that case, we should take statements from everyone. That would be 900 pre-cognitions. And possibly 900 summonses." He was almost overcome.

"Nine hundred formal statements at least ten quid a time *to begin with.*" Odhar tore off his pince-nez in his excitement, his avarice completely apparent. "We've struck gold. Nearly a thousand precogs. Think of the MONEY."

*   *   *

Monitored phone call 17306880:

"He saw in the newspapers that this one was a sort of doctors' leader and he thought he must be good. Doctors' leaders are good doctors, aren't they, Digby? I suppose they must be if doctors get them to represent them on all these committees and things?"

"What did he do?"

"He poked about and told Torquil there was nothing the

matter with him again. He told him to pull himself together. Shouted at him, in fact, just like the local doctor: then he charged fifty guineas and left."

"How's Torquil?"

"Unchanged . . . About this other thing . . ."

6

In a pink stucco suburb of Lahore, in Pakistan, the Airmail *Times* was carried reverentially into the study of Dun-strumpet House by the butler, Ali Ahmed, on a worn silver salver of great age on which could still be discerned "The Governor and Company of the Merchants of London trading into the East Indies," and very faintly, the date, "1660". The servant bowed and presented the flimsy newspaper to Duncan Strumpet, a retired Government official. It was late morning. He had just listened to the 1,000-strong pipes and drums of the Pakistan Army School of Piping, the dust from the parade ground rising above their puttees, as they completed morning practice with the retreat air, "The Heroes of Dunkirk", which he found peculiarly affecting. He shook the creases from the newspaper and began to read, appreciating it as the last link with home and also providing a welcome break between his literary and genealogical studies, and tiffin.

Duncan Strumpet had retired to Lahore, partly to enjoy the constant feast of Highland music provided by the Pakistani pipers, and also to continue work on his thesis, over which he had laboured for seventeen years, and which led to the inescapable conclusion that he was the rightful Marquis of Strummet and 29th chief of the clan.

His claim was well-founded. In 1652, the eighth earl had

two sons and one daughter. The younger son, Duncan, who had worked as a double agent, had fought with the Royalists against Cromwell in Scotland and had simultaneously intrigued with General Monk to try to abscond with the Scottish Crown jewels which were hidden in Dunottar Castle. Dressed as a serving girl he had the sword of state, presented to James IV in 1507 by Pope Julius II, wrapped in a bundle of flax, and the sceptre, with the older rock crystal of the earlier sceptre set in its head, similarly hidden. The real serving girl he had stripped, and raped, in the dungeons of the fortress of the Keiths, built the previous century, and had tried to leave the castle with the girl's employer, Mrs Granger, wife of the minister of Kinneff, who had the crown, once worn by Robert the Bruce, concealed in her lap. His plan was to overpower the minister's wife and later flee to Monk's headquarters with the Honours of Scotland. When he was unmasked, he talked his way glibly from mandatory and almost instant beheading by claiming that he was acting in the best interests of Scotland by not leaving the priceless jewels in the hands of a serving wench, but safeguarding them behind the point of a skilled swordsman. His eloquent plea meant a grudging and conditional release, but as his father told him before he was banished in disgrace, his sin was not in being caught, but in being caught by the wrong side.

Duncan Strumpet had made his way to London with a letter to a Scots-born banker, who arranged an introduction to the East India Company. He was given a lowly position on the Coromandel Coast and sailed to Pondicherry the following autumn in a merchantman. His voyage was uneventful. When he disembarked, however, he discovered the ship had carried a confidential memorandum advising of his record of duplicity, attempted malfeasance and military accomplishments. He was straightaway put in charge of a force of natives, which was primely required to ascertain the whereabouts of precious stones and metals in the various States, with a view to acquiring them. Eight years later, in the course of his duties, he entered the State of Huzpoor and had occasion to make his way to the palace of the reigning family. There, at first sight, he fell in love with Jazbir, the slim and lovely daughter of the Royal House of Huzpoor. They married and he vanished into palace life in the isolated State. His only memento of the Company, which presumed him dead, was the silver salver which was still in use in Lahore almost three centuries later.

At home in Scotland, the fortunes of the Strumpet family had fallen to a low ebb. The elder son, Iain, had died of mercury poisoning three years after Duncan was exiled, and as he could not be traced, the succession was endangered. The earl, who was 67, discovered that his wife had become barren, and one summer evening, tied her by her hair to a rock below highwater mark in the Sound of Strummet, and went home to carouse with his new bride while the sea first drowned his wife, then swept away her body. Doubts assailed him when his new wife gave birth to a son seven months after the nuptials, and he wrongly thought he had been cuckolded. To ensure that the title stayed with the blood, he had the boy married on his sixteenth birthday to his own step-sister, Margaret, a hare-lipped prematurely obese woman of forty-four. She conceived quickly and, on his death-bed, the old earl—the marquisate came in the 19th century—saw his grandchild safe alive, then turned his face to the wall and expired.

Later Margaret was passed off as her husband's cousin, but could never again bear to use the name Strumpet, because of the obscene remarks addressed to her by her distant kinsfolk, and she altered her patronym to Strummet.

Margaret was the person to whom the marquis referred when he gave evidence to the Royal Commission on Parliamentary (Lords and Commons) Morals. He told the Commission, "An ancestress of mine dropped the 'p' from the family name in the 17th century and none of us had the moral fibre to pick it up again."

The consequent in-breeding irrevocably fixed certain genetic traits in the family. Although a high intelligence quotient was normally found, other and more dubious characteristics were apt to emerge. Unknown to Torquil, he had an elder half-cousin whose mother had been a castle scullery maid and who lived in a cell behind the water gate of Strummet Castle. He was excessively tall, almost six feet seven inches in height, and although he was of insignificant intellectual powers, he normally had an affectionate and playful nature, except when a change took place in the electrical impulses and rhythms of his brain. He then developed ungovernable urges to destroy by fire, and also to attack visitors to the estate who chanced to walk in the castle park. On several occasions he had started large bonfires of dried leaves and branches in the castle cellars and had several times attempted to strangle the Chamberpot as he slipped covertly down to the village, for an evening dram. The mysterious posts which Gerontian-ffylde had observed in the games field were used by the giant as scratching posts in the gloaming, his great shoulders shuddering and heaving against the Scots pine as he sought relief from the itch; possibly caused by a skin exudate of the same chemical family which provokes deep scratching and self-laceration in schizophrenics. Or it may have been brought on by his almost permanent diet of raw rabbit meat, eked out by whatever wild fowl he could snare. His fire-raising propensities had meant that he was kept completely without matches or any other source of combustion, and he had no means of cooking.

A geneticist on holiday in Dunstrummet had been cornered in the castle grounds by Torquil's half-cousin one dark night and had the presence of mind to inject the giant figure with a syringe of methedrine which he had been about to use on himself. He had insisted, the following day, on interviewing the marquis (he otherwise threatened a civil suit for damages and possible criminal charges) and had obtained permission to take blood samples and certain measurements of the half-cousin.

To his astonishment and professional delight, the geneticist realised that he had found the first case in Scotland of the extra "Y" sex chromosome, which was subsequently claimed to cause criminal violence: the first time that a genetic cause of crime had been discovered.

Another adventurous member of the Strummet family was recorded in a Nasmyth in the Castle portrait gallery as having the condition known as the hairy ears syndrome, a self-explanatory type of hirsutism, previously discovered only in a small tribe of inter-related Japanese fishermen. After considerable research it was discovered that the

Strummet in question had indeed been shipwrecked in Japanese waters during a gun-running expedition in the early 19th century, and had reappeared seven years later with a little son. The episode caused intense speculation as to whether the Strummets had inherited the characteristic from the Japanese fishermen or had, in fact given it to them. Even Torquil, or so his father believed, suffered from a congenital condition, for many famous physicians from Harley Street, Glasgow, and as a last resort, Edinburgh, had failed to dislodge his general malaise.

In Lahore, Duncan Strumpet was unaware of these facets of the genetic make-up of his kinsmen, and, indeed, his side of the family seemed remarkably free of aberrations. He read the front page, the personal columns and the foreign news section of *The Times*, and decided to leave the remainder of the newspaper until after tiffin, when he could read and relax simultaneously.

Before leaving the study, he crossed to his desk and tried to make up his mind about the letter which had arrived from Scotland the previous day. It was from a man called James MacStrummet, who signed himself as chairman of the Strummet Clan Society.

The letter read:

Dear Chief,

After considerable search through the records and papers of the Strummet family which are available to me, I have come to the ineradicable conclusion that you are the rightful chief of Clan Strummet.

I may say that I am not unconnected with the laws of genealogy and I urge you on behalf of myself and all loyal clansmen to make immediate representations to the Lord Lyon King of Arms, who must support your claim. I have taken the liberty of calling on Lyon who admits that he will accept that you are the rightful chief, provided you can furnish some form of written proof of your birth during your family's long exile.

Meanwhile it would be a great honour to us if you would accept the office of President and Chief of our Society, which will now replace all previous societies of the *true* Clan Strummet. Do not be misled by any other impostors who claim to have authentic societies relating to our glorious clan. Their society should be ours.

Yours in clan brotherhood,
James MacStrummet.

P.S. After your long exile you may not be up-to-date with the modern spelling of your name. I wonder if you would be kind enough to conform to this spelling in future as it will mean otherwise that we will have to have our stationery reprinted.

James MacStrummet had been elected chairman of the new Strummet Clan Society after the break-up and re-formation of the Clan Strummet Society. This had occurred after his brother and family had been made homeless by the marquis, himself president of the society which existed, according to its constitution, to multiply, aid and succour all clansmen in the traditional ways of history and the clan. James MacStrummet's brother had farmed the green and fertile holding of Strummetbeg, reclaimed from the sea loch by judicious and expert dyke-making in the 1850s. The farm had been made so rich and bountiful by succeeding generations of MacStrummets that the marquis had begun to covet its level fields and rich dark soil. When the owner refused to sell, the marquis had the dykes, which, by a legal quirk, were owned by him, broken down on the grounds that they were unsafe and that he no longer wished to be put to the expense of maintaining them. Later he bought the abandoned and flooded farm for a few hundred pounds.

When an extraordinary meeting of the Clan Society had demanded the marquis's resignation from office as president and chief, he refused and said that he would instead dissolve the society. This he did and formed a new society with the name merely transposed, calling it the Society of Clan Strummet and installing the Chamberpot as secretary.

The breakaway Society had cast around for a chief and president, and only then did an elderly member speak hesitatingly from his failing and unreliable memory of the legendary tale of the Strumpet who had gone to India. Research had been instituted, and Duncan Strumpet had been found in retirement in Lahore.

The retired civil servant put down the letter, and realised that he was still holding the *Times* which had half-opened at the home news section. A small item caught his eye, headed "New Regiment at Clan Gathering".

A photograph between the headline and the body of the short article looked vaguely familiar. With a start of curious pleasure and anticipation, he saw that it was of the marquis's face. The article read, "The newly-reformed Strummet Foot will parade for the first time at the annual gathering of Clan Strummet on October 29 in the presence of the Marquis of Strummet, their colonel-in-chief.

"The gathering, which is taking place late in the year in the hope that the regiment will be up to strength by that time, has attracted the interest of clansmen the world over, a correspondent writes . . ."

It was the article which finally made up Duncan Strumpet's mind for him. When his family gathered in the lounge for pre-tiffin glasses of iced and sweetened lemon juice, he decided to make the announcement immediately. He felt a glow of pride as he gazed at their smiling and attentive faces. "I have decided after long and careful thought," he said, "to go home and claim our rightful heritage. You will of course accompany me. Perhaps you would all care to read this?" He passed the letter to his eldest daughter, Emerald Jasbir, who read it and handed it in turn to Daisy Belle, Rosie, Reita Habib, Jasmine Jasbir, Maggie Jewel, Poppy Habib, Rachel Jasbir and Pixie Delight.

For the clan society had neglected to secure two vital pieces of information. The full name of their new chief was Duncan Jasbir Habib Strumpet, and the complexion of this highly principled, intelligent and sensitive man was as rare and refined as sandalwood. Not black, nor even dark brown, but still perceptibly and undeniably coloured.

*　　*　　*

Monitored phone call 193517880:

"He's got a South African up here with a chimpanzee's heart in a bottle. He says he could cure Torquil by giving him a heart transplant. An allograft he called it. He believes the loss of heart function is causing a general deterioration in Torquil's condition."

"Oh my god," said Digby. "Why don't you send for the police?"

7

Mr Odhar paused inside the courthouse door and inspected the formal notice of interdict pierced on the hook, already bloated with legal documents. It read simply that the petitioner, the Marquis of Strummet, was seeking interdict against his wife, the Marchioness of Strummet, and that seven days were allowed for her to enter answers, when a Judge would hear the action. He walked away across the quadrangle, his small feet striking tinnily on the cobbles and echoing back from the historic stone walls. How nice, he thought, to keep up the traditions of the Scottish court. On the pavement, he joined his wife, a fat squat woman with fine lines bisecting the planes and sagging angles of her ponderous jaw, linking with deeper grooves and channels which ran contrarily from her mouth to her ear lobes. She was wearing thick white pancake make-up. Digby thought her face was cross-hatched, like a map. He stepped aside to let them pass, and the woman deliberately bumped into him. Odhar glared, but did not speak. Digby said to a shrunken reporter, so that Odhar could hear, "The natives are a trifle restless today, aren't they?" The woman's back stiffened.

The shrunken reporter said, "I don't think it's safe to be seen with you, not with the Establishment's views about how you behave. You'll get me into trouble. We want to be friendly with these people, otherwise we would get nothing to print. No stories, nothing." He blinked, thinking of his neo-Civil-Service life on the *Scottish Sentinel*, one of the rash of web-offset newspapers that started up in the late seventies.

"I always did think that everything you lot wrote was approved by the Establishment. No wonder this country's still in such a mess."

"You can't say that about us journalists on the quality Press. We're not censored. We only check to see what we're printing is respectable. We're not like you popular newspapers where the proprietor controls every word you write."

Digby started to grin loathsomely, visualising Lord Acarid reading every word of the forty-eight editions of his newspapers. He decided to cherish the remark as a testament to the accuracy of his competitors. On the surface he ignored the shrunken reporter, and idled silently across the quadrangle and entered the courthouse to look at the notice of petition. Another reporter called Kimble had arrived from the *Daily Flute*.

"It doesn't say much," Digby said to him, introducing himself.

"I don't suppose it does." Kimble was guarded. "How did you know this was coming up anyway?"

"It doesn't really matter. If you're really interested I'll buy you a drink." They walked out on to the main road and went into a small oak-panelled bar. Digby said, "Who gave you the copy of the petition?"

"How did you know about that?"

"Look, old son, I don't want to sound like your grand-dad, but I used to work in Scotland. Their clumsy methods don't change very much."

"This is supposed to be an exclusive," said Kimble. "For god's sake, don't steal it or I'll get fired. This newsdesk man we've got. He's dangerous." He told Digby about the chimney incident. "I just put the phone down on him and went back to resign, but everything had blown over."

Digby decided against telling Kimble that he knew about it. Instead he said, "Even if you don't tell me who gave you the petition, why don't you drop it on the table so I can read it? I promise you I'm not going to use it." Kimble hesitated. "Look," said Digby, "if I wanted a copy, I could get one. All this is going to do is save me a lot of trouble. I don't even want to pick it up . . . If there's any noise, you can come across to the *Tentacle;* you'd be far better off there anyway. You want to avoid newsdesk men like that: they can damage you professionally."

The petition read:

> The petitioner craves the court to grant him interdict against his wife, the Marchioness of Strummet, hereinafter described as the defender, preventing her from entering Strummet Castle and coming in contact with Torquil, Earl of Pumphrey, and Lady Sheila Strummet on the grounds that the defender had conducted herself in a shameless and libidinous manner with recruits to the petitioner's private regiment, the Strummet Foot, and is in a position of trust regarding the children and is in a position to corrupt the morals of the aforementioned children of the pursuer . . . .

Digby lit a cigarette and leaned back. "I wouldn't touch that with a swab from Lambarene," he said. "I heard the petition was coming up, but I didn't realise it would be as poisonous as this . . . Still, what else can you expect from a man like Odhar?" He added with a trace of malice, "Anyone who would marry an old boiler like that would be capable of anything. I wonder if it's some type of sexual frustration, or even deviation, on his part?"

"You seem to know him pretty well."

"Perhaps that's why he doesn't like me."

In a Pavlovian reflex, Kimble was impelled to ask, "Why should that be?"

Digby surprisingly replied, "I asked him if he would represent my wife in our divorce action."

"Your wife? No-one in these parts knows you've got a wife. Why should that upset him anyway?"

Digby decided to ignore the second question. The fewer people who knew, the less likelihood of a mishap. "A youthful folly, chum. I'd gone abroad to get away from her, and some drunk cabled her the number of the flight I was coming home on, and she met me at the airport. She gave me such a heart-breaking tale that I married her with a special licence. She said she was pregnant to a married man who had gone back to his wife, that she had just been sacked, and that she was desperately ill. . . . The marriage lasted a fortnight."

"And you were such a gentlemanly twit you believed her?" Kimble was incredulous. "If all the people who think you're a hard bastard knew that, possibly they'd revise their opinion of you."

"Who cares now? They could have found out for themselves, but they decided to specialise in slander instead. Anyway, I came up to Scotland on a story a month ago and went to see her about arranging a divorce, and found her in bed with a cut-price wine salesman. Fortuitous, to say the least."

"It doesn't look as if Odhar has much of a case to defend."

Digby laughed. "I didn't tell him that she's supposed to be the guilty party. He thought it was me. I merely passed on the message from the trollop concerned. She had asked if I could find her an Edinburgh lawyer to cut down the expense. For old times' sake, as she put it, which automatically made me suspicious."

"Why pick on Odhar if you're suspicious?"

Digby's voice became remote. "Let's say I thought he needed the business after I heard he was reduced to scheming slimy petitions through the court."

"Slimy?" The ugly connotation of the word intensified the doubts already in Kimble's mind.

"Yes, slimy."

"Why do you think I was given the petition anyway?"

"Probably hoping you would publish it. If I were you, I'd go straight to the office lawyer, then straight into a bath."

"It's all right for you. You're four hundred miles from your news desk . . . that's if you even work through one. I've got to go back and convince that stupid bastard. . . ." Two hours later he was back in his office and the newsdesk man, who always conducted his business in a shout, shouted: "Careful? What do you mean: be careful? Who the hell are you to decide what I publish?"

He went on shouting. "I've had just about as much of you as I can stand. You're the fellow who caused all that trouble over the family picture I wanted taken at that falling chimney. You're a knocker, a filthy knocker; that's what you are. If I have any more trouble from you, I'll suspend you. I'll fire you. . . ."

The reporter said, "I think I should speak to the lawyer before I start writing. . . ."

"What do you mean: lawyer? Get down to that typewriter at once. I'll decide round here what's legal and what isn't. Sit down and write my story. The editor and I will decide what we'll publish and what we won't. You write the story or I'll get rid of you and spread the word round the other papers that you're no use."

The newsdesk man stopped shouting. Silence flooded back. The reporter sat down and put a top folio and three folio copies interleaved with carbon paper into his typewriter. He typed across the first sheet, "MUST—FOR LAWYER'S ATTENTION."

He began to write, "The Marquis of Strummet has brought an action against his wife, attempting to ban her from the family home at Strummet Castle, Drumshire. . . ." He translated the petition into English and assembled its facts in an order of decreasing importance. As he finished each sheet, the newsdesk man ripped the copy paper from the machine and took the top three copies. He did not see the fourth. When the article was complete, the newsdesk man hurried into the editor's room, pausing only to assume a boyish, devil-may-care smile and simultaneously score out the instruction to the lawyer with a 12B pencil, which obliterated all trace of the words.

"I've got a great story, chief. An exclusive that'll wipe the smile off the opposition's face. This'll pay back that thug Digby for his scoop. This is big stuff, chief."

He thrust the bundle of fawn copy paper at the editor. "Are you sure we can publish this?" the editor asked diffidently. "It looks highly actionable to me; too one-sided; too vicious; somehow not journalistically correct. Why don't you get her side of the story, before we decide what to do with it?" He wondered where on earth the newsdesk man got his archaic expressions.

"If we do that she might phone the *Tentacle*. We've published these petitions before; they're dead safe." He thumped his fist reassuringly on the editor's desk. "And they're g-r-e-a-t copy . . . stupendous . . . splendiferous. . . ." He added, "I think we should make it the splash."

*   *   *

"Hello. They've bitten, I think. I gave the petition to Kimble as arranged. He was speaking to that English reporter later . . . I don't know what he was doing there. How should I know. . . ? He did look dubious until the English chap told him something. . . . Yes, I'll buy a dozen copies of the first edition as soon as it's out tonight . . . Ha-ha. Yes, indeed. They should thank us for putting their circulation up. You're sure twelve copies will be enough?"

The editor was wearing his newest Savile Row, go-to-important-meetings suit. It was in grey mohair. His face was grey. He had been called to the court and icily told that he was guilty of contempt and was fined £27,000. There was no trial. He was indeed fortunate that he was not being sent to prison for a year, he was informed by the judges. . . . The editor stared at the newsdesk man. "You," he said in his neutral voice, "You are a balls-aching crud. You are the original pain up my tits. You are lower than the man who scrubs the snake's ballocks." His voice remained neutral. "I don't want to kill you: I want to maim you every day for ever. Come into my office. Bring your contract, and bring Kimble."

The newsdesk man said, "I hope you're not going to blame this on me. Kimble talked me into letting you see the story. I told him not to even commit it to paper, but he insisted. He told me he had talked it over with the office lawyer and claimed the lawyer said it was as safe as houses."

The editor moved behind the desk. He pointed a paper-knife at Kimble and said, "Kimble, before I tell you what the judge told me this morning, you tell me what you told him." He pointed the paper-knife at the newsdesk man.

"Before I tell you that, let me make one thing clear."

"By all means."

"This lying bastard should be strung up by the throat."

The newsdesk man screamed, "Don't you speak about me like that." He rounded on the editor. "You're not going to let him talk like that about his superiors? It's either him or me."

The editor ignored him. "Go on, Kimble."

"I told this fellow that it wasn't safe. I typed on top of my copy that it was a must for the lawyer."

"He's a liar. He typed nothing on top of his copy."

Kimble held out the fourth copy. "I took this extra black and kept it in case this happened. . . . It doesn't matter to me. I'm leaving anyway. This isn't journalism. This is the Keystone Cops. I'm going to join the *Tentacle*."

The editor said, "We could send this fellow to join the *Tentacle* instead, Kimble. Have you any newsdesk experience?"

"Has he?" Kimble did not even smile.

The editor appeared not to hear. He put down the paper-knife and enquiringly held out his hand to the newsdesk man. "Is that your contract?"

He took it. "Regard the world as a type of griddle," he said. "On to it fall big chestnuts and little chestnuts. When the griddle shakes, the big chestnuts stay on top, and the little chestnuts fall through."

He tore up the contract and threw the pieces on the floor. "You," he said in the same neutral voice, "are a little chestnut. Go away while I talk to my new man."

He told Kimble, "There is a newspaper apothegm which you would do well to remember. It states, 'Never kick the office cat: It may be editor tomorrow.' I should remember that, if I were you."

*　　*　　*

Basil Makebelieve tried to avoid showing the anxiety which was almost forcing him to scream. His small feet were moving incredibly fast as he made his way through the corridors of the Palace of Westminster to Tony Pleasance's office. To his horror, he had been informed by the Special Branch early that morning that private detectives were interviewing witnesses about his movements, both at

Strummet Castle and in London. They were employed by the Marquis of Strummet, he had been told by the hard-faced inspector who had called on him at his flat on the far side of Victoria Bridge. Their object seemed to be to obtain evidence that would show he had been committing adultery with the marchioness.

"It's so bizarre," he said to the Minister of Aggression. "Why should Bodkin want to pin me over his wife? Not physically but psychically, as it were. She's screwing half the regiment, according to Wherry. We had a very chilly interview."

"Can he prove anything?" Pleasance's voice and manner became formal and almost hostile.

"Is this a set question? Do you think I should see the Prime Minister?"

Pleasance said quickly, leaning over his desk, "Come now, Basil; little would be served by seeing the Prime Minister at this stage. He doesn't know about it officially."

"But unofficially?"

"You know the convention as well as I do. If you see the Prime Minister, you've got to tell him the truth. You can't leave him exposed in the House."

"And if the allegations are true: what then?"

"The point is: can Strummet prove them?"

Basil Makebelieve said, "I can swear on oath that I have never committed misconduct with the Marchioness of Strummet." He was adamant and slightly flushed.

"You look beady, Basil. What are you hiding?"

"I repeat: I have never committed misconduct with her."

Pleasance's face began to clear of doubt. "I think I get your drift. You mean: with *her*."

"Of course that's what I mean. We don't have to run about Westminster shouting what I have or have not done with anyone else."

"Why should he want to name you in the divorce then?"

"I don't know. He's cranky. He may be being bloody-minded."

"You don't think he found out we were tricking him over the use this new brigade was to be put to?" Pleasance's voice became urgent. He desperately wanted to put his hand in his pocket.

"Definitely not. There has been no leak-back of information, whatsoever, according to Wherry."

"Why else should he be jealous? There isn't someone else, Basil? Not another victim of your strange little whims?"

Basil exploded within. He thought it was as if he had been given a revelation. "Christ. . . ." He darted to his feet in anguish. "It was that filthy picture in the *Sunday Tentacle*. That bloody, two-timing, dealing-off-the-bottom toad, Acarid, trying to stir up trouble." He began to laugh, deciding to inject the correct note of desperation into the thin vocal sounds. "I've made Strummet jealous of his wife."

Pleasance looked at him without sympathy. "I think you'd better fly up there immediately. This morning, in fact, and sort the whole sordid affair out. You can take my heliplane. I'll buzz my p.a. to lay it on for you at once."

*   *   *

The green troop carrier sped through the village, the section of ten men upright in the back, with the muzzles of the new Stirling-Levi machine pistols level with their knees. Their helmets dwarfed their faces into shadowed ugliness. In the cab Lieut. Smith, seconded from the 1st Battalion to the 3rd, was seated beside the marchioness, chic in a quilted Strummet tartan jacket, with a tailored waist. From her zip toggle hung a silver replica of the regimental cap badge. Her slim-fitting jeans were also of tartan and she wore a green slouch hat, with a peregrine falcon feather secured to the felt by an unencircled Strummet Clan crest. Her face was excited. "Almost there," she whispered in Smith's ear. He was in a camouflage smock, and had shoved twigs into the netting over his helmet. He was nervous. Colonel Strachan had told him before they left, "I want you to exercise your discretion in this matter, Smith. Officially this is an exercise in entering and breaking into nuclear power plants and assault stations in enemy territory. You will obtain certain information which you will give to Lady Jayne who has kindly agreed to act as umpire. She will direct your movements and point out targets. It is very good of her to lend her services in this way." Colonel Strachan turned on his heel and walked into the ante-room of the mess. He drank a large whisky, and told the mess waiter to bring another one. Gerontian-ffylde was amused. "Don't smile, Puff," said the colonel. "If this is discovered, I'll be cashiered. I don't know where my loyalties are any more."

The games park was empty when the heliplane dropped swiftly from the grey sky on to the wind-bleached grass. Basil, in Devonshire tweeds and crocodile-skin chukka boots, walked daintily across the field. The castle door was bolted. Torquil slid from the archway leading to the stables, and said contemptuously, "They've gone that way." He jerked his thumb towards a dark spruce forest rising softly almost from the castle walls to the summit of Ben Odhar. "You'll find them on the second ride."

Basil thought he would be amusing. "Wasn't the first good enough?"

Torquil shrugged and started to walk away. He said over his shoulder, "A ride in the forest is a road left as a firebreak. It's an ancient word meaning boundary. You'll find them on the second roadway on the left. That's all." He drifted silently through the arch.

Before Basil had picked his way for a half-mile up the sloping forest road, he heard the shrill screams of pleasure, occasionally piercing the calm screen of evergreens. A roe deer, its sculptured ebony hoofs glittering in the sunlight, swirled across the ride in a profusion of fawn dapples, its white bobtail barrelling into the green darkness. He came to the corner of the second lateral ride. The ground fell away on the left, and there, he could see the marquis in riding breeches surrounded by the *au pair* girls, dressed in shorts and tight poplin shirts. They were giggling and gazing at a cariole, a two-wheeled light dog-cart, which was parked on the grassy ride. The marquis was cutting the air with a riding crop, and talking to Professor Knapbone. There was no pony.

"What ho, here's Basil."

"Could I speak to you, Bodkin, on a matter of some urgency."

"You mean about the divorce, presumably." The marquis

was quite disinterested. "And the unsavoury part you play in it, I suppose. Why did you do it to me, Basil?"

Professor Knapbone, scrawnier than ever, extended a polythene bag of peanuts. "Have some," he said. Bonhomie oozed militantly from him. "Do you like peanuts?"

"I think you're being most unfair."

"I don't think so: they're not from Uganda."

"If you play with fire you must expect to get your tiny pecker scorched."

"I suppose you're referring to that objectionable photograph in the *Tentacle*."

"Perhaps you mean the microphotographs of *aspergillus*. Very revelatory."

"Which one?"

"I'm terribly sorry about the effects. It was Acarid who deliberately tried to balls it up. We understand he's assembling a dirty file to drop before the next election. He's poisonous; he's a spider figure. He's trying to infect the country against us."

"Don't you mean inoculate? Try one of these: they're American."

Basil Makebelieve shouted at Knapbone, "For God's sake, take your bloody peanuts away. What the hell are you talking about?"

"I thought you were fond of sociologists?" The marquis linked arms with Professor Knapbone, whose face was flushed. "*I* certainly am: they've a lot to offer."

"So I see," Makebelieve hissed.

"There is no need to shout at me, minister," said Knapbone. "I was merely pointing out the hazards of eating Ugandese peanuts. My latest information is that they are infected with *aspergillus* which, as its name implies, is a mould. The peanuts become carcinogenic. In lay language, they promote cancer." He smiled shakily. "I always eat American peanuts nowadays. They're wholesome. . . . Won't you have one?"

Basil ate a peanut, his face white with anger. "When could I see you alone, Bodkin? A great deal depends on this."

"Is it safe?" The marquis had made a hellish simper, which gave his face the appearance of a Notre Dame gargoyle. "Is it safe to be alone with you? My lawyers say you would compromise me. Shall we see about it later? Knapbone and I are rather busy . . . unless you would care to join in?"

The troop carrier slewed through the gates of Strummet Castle, knocking a granite pediment from the gate post on to the scattering gravel, and its engine bellowing in effort, sped up the drive to the castle.

The marquis beckoned to the *au pair* girls who had fallen nervously back from the angry group, and stood in silence at the edge of the forest. They smiled and made indecisive movements forward. One of them bent down and picked up a pair of leather traces. Another lifted a padded collar which was lying on the mossy grass beside the cariole. Professor Knapbone's smile became toothy. "My investigations in the sauna bath have given rise to considerable thought on my *rôle* as a sociologist. I felt it incumbent upon me to research the integrals with which group activity combine to evoke a therapeutic and meaningful effect on narcissism and indeterminate work-tasks and aligned manifestations of pleasure."

Basil Makebelieve said in a surly voice, "You mean you like being thrashed."

"That is an over-simplification, quite common with lay-people. I mean the randomisation of experience must be supra-analysed at the grass roots." He removed his shirt and began to unbutton his trousers.

The marquis took the padded collar from one of the *au pair* girls.

"What Professor Knapbone is trying to say is that we're going to harness him into the cariole and the girls are going to whip him up and down the rides to see if exhaustion occurs before satiation . . . I got the idea from a friend of mine," he added. "Isn't that so, Knapbone?" He slipped the collar, upside down, over the sociologist's head, then spun it into the correct position.

Basil Makebelieve was curious. "Wasn't there a peer up here who used to do this sort of thing?"

"Yes, indeed. With his wife, or rather, his wife with him.

She used to harness him naked into a dog-cart and leather him up and down the estate rides. Demned appropriate, what? Rides? He got a divorce.''

"What for?"

"Cruelty, oddly enough."

The earth shuddered and a vast rush of air swept through the forest ride. Birds shrieked into a momentary silence. Booming and cracking the penetrative impact of an explosion sucked in the atmosphere, then in a blustering torrent of sound, burst over them like water crashing from a river dam.

The explosion caused the bottles and glasses to tremor on the bar of the Strummet Cave Hotel and Digby lifted his whisky. "There she blows," he remarked and swiftly finished it. "I'm sorry, I'll have to go up to the castle and see how it went."

"Wait a moment," said the proprietor, pouring another drink. "I've almost finished, and you're the only person who can help me now. I told you old Strummet was the feudal superior. But I didn't say what happened after they started to take out interim interdict to stop me selling drink because of the feu charter. Nothing else happened." The legal phrase held Digby's attention. "Because I know legal proceedings have started, it's all *sub judice* and I can't mention it in public, or even talk about it, I suppose, or I'm in contempt of court and could be sent to jail."

"Why should he want to stop you selling drink? I thought this was a tourist area. He hasn't got another hotel, has he?"

The owner poured himself a drink. "Not the marquis," he said. He was sad. "No, not the marquis. But his aunt owns the Strummet Arms."

Digby was astounded. "You mean the magistrates legally empower you to sell drink, and he rides roughshod over their wishes because his auntie owns the next hotel, which has a bar. Why don't they do *him* for contempt of court?"

"No one's thought of that. We're not much good at protesting up here."

"Take the old bastard to the Monopolies Commission. That would drag him into the twentieth century."

He drove up the castle drive and stopped at a safe distance from the troop carrier. He shouted to the guards,

"How's it going, mac?" They grinned and waved him onwards.

Through a cloud of dense black smoke, he could see that the massive door of the castle had buckled outwards and was hanging from a single hinge. Dead pigeons from the shattered chimney and ceremonial pikes lay scattered over the Great Hall. A boulder had fallen into the open fireplace, and the turbulence had carried miasmic dust over the tapestries and furniture. An excited voice rose. "Wadye-fuckenlookythathen," said Private McEntee. He was clearly impressed as he stepped over the bird carcases and the ancient weapons which the marquis claimed had been used by his ancestors to thrash his traditional apostate enemies, the Campbells, at the Second Battle of Inverlochy in 1645.

Private McEntee, of Irish-Catholic parents, was not aware of the religious significance of the shattered weapons. "Whit-dae-ye-think-y-that-bloody-jelly?" He tried to portray the depth of his emotions by separating each word. His eyes darted around the desolated hall. "A only useda haunfie." He held up his hand. In it was a lump of putty-like material, approximately half the size of a pullet's egg. He gestured at the wreckage. "Whaur's the fucken peteren?"

Lieut. Smith dusted down his camouflage smock and translated for the marchioness who was standing beside him, thrilled and rigidified by the devastation. "He is asking what you think of the power of the new explosive. He says he only used a handful. He is most impressed."

He turned to McEntee. "Hurry up now. Find the safe for Lady Jayne."

"Swhat a'm fucken asken you. Whaursapeter?"

"Call me sir, McEntee."

"Away or a'll fucken cawra feet frae ye. Whaursa peter. Ra safe, you daft bastard."

The day before Private McEntee had joined the Strummet Foot, he had been released from Perth Prison after serving seven years of a nine-year sentence for safe-blowing, losing a year's remission for attacking a warder with a sharpened cold chisel. This, the authorities decided, was caused by too authoritarian a regime for so many years, and they had begun to allow McEntee to train for freedom, working in a ship chandler's by day, living in a hostel, and breaking safes at night. When news of the reorganisation of the Strummet Foot seeped into the underworld, which is closely connected with the surface world of Glasgow, many thugs, including McEntee, decided to join the regiment to provide themselves with an excellent cover for criminal activities. Discipline, they were told, was slack, and a blind eye was turned to minor offences.

"Watch your language, McEntee. There's a lady present."

McEntee turned crimson and came to attention, a movement which he had cultivated after a study of war films shown on both TV and in the cinema. "Beg your pardon, Lady. A didnae see you there. A wantit to ken where the safe is." His voice was stilted. He added, "Sir."

"It's this way, darlings," cried the marchioness, directing the section of men towards the door leading to the turret. They charged up the worn stone stairs.

By the time that Lieut. Smith panted up to the turret room, McEntee was already examining the safe, which was concealed behind a bronze Buddha with the keyhole disguised and set in the navel of the statue. McEntee ordered the men, mostly experienced in the practice of safeblowing, to drag the immense circular divan over to the Buddha, while he packed plastic explosive into the metal navel. He located the reverse hinges and patted a knob of the explosive over a detonator and stuck one over each hinge. Then he taped a detonator over the keyhole and inserted a length of wire which he connected to a standard lamp.

The men discovered they could lift out only the table top of the divan and tilted it against the statue. Then they ripped down the long crimson velvet drapes from the slit-windows and muffled them over the safe. An interlocking pattern of chairs and tables jammed the upended divan-table against the statue. They finally dropped the circular mattress over the furniture and stressed their backs against it. McEntee grinned. "It'll drap aff, just fucken drap aff, A tell ye." He pressed the lamp switch.

The entire room moved and became wild. Disintegrating furniture burst across the room in a fusillade of violent splinters. There was a suck, a great tumult of air, and the men were lifted like babes and heaved against the walls. Feathers and swansdown from burst cushions rained over them. Someone flung on to his back screamed, "Christ It's comin' down. Watch your eyes."

Jagged frets appeared in a cobweb pattern over the circular ceiling mirror. It bellied out, in a grotesque swelling, then crashed down on the men. Above it, seeming to linger in space, the naked bodies of Cinnamon and Griselda were revealed, then they fell in a disembodied tangle of arms and fear-frozen legs into the wreckage of the mattress.

"The dirty bastards," said Private Neilly. He walked over to Cinnamon and kicked him in the groin. "Thae dirty bastards were havin' it aff an' watchin' us at the same time. I canny staun thae perverts. I've read about thae mirrors."

He was interrupted by the marchioness who straightened up from the aborted Buddha, its flacid belly gaping. She was radiant. "My darlings," she said mistily. "My very own darlings." She tore open a strong brown envelope marked Makebelieve. Inside was a selection of photographs, showing Basil and the marquis naked in the sauna bath, but while the naked marquis stood with his hands down by his sides, the Cabinet minister appeared to be touching his host's genitals. "What treasures," she breathed. "No court in the country would refuse me revenge now."

There was a rattle of small-arms fire below. Lieut. Smith screamed at his men and they swarmed downstairs, carrying the marchioness on their shoulders. They jumped into the troop carrier, where the guards self-consciously blew down their machine-pistol barrels, like cowboys after a cinema gunfight, and the carrier whirled round and disappeared down the drive.

"We thought they were coming at us," said the guards. Digby drove after them.

Far down the forest ride the marquis slashed at the naked shoulders of Professor Knapbone. "After them," he shouted. "You aren't going to let them get away, are you?"

"I think you'll have to abandon your experiment," Basil

Makebelieve said viciously. "Exhaustion and satiation appear to have arrived coincidentally." Professor Knapbone collapsed and lay on the mossy grass, twitching.

8

The meeting in the lawyer's office was short and ugly. Odhar's sibilant antagonism caused the Marquis of Strummet's lip to inflate, purple and obtuse, in a customary prelude to anger, as the spindly, crouch-backed lawyer extorted details of how the marchioness had absconded with the photographs.

Odhar was outraged. "You mean you allowed these photographs to actually show you in an indecent posture with Mr Makebelieve?"

"I don't know about indecency, what." The marquis made a weak attempt to gloss over the situation. "It was all quite clean, actually. . . . They were taken in a sauna bath."

Odhar asked chillingly, "You allowed your face to be exposed?"

"Not quite, I suppose. Cinnamon did try to shield my face." He grasped at the straw. "Would that make much difference: if my face couldn't be seen?"

"Not entirely, if it could be proved to be you by other means. We have seen several precedents to guide us in that eventuality."

"You mean, by. . . ."

"Yes, by measurements, perhaps, or by comparison with other physical attributes."

"I don't know if I like the sound of that."

"Come, come, my lord. Legal photographers are most discreet, quite impersonal."

"Perhaps you can see my face after all."

"What relationship in space does Mr Makebelieve then bear to you?"

"He is, ah . . ." The marquis looked temporarily shame-faced. ". . . facing me."

"At what distance?"

"About six inches."

"Almost touching, in fact?" Mr Odhar appeared revulsed. "This is monstrous."

"He only looks as if he's touching, dammit."

"You mean he's touching you?" Odhar's mouth screwed into a moue of distaste. "You mean that his hand was outstretched, touching you?"

"I don't see why you should be so bloody moral about it. It happens all the time in Edinburgh lavatories."

"Please let me get this clear in my mind. You and Makebelieve are facing each other at a distance of six inches. Your face is clearly visible, and he appears to be touching you. . . ." He said faintly, "Not in the region of your genitals, I trust?"

"No, not in the region of," snarled the marquis. "On them."

Mr Odhar crossed his office to a deed-box marked, "Earl of Keith, decd." He opened it and poured himself a stiff brandy. His voice was shaken. "I don't know what to say."

"Why the hell should you say anything? Why should you have the impertinence to be my moral censor?"

"Morals?" demanded Mr Odhar, as the brandy took effect. He poured another. "Who the hell is talking about morals? You've ruined our case."

"Pour me one, too."

Odhar ignored him. "Morals are the last thing I'm worried about." Eventually he gave the marquis a dribble of brandy in a toothglass which he found in the bottom of the deed-box. He said swiftly, "You'll still have to pay for all the precognitions. We've done 349 so far and 250 more are pending."

Odhar scarcely waited for the marquis to finish his brandy before seizing the glass and locking it back in the deed-box. He put on his black gaberdine overcoat and picked up his silver-handled umbrella. His manner was discourteous and cold. "I suppose your car is waiting. I want to see Mr McPhuig immediately." Odhar had the impertinence to walk in front of the marquis and get into the car first. Cinnamon remained in the driving seat, dressed in a kilt to cover the bandages where Private Neilly had kicked him. They drove along Queen Street and again turned down Dundas Street. McPhuig, his head bowed against the biting August wind, was struggling up the hill.

"There he is," said Odhar. He rapped on the glass partition with his umbrella and motioned to Cinnamon to swing the car round. "Walking up to Parliament House most likely. He must have some vacation business."

"Why doesn't he buy his own car?" The marquis felt the heavy smouldering taste of anger rise in his mouth at Odhar's presumption.

"Parking problems," intoned Odhar.

"Well, he can't be too poor to afford a bus?"

"You'd be surprised," replied the lawyer. He decided to let the marquis into one of the secrets of the profession. "It can be most impoverishing for a senior man like McPhuig. It's an ancient tradition, you see, like not shaking hands. The most senior advocate on the bus has to pay every other advocate's fare. It all mounts up; that's why so many walk. Even judges walk up the hill."

"Good god," exploded the marquis. "He must be extorting £30,000 a year from the Scottish public. He could afford to buy a bus . . . and what's so ancient about it anyway. . . ? He drew on his encyclopaedic and global knowledge of transport timetables. "The last tram ran up this street past the law courts on November the sixteenth, 1956. Buses followed."

"It began with tramcars," snapped Odhar.

"Cable cars only began on January the twenty-eighth, 1888," retorted the marquis, and felt his anger melt gloriously away before his impending victory. "It seems a pretty bogus tradition to me, like the rest of your rubbish.

I never consider a habit to become a tradition until it's at least five hundred years old."

Odhar's mouth was white at the corners. He ignored the marquis, and tapped on the car window to attract McPhuig's attention, and the advocate climbed into the back seat, his breath short and jerky. He did not shake hands, nor discuss the case. Cinnamon reversed into the traffic stream, which automatically made way for the Rolls-Royce, and they drove back to McPhuig's chambers.

Once they were inside, McPhuig said, "How pleasant to see you again, marquis. I believe Mr Odhar's staff has already precognosed three hundred and forty-nine recruits. We decided not to question the First Battalion. It must be quite a record. I'm sure you will be glad to know how avid everyone is to bring the case to court." His junior, Lorimer, came in silently, and the three legal heads went together. A discordant babble of voices rose. "All those precogs wasted . . . how can we keep it up now . . . can't condone this behaviour . . . diabolical to think of it all going down the drain . . . ten thousand off . . . we should drop him. . . ."

"I'm sorry if I've caused you extra work," shouted the marquis, his anger returning at being ignored.

"Not at all," said McPhuig smoothly, turning away from Odhar and Lorimer who went on whispering to each other. "It's all in an advocate's day. We always put service to our clients before our own interests and comfort. Let me explain. . . ."

Under cover of McPhuig's unctuous voice, Odhar hissed at Lorimer, "No chance of getting your brother to use his influence with the Minister and get the regiment flown abroad somewhere? We could all go out and precog. them in the sun for a change."

Lorimer hissed back, "Not a chance. The Secretary's out of his mind with rage. He's found out about the sauna bath. The reactionary old swine threatens to sack him."

"Why is he so upset? His morals can't be so strict as all that."

"It isn't his morals—he's jealous."

". . . it is an arduous and demanding life, made no less comfortable by the fact that we are constantly in public scrutiny living as we do in the New Town. But to your case . . . I think we are all agreed on the seriousness of the matter." The marquis looked abashed. "I don't see why you're all so worried."

"It's the marchioness," McPhuig said. "She's got the whip hand on you." The marquis stared at him suspiciously. Was the bastard having the impudence to make a fool of him? But McPhuig was unaware of any innuendo.

"And there's nothing we can do about this?"

"You can't raid her, if that's what you mean, or steal the photographs. Her solicitors probably have them in the strongroom by now."

"Is there nothing else we can do?"

"Fuck her," said McPhuig conversationally.

"I reciprocate entirely. I've been saying that for years."

McPhuig was outraged, presumably by the implication that he would use such a word vulgarly as a mere expletive. "I was offering you professional advice," he said stiffly. "I mean have sexual intercourse with her."

"With her?" The marquis was appalled. "Do I have to?"

"Yes, you will," said Lorimer. "You'll have to lay her so that she condones your conduct."

"But then I'll condone hers."

"We'll wriggle round that, dear boy, never fear," said Lorimer, in an access of familiarity. "Just you go and fuck her, if you're still capable that is . . . and don't forget the witnesses."

*　　*　　*

Angela Proof flashed through to the extension in Gerontian-ffylde's office. "It's Genital Jayne again," she said. Before she slammed down her receiver with the maximum impact so that she could temporarily deafen him, she added, "Do Chanel make a scent called Nymphomania, or do I merely imagine she exudes it?"

"Darling," said the marchioness. "Have you confirmed the bookings? Have you absolutely positively confirmed them? I refuse to travel British Airways despite what your department orders."

"My secretary has confirmed the flight at 1.40 tomorrow

morning. We are flying by independent airline."

It was the seventeenth time the conversation had taken place. He sounded jaded. He picked up his *sgian dhu*, the traditional stomach knife of the Highlands, which he had kept as a souvenir of his schoolboy holidays, and used as a paper knife. As her voice babbled on, he absently nicked his thumb along the grooves on the blunt edge of the blade, historically and deliberately notched to hold an enemy's blood which then coagulated and became toxic in time for the next victim. "Yes, Lady Jayne," he kept on saying.

"I've phoned Mr Aziz at the St Andrews. He's so sweet. He would do absolutely anything for me. We'll have such fun. I'm so glad it's a night flight."

"This"—he tried to stiffen the tone of the word—"*is* an official visit, Lady Jayne." He slid the tip of the *sgian dhu* into a manilla envelope and sliced it open.

"All work and no play makes Puff far from gay," she babbled. "Isn't that a delicious thought, darling. Not that I hope for a moment you are gay. You aren't like Basil are you?"

He thought he heard Angela Proof titter on the master receiver. He adopted his official manner. "I have just received a signal from Colonel Khan-Ali of the Defence Force. His car is meeting us at the airport."

"Don't you think we should be less formal? Stealing in and out like Arabs with their tents and all that? How else can we discover how they are raised? Perhaps we may discover an entirely new way to raise troops."

The marchioness had been so spectacularly successful in her kisses-for-recruits campaign that she had demanded to be allowed to undertake a fact-finding trip to assess the comparative values of other recruiting campaigns. "Kushta," she had snapped at the under-secretary who had questioned her on her intended itinerary, naming the small dependency lying between Pakistan and Iran, and stretching inland to the mountains of Afghanistan. The international set, tiring of Beirut and Corsica, had ostensibly allowed themselves to be persuaded to move to the dependency by certain Greek millionaires who had somehow acquired and transformed it into a sybaritic and exclusive holiday resort, which had become so successful that even the casino had begun to employ a Press officer.

"I want to see how the local levies are raised. I'm sure there must be a parallel somewhere between how they do it and how we do it." The under-secretary had been hideously embarrassed, but the marchioness appeared not to notice the ambiguous meaning of her remarks. "And I insist that Colonel Gerontian-ffylde accompanies me. He is indispensable to my plans and intended discoveries."

Tony Pleasance himself had given the news to Gerontian-ffylde, on the inter-office telephone. "I thought I would break it to you personally. I always like to let the chaps know the worst from me in person. I never like to shirk my responsibilities to the chaps. The marchioness insists that you go with her on some damn-fool fact-finding trip or other. She's been so successful we daren't refuse her. I'm afraid you'll have to accompany her as a chaperon. It's her rank in society, actually. You and I understand it and can cope with it, but the others . . . I hope you don't mind. I can't think why she insists on Kushta, but there it is. Get your secretary to book flights. Try to fly British Airways of course, in case the Press gets hold of it."

"Chaperon, indeed," Gerontian-ffylde said to Angela Proof. "I feel more like a procurer."

"Why not relent darling, and go as her pimp?"

He said nothing.

"Your plane leaves at 1.40, Colonel Gerontian-ffylde," she mimicked.

"I'm sorry, Angela. I shouldn't have been so rude, but how vicious can it get? She seems to be seducing the entire contents of two new battalions, and now she wants to start on me." He moodily poured a sherry for both of them. "Going off with a love-starved peeress to Kushta . . . I like Kushta. I don't want to go there and catch the clap."

"Didn't they have Jordan Highlanders or something around there once? She could always find out what they wear under their kilts."

"I think your memory is far too vivid, Angela. It must be months since I told you what happened in that tent. . . I only wish you were coming with me." She looked at him strangely, and finished her sherry.

He took the high-speed lift to the basement and after shuttling between floors fifteen and twenty-four for several minutes, escaped at the first floor, which he inexplicably reached, and walked down to the basement car park. He drove home silently and packed.

*   *   *

Monitored phone call 1640 3980:

"He's got plumbers ripping out all the lead piping in the castle. A great beaky man came down and took about a quart of Torquil's blood. The poor boy was grey for days afterwards. This one thinks he's got lead poisoning. It's something to do with the water supply being acid after it rains and making the lead soluble in the pipes."

"How's the marquis taking it?"

"He's poured about two hundred tons of lime into the reservoir. It's just like drinking water in Cheddar Gorge, all chalky. He's had to import bottles of water from Glasgow for his whisky."

"And Torquil?

"He's anaemic, poor thing. You'll have to hurry, by the way."

*   *   *

The super-jet, a crimson cockerel emblazoned on its tailplane, rose like an arrow fired from a god's bow, soaring into the sky and over France and Italy. At 20,000 feet, the dawn Mediterranean was a corrugated sheet of gun-metal. They began the descent into Kushta, where Col. Khan-Ali's limousine was waiting at the airport, and they drove to the St Andrews, facing the sea on the main boulevard.

Mr Abdul Aziz, the resident manager, was almost prostrate with delight. "Your favourite suite, your highness," he said, his slim face beaming, his hands weaving and interlacing, and occasionally brushing his luxuriant, full moustache. "Overlooking the yacht harbour and the bathing beach, of course. How very splendid to see you again. How entranced I am . . ." Graciously he turned to Gerontian-ffylde, somehow contriving not to show his back to the marchioness. "And you, lord, I have reserved the guest bedroom of the suite on the marchioness's orders." He seemed to wink, his eyelid dipping like a sea swallow. "You will have every comfort, my lord." He ushered them towards the lift. "Permit me to show you."

Through the archway leading to the marble-fitted bathroom was the guest bedroom, its door slatted to allow free movement of any breeze from the sea. To his dismay, Gerontian-ffylde discovered that, like most inter-connecting doors in Eastern hotels, it had no lock. There was another, more formal, door leading to the corridor.

"Do you like your room, darling?" Lady Jayne's voice carried clearly along the passage.

"We must be ready to leave at one o'clock." Gerontian-ffylde replied, as roughly as he dared. He wondered how he could jam the door shut. "Don't forget our appointment with Colonel Khan-Ali." He opened his document case to extract a courtesy letter to the colonel from the Minister of Aggression. His paper knife fell out. "Perfect," he said aloud. He rammed the *sgian dhu* between the door and its jamb, effectively securing it. "Not even a queen could force her way through that," he said aloud. "Of either sex." He pulled out the knife and put it back into his case.

The colonel's Daimler was waiting beneath the patio, and they drove at breakneck speed up the Kornet Gorge, between massive red and grey spurs of rock, which burst against the skyline like great sea breakers, to the télésiège under the mountains, where Colonel Khan-Ali's troops were taking part in a ski exercise. The small party rose even higher over the jagged rocks.

"It's awfully cold," said Lady Jayne. "I feel as if I'm turning blue."

"You are 8,000 feet up," said Colonel Khan-Ali, his eagle nose hooking from his bearded, warlike face. He was not at ease.

"I've never been as far up as that before," she said. She attempted to look provocative.

"I think you are blue." Gerontian-ffylde began to tire of the continual sexual allusions, which were clearly embarrassing the colonel.

"Even the trees are blue. What are those funny trees over there?" She pointed to the open grove of dark-green cedars, their massive fluted trunks as permanent and as restful as time.

"Those are the Cedars of the Lord," said Colonel Khan-Ali gravely. He still wore the old-fashioned twin-pointed beard. "They are three thousand years of age, a few even six thousand years old. They are older than the forests of Lebanon from the days when King Solomon commanded the people to hew him their trees for his great temple."

"How frightfully phallic," said Lady Jayne brightly. "I think I feel randy."

Colonel Khan-Ali's face discoloured with mortification at hearing a woman speak about male sexual parts. Gerontian-ffylde caught his eye and attempted to convey his apologies and sympathy without speaking. Stiffly the colonel escorted them to the car and walked away as soon as courtesy permitted.

They hurtled down the gorge towards the coast. "You aren't being very friendly," the marchioness said. "You've hardly spoken a word to me." She snuggled beside him and asked him to light a cigarette for her. "I think you should take me to dinner tonight. I think we should go to that funny restaurant place at Bulbul Rocks. I love to hear the sea, calling softly as I eat . . . I love sea food, too. It has the most disastrous effect on me." She cupped her hands to shield his lighter flame and her fore-finger somehow scratched the palm of his hand. She looked at him intently. "Then we have all night to talk about raising things."

They were into the city, driving between the rows of shanties, knocked together from flattened four-gallon petrol cans. "What dreadful houses," she said. "Do people actually stay there? They make me feel quite grubby just looking at them. I must bathe as soon as I get in."

He heard her singing in the marble bathroom, the notes bouncing off the gold-leaf cupids and angels decorating the frieze. He discovered that he loathed her. The noise cloaked his movements as he took out his *sgian dhu* and jammed it into the door. He tugged the door handle. It did not budge. He went deeper into his document case and pulled out a bottle of blended malt whisky. As he was pouring himself a drink, he heard water swirling and gurgling, and realised she was out of the bath. There was a rustle of silk and a familiar, musky scent at his door.

"Puff, darling." Her voice was enticing.

"I'm very busy."

"Be a darling and zip me up." He felt the door shake.

"I don't think I should. Ring for room service."

"They might send a waiter."

"Ask for a lady's maid." Her weight was against the door, steadily. He could feel his flesh prickle.

"I don't think you're being very flattering."

"I'm tired. I want to have a quick kip."

"Can I come in and tuck you up?" She began flinging herself at the door. "Don't be mean, darling. Let me in." Her fists were banging on the slats. The knife was vibrating, its black haft the epitome of treachery.

He heard himself say, "If you don't go away I think I'm going to cut your fucking throat."

"Darling, how exciting." Her voice was shrill, with uncontrolled darting overtones. The door was shuddering. "I'm dying for you. I want you. I'm melting for you."

In a sudden craziness he wrenched the black knife out with his right hand and sprang back straddle-footed, the knife tip outstretched at belly level as she plunged through the door. His eyes were glazed with hatred, his elbows and forearms turned out in a primeval fighting stance. She screamed and went on screaming in fear as his arm came up in a killing sweep to rip her open from her crutch to her breastbone, in the Highland method.

Digby opened the corridor door and said, "I can see it now: 'Peeress dies in sex-city knife fight.' What a headline."

Gerontian-ffylde jerked back as if he had been slashed with a whip. Through his mind swept a kaleidoscopic series of pictures of headlines, scandals, broken homes, Angela Proof. He was too enraged to restrain his violence. Uncontrollably he switched the knife into his left hand and punched the marchioness across her left jawbone. She was lifted from her feet and skidded backwards along the tiled corridor to the bathroom. The door cracked with the impact and she slid to the floor, her legs crumpling like paper curving.

Before he could turn, Digby had locked his left wrist and wrenched his hand inwards. Gerontian-ffylde shrieked in agony. The knife dropped to the floor and Digby kicked it under the bed. The shriek released Gerontian-ffylde from his blood-trance.

"I think we need a drink," he said. He attempted to speak lightly, but his voice was uncontrollably undulating. "Let's go down to the bar for a drink."

"If you say so." Digby handed him his jacket.

Gerontian-ffylde's hands were shaking with the release from tension. He began to snarl in reaction, "What the hell are you doing here? Now what, Digby?" He came fully to his senses. "For Christ's sake, Digby, how did you get out here? What are you up to now?" He shook him by the arm. "You're not going to report on this, are you?"

Together they walked along the corridor. Digby pushed him past the lift. "Discretion," he said. "I came out on the same plane as the marquis. I gather he's on his way up to screw her for reasons best known to himself. Someone else wants to see you, too."

As they disappeared down the staircase, the lift door opened and Mr Aziz stood, his hands fluttering in desolation. "Are you sure her ladyship is expecting you, Lord Strummet?" He tried to restrain the marquis, dressed in a fawn linen suit and carrying a gold-topped ebony cane.

"Out of my way, you little wog." The marquis thrust his cane into Mr Aziz's stomach. "Out of my way—and send a lackey up with champagne in an hour. And some brandy," he added loudly. "And send another of your lackeys up to mix the drinks. On the hour, you understand?"

He shepherded Mr Aziz back into the lift, pressing the "down" button, and as the manager sank from sight, his voice still echoing from the lift shaft, the marquis raised his long head and stared down the corridor. With precise steps he arrived at the marchioness's door and barged in. She was still lying at the bathroom door, her peignoir open and her legs sprawled woodenly apart. The mark on her jaw was already rising into a livid crescent, with four definite welts where Gerontian-ffylde's knuckles had caught her.

In a semi-coma she whispered, "Darling, how wonderful . . . what wonderful violence . . ." Her head was lolling as he dragged her towards the bedroom, the peignoir bunching under her shoulders and acting as a silken toboggan. Fastidiously the marquis removed his clothes and threw them on the floor. He slipped her left foot under her right ankle and used it as a lever to jerk her face-down. Astride her he grasped her by the waist and flopped her on to the bed. Her legs came up and he again levered her round, made sure her peignoir was open, and crawled on to the bed beside her and settled back, naked, to wait.

Exactly an hour later, the discreet tapping at the door disturbed her. Hazily she looked round. She burst out, "Bodkin. You haven't . . . not when I was unconscious . . . my lawyer warned me . . ."

The door opened and two Lebanese waiters pushed a chromium-plated trolley into the room. On it sat an ice-bucket containing a bottle of champagne. Behind them a camera flash-gun whitely blinded the room.

The marchioness rushed from the bed, the waiters and photographer fleeing before her, and seized the champagne bottle. Screaming like an alley cat she hit the marquis on the head with the concave butt, the cork detonating off and a curtain of wine foaming from the neck. "You swine, you treacherous swine," she shrieked. Frothing champagne intermingled with the blood running down the marquis's forehead. He nodded his head. "Worth it," he mumbled. "Every drop was worth it." He struggled into his clothes and stumbled down to the bar.

"And if you think I was going to let you spend a few nights in Kushta with that tart," said Angela Proof, "you are gravely mistaken." She picked up her purse. "I'm sure Digby won't mind if we vanish. I told him on the way out what I was going to do, and he agreed. I've booked a double room for us in the Salamander and we're going to stay there until it's time to leave. And I'm not going to take my eyes off you for a second. Someone has to protect your honour, or what's left of it."

Gerontian-ffylde was still dazed. He allowed Angela Proof to lead him out. As he was going through the bar door, the marquis came in.

Gerontian-ffylde, still unsteady, said, "Good evening, sir."

"I know you," said the marquis. "You're the Army fellow. I meant to tell you something . . . Yes, that's it. I remember it now. Haw, haw. I buggered your second cousin Bertie in a shell hole at Tobruk, haw, haw, haw."

Digby gazed at him with revulsion.

"Ah, the gutter Press," said the marquis.

"I find that only guttersnipes use that expression." Digby turned coldly away and ordered a John Collins. To upstage the marquis, he spoke in Arabic to the Persian barman.

The marquis trumpeted, "How dare you speak to me like that. Don't you know who you are speaking to, you . . . you . . . impertinent . . ." The marquis's upper lips swelled and became empurpled, giving him the look of a bursting rubber balloon. He could no longer control his sentences.

Digby looked over his shoulder. He said, "Yes, you're the fellow with the johnny-come-lately title." He added, "Your face is swelling up."

The marquis could barely speak. "You wretch . . . you objectio . . ." He made gobbling sounds. "How dare . . ."

Digby said, "I dare for the very simple reason that I dislike people who usurp privilege behind the protection of phoney titles."

"I can trace my ancestors back to Bannockburn," shrieked the marquis.

"I know you can." Digby's unexpected answer silenced the marquis. "I know exactly that you can. Your lot was pimping for the Duke of Atholl's ancestors, weren't they? Wasn't that when the Atholls and your lot waited till the Scots army was fighting for its life, then crept in at their backs like jackals to loot the supply camp?"

Furiously the marquis retorted, "How would a guttersnipe reporter know about that?"

"Tut, tut," said Digby. "My ancestor was at Bannockburn, too, you know."

"Your ancestor? Probably some nasty little camp follower."

"He was commander of the Scottish mounted axemen, actually . . . ." Digby was staring oddly at the marquis. "You know, the man that routed the English archers . . ."

He stood erect, staring at the marquis as if he was a backward child to whom he was explaining a problem. He was suddenly aware of the past and very proud of it. Unwittingly his left foot began to arch away from his ankle, as if a type of genetic message had been transmitted to it. He was pointing like a hound. The Persian barman, in the spherical silence, was gazing at him in a rapt pleasure, the glass in his left hand forgotten and the brilliant white towel in his right suspended like a starter's flag. Digby's voice altered. "It was my ancestor who broke them and turned the English flank and began the rout. He fought his way to King Edward's side and seized his bridle to unhorse him and capture the sovereign of England . . . and ten of your filthy turncoats attacked him from behind." Digby put down his glass as if he had a sudden distaste for alcohol. "He killed them in single combat, all of them . . . For his exploits, King Robert Bruce made him Great Officer of Scotland on the battlefield, a title which our family bore honourably until 1715 when they were attainted for proclaiming a Stuart King, not because they loved Stuarts or papism, but to defend their country against the excesses of Calvinism which you lot introduced to get the pickings from the Catholics. They went away then, because they could not bear to see what your kind had done to their beloved."

Digby's face had become hard, his cheek bones pronounced and a faint flush mantling them. "You had your title by then, hadn't you? With your original name reflecting your calling. The first Earl of Strumpet, chief pimp to King James II and procurer to the Royal Court."

He said to the barman, "Give this fellow a drink. I think he needs one."

He began to walk from the bar. The marquis's voice screamed after him, "I'll ruin you. I'll write to your proprietor. I'll finish you."

Digby rounded on him. "O, shut up, or I'll write an accurate history of Scotland and you'll be executed for treason." He felt slightly better after his outburst. He pushed through the gilt and white enamel doors and went down to the casino for a drink. The Press officer used to work with him on the *Tentacle*. Charlie would buy him one, he thought.

9

It was an enterprising September. An international medical team from the World Health Organisation landed on the moon and declared there was no hazard from silicosis. A medinaut named More extracted a tin of Earth dust from his space-suit and wrote on it, "Dust from moon". He was quoted as saying, "This stuff's still worth 11,000 dollars a pound at Berkeley." A counter-statement from the Astrologer Royal, Edinburgh, denounced the team for sensationalism, mis-reporting, and tarnishing the scientific image by recalling the scientific fact that dust was previously believed to have covered the moon to a depth of eight feet. The breakaway State of Sibergolia initiated a series of nuclear tests which Western observers claimed were intended to alter the course of the Gulf Stream, diverting the warm currents by underground tunnel to Lake Oz Baikal, bringing to the new capital, Irkutsk, a sub-tropical climate. Britain, Russia and China entered a tri-partite agreement, denouncing the avant-garde socialism of emergent and immature states, pledging non-aggressive and mutual force to overcome hazards to world peace. The Americans installed a lady quadroon in the Brown House, recently renamed to reduce inter-racial hostility, which the Russians subsequently claimed was a blatant resurgence of American Nazism. South Africa went on to the Gold Standard. In Scotland,

Seumas McPratt won the premier piping awards at Oban and Inverness, and was hailed by a leader page article in the *Scots Sentinel* as "the greatest piper since the MacCrimmons".

Other events took place. It was briefly reported that the Strummet Foot lost two men in grenade explosions. Mr Duncan Habib Strumpet arrived, with his family, in Edinburgh to lay rightful claim to the Strummet titles and chiefship. And the Marquis of Strummet was asked to call unostentatiously at the Chromatic Club on the 17th at three p.m.

Lord Strummet threaded his way through the leather smell and must of the Chromatic Club smoking room. Isolated patches of members stirred beneath newspapers in the uncertain yellow light. The meeting was meant to appear accidental.

"I'm so glad you could come, Lord Strummet," said Tony Pleasance, half-hidden in the depths of a cavernous arm-chair, paired in seclusion with another chair, purposely placed side-by-side for the marquis, and separated by a low occasional table on which was placed a decanter of port and glasses. "I appreciate how busy you must be . . . I never did have the opportunity of thanking you in person for that delightful week-end in your home."

"If you think I'm going to let that slimy toad Makebelieve off the hook, you're mistaken." The marquis saw no reason for equivocation.

Pleasance decided to give the impression of being frank. "It had occurred to us that we should enter a plea of mercy to you. Not for Makebelieve; not on his behalf, I assure you." He raised his glass and gazed intently through the faint limning of deep umber which embraced the crimson lambency of the port. He said, with ministerial resonance, as if it was the implacable word of God, "I do hope this port isn't going off. It seems somewhat discoloured."

The marquis said, "What an astonishing thing to say."

"That we should be so lenient? I fear not, marquis. If Makebelieve can not behave like a gentleman"—he smiled inclusively towards the marquis—"he must be treated in a fitting manner."

The marquis held up his own glass for scrutiny to the dim light percolating through the leaded windows. "Goddammit, man, it's perfect."

"Our revenge, you mean?" asked Pleasance, without turning his head. "We do have means of subjugating people like Basil. I think we may pass him over in the next Cabinet reshuffle, or offer him a job so far beneath even his meagre talents that he will be forced to refuse it."

"I hope you aren't counting on me to help you out in your bloody manoeuvring?" The marquis had decided to investigate the possible reward for co-operation.

Tony Pleasance sat forward, half turning towards the marquis who lay flattened and almost lost in the shell of the armchair. "I know I can speak in confidence, sir. I have already discussed the matter with the Prime Minister. There was no other course; we must always keep the leader informed of the peccadilloes of his team, no matter how unpleasant the telling may be. The Prime Minister took it well: Makebelieve broke down under the questioning and confessed to certain *things*,"—he dwelt on the implications of the word—"but he was adamant that he had not committed misconduct with your wife. The Prime Minister knows all about the unsavoury episode, however, and is most perturbed. Not for the sake of the party, but for the sake of the country, which is of paramount importance at this juncture in world affairs."

The Minister of Aggression smiled slightly, as if he was in perfect control of the interview. "He did not ask me to approach you, you understand. As gentlemen we can understand his position in the matter. He did not so much as hint that a meeting was desirable, but I received the impression, the distinct impression, that if you drop Makebelieve from the case and leave him to us to discipline, we should not be unappreciative."

"Poisonous little man . . ." The marquis was deep in thought. "Go on Pleasance. What have you got to offer? What's the bait?"

All that Pleasance could see was the silvery top of the marquis's head, rising like a rounded hill crest through morning mist. He moistened his lips. He said, "Could we discuss that after we discuss the Strummet Foot?"

The marquis lunged upwards. He said viciously, "Under no circumstances will anyone who has so disgraced my tartan go unpunished. My clan tartan is sacred and must be unsullied. They aren't real Highlanders anyway, those riff-raff and gutter scum you dredged up for the second and third battalions. Or rather that she recruited with her bloody mouth open and her tongue halfway down their throats. Or wherever it was."

"But, marquis, these are the men who were to be the spearhead of the new Army."

"They shouldn't have spearheaded my wife. Damn every one of them. I'm tired of being cuckolded by that slut. This time I'm going to have my own revenge. Having my wife poked by a pack of half-Irish gangsters, indeed." He banged his glass on the table and indicated that Pleasance should refill it. "Having them in the regiment was bad enough. Having them through my wife was intolerable."

Tony Pleasance became ugly. "I understood there were difficulties about calling these men in the divorce. I heard from a certain source there had been some measure of condonation."

The marquis was furious. "Who told you that?" A first tendril of colour suffused his cheek. "I demand to know. Who was the bastard who's been spying and gossiping about me?"

"I merely heard this from a source. For that reason alone, provided we can muzzle the Press, we are not so worried about the eventual outcome of this chapter of the case. If you even hint that our information is correct it will suffice. What we are worried about is Makebelieve. The inexcusable trouble about Makebelieve is that he was not brought up to respect a gentlemanly code of conduct." Again he smiled inclusively at the marquis. "We all know about people like that. But his fall could have serious repercussions on the Government, and although we are man enough to accept that eventuality without fear or recriminations"—his elongated tongue brushed over his crimson lips once more and he discovered he was sweating—"we are perturbed about the effects this would have on the well-being of the world . . ." His voice became pleading. "Is there no way in which we can come to some agreement?"

"I suppose there are one or two things I could do with."
The marquis realised that Pleasance was in no position to
refuse him anything within reason. He idly wondered what
would give him most pleasure. He was immensely rich; he
had no need for further honours; his life was singularly
barren since his potency had almost failed. "I did have a
little trouble with work permits for my *au pair* girls." He was
tentative. "Do you think," he asked, "I could have them
renewed? You know the sauna bath has had to be closed?"

"O my god, marquis, even with Makebelieve involved,
it's out of the question. The Church of Scotland has been
talking about the morals of Parliament and the aristocracy
again. I think they may even press for another Royal
Commission."

"Pity about Makebelieve," said the marquis. "Pity he's
going to cost you so many seats. I suppose it will lose you
the election."

"Why don't you confound them?" Pleasance decided it
was time to reveal his final and strongest lure. "I could
arrange it so you could take in refugees. What about forty
Laotian schoolgirls? The Church wouldn't dare criticise you
over them, for fear of counter-charges of bigotry. The girls
are all Catholics."

"Schoolgirls?" The marquis's fingers curled around the
stem of his glass, which Pleasance hurriedly refilled. "You
mean I could get forty schoolgirls?" His voice thickened. He
began to salivate. "All in gym tunics and those tight blue
knickers with elastic round the legs?" He pulled himself from
his armchair. "You can forget bloody Makebelieve," he said.
"Excuse me." He disappeared towards the lavatory.

*   *   *

Three weeks before the divorce action was to be called at
Glasgow, the new battalions of the Strummet Foot were lying
at their barracks at Malvaig, rejoicing in the regimental
traditions of Christian tolerance and brotherly love.

The 3rd Battalion (Lady Jayne's Own), recruited mainly
from the Catholic areas of Glasgow, was allocated the East,
or Claverhouse Block, named after the Scottish General who

had hunted down, tortured and murdered the Protestant Covenanters, with the aid of the Strummet Foot.

The 2nd Battalion (The Derry Mutineers), drawn from the Bridgeton and other Protestant districts of the city, was allocated the West, or Culloden Block. This was named after the last battle fought on British soil, and commemorated the glorious role of the Foot in executing and often incinerating Catholic Jacobite fugitives from the battlefield, under the general command of the Duke of Cumberland, and also marked the regiment's subsequent skill in the official campaign of rape, fire and looting in designated Highland glens. For its loyalty, the Foot had been granted the unique honour of carrying "Culloden" on its colours, a distinction surprisingly declined by every other formation which fought there on the Government side.

On the north of the square stood the Headquarters, or Sheriffmuir Block, in which was normally quartered the 1st Battalion. The block stood as empty as the original battlefield (where both sides ran away in the transitional period between Papacy and Presbyterianism) for the entire battalion had unaccountably been sent on so-called embarkation leave in a mysterious signal signed by the Minister of Aggression himself.

Perhaps the boredom of country life had contributed to the sporadic outbreaks of barrackroom violence, for only the previous evening, a 3rd Battalion sentry had been found unconscious with a capital C for Culloden ripped open on both cheeks. Later that night, Private McEntee left a symbolic bottle of orange squash in a Culloden sentry box in retaliation. When the sentry unscrewed the cap, it blew off his right hand. Apart from a shout of "Away ye Orange bastard," no evidence was found, and none was forthcoming, because Army regulations did not permit payment for information.

Colonel Strachan was speaking to Major John Drob, of the Judge Advocate General's office, about the difficulties of combatting criminals with outmoded legal procedures, when Lieut. Rossetti marched into the battalion office and saluted. "Third Battalion ready for inspection, sir," he said, barely unclenching his teeth.

The 3rd Battalion (Lady Jayne's Own) had paraded in

their new black and yellow kilts, but had decided that morning to appear with emerald green hackles, replacing the blue bonnet plumes of the original regiment. This was in revenge against the 2nd Battalion who had retained the blue hackles, which to them had a Protestant and Orange symbolism, but had also insisted on the right of their battalion commander to inspect them on a white horse, out of deference to King William of Orange, who had, according to legend, led an army of Dutchmen to victory against an army of Jacobite French at the Battle of the Boyne in Ireland, so impressing the free world in 1690 that the Pope of the day had ordered a peal of bells to be rung in thanksgiving and praise in the churches of Paris.

Colonel Strachan listened as Lieut. Rossetti outlined the latest affront to regimental tradition. He turned to Lorimer, the Minister for Internal Security (Scotland). "Quite frankly, Lorimer, I don't see the reason for this nonsense. I can't see furthermore why we should have to put up with such tripe. This is a Highland regiment, not a rag-taggle of Dutch and French-Irish tinkers."

Lorimer went white. "Don't ever say that, colonel," he breathed. "Don't let any of these men even hear you saying that, I implore you. This latest sociological experiment has worked so well. All this nonsense, as you put it, was the basis for all the trouble in Glasgow. One of our dynamic new psychiatrists has come up with the theory that a trigger-excuse, as he puts it, was all that that was needed to set off these men into unrestrainable violence. The religious feelings of these men had so often been fanned to fever pitch by the accentuated difference between the religions and by certain football teams which were surrogate influences, that once we removed the ring-leaders, violence came to an end. Or almost. Protestant and Catholic strife was rooted in the unrest."

"Don't be so damned stupid, man," snapped Colonel Strachan. "If the Pope's a Catholic, why did he order the bells of Paris to be rung for a Protestant?"

"I don't know. I haven't had the time to go into it. All I know is that the Press is off my back, and that since we have these six hundred or so men out of the city, violence has almost vanished and Glasgow is almost possible to live in. Apart from the slums, of course, but we hope to have those cleared in the next fifty years."

"I still don't know." Colonel Strachan could barely understand the psychiatric jargon. "I only know I've the highest crime rate in the British Army. I don't even know if this latest scheme will work with these hoodlums."

"I'm sure your manner will carry it off perfectly, colonel." Lorimer handed him the envelope. "Be as tough as you like in this. You have our full support."

"I still don't see it." Colonel Strachan was distinctly nervous. "I don't see how the Official Secrets Act can be used for such a purpose."

Lorimer buttoned up his black vicuna overcoat and put on his hat. "It is simply being done in the best interests of national security and to retain confidence in the integrity of the armed forces. I also have a confidential message from interested parties which may help to influence your feelings." He had become covert. "Your promotion to brigadier will be through any day now. . . ."

There was a polite cough, virtually a clearing of the throat, behind them. "I'm coming, Rossetti," snarled Colonel Strachan, appalled by Lorimer's insult. He picked up his cane, and the small party left the office and walked across the square to a wooden podium, which had been equipped with a microphone. Far across the loch, the standard of the Marquis of Strummet was being run up on the castle tower.

"Men of the 3rd Battalion The Strummet Foot." The colonel's voice boomed over the parade ground. "This is your first C.O.'s parade since your battalion has been brought up to strength as the spearhead of the new Army. It is a proud and illustrious moment in the annals of our regiment, once the private property of our Colonel-in-chief . . ."—he paused while the sergeants growled up and down the ranks like terriers, and a customary cheer, ragged and disinterested, rose at the mention of the founder of the regiment—". . . that we should be in the forefront of the newest battle in these days of approaching peril."

In a practised movement, he hunched his shoulders forward and smiled in a spirit of comradeship. "But we're all soldiers together. We face danger without flinching and fear, and we take our pleasures in the same way." The men began to smirk self-consciously. Private McEntee said out of the side of his mouth, "You'd think he'd been hangin' outy her an a'." Colonel Strachan's voice changed yet again. He became harsh. "But if any man here thinks that his pleasure or his behaviour is going to place the name of my regiment in jeopardy, he is mistaken. He is vastly mistaken. While you have been settling in, I have been lenient with you. These days are now over. For this reason I am going to read you the Official Secrets Act. When you joined the colours of this regiment, you swore yourself to secrecy under the Act, and over the conduct and activities of this regiment, and over revealing any information which would be of comfort or aid to an enemy."

His hawk nose was white along the cartilage in an assumed fury. "If news of your activities are ever revealed outside these barracks, I shall have you brought up in front of me on a charge under the Act." He leaned towards them and pulled a copy of the Act from the envelope which Lorimer had handed to him. He read it out in a terrible voice.

"I'll see that the men responsible—and I'll pick every tenth man until you break and confess—are court-martialled and found guilty, and there won't be much doubt of that, and I'll see that these men are sent, not to one of your cushy civilian jails like Peterhead or Barlinnie, but to a military prison for thirty years." He repeated in a loud, icy voice, "For thirty years—at least. And there will be no remission, and no review of sentences, and I can say that, backed by the highest authority of Government—so don't go writing to your smelly MPs . . . that's if you even know how to write, or who they are."

The men stood in shocked silence, McEntee was suddenly incapable of speech. A sudden squall of wind caught the colonel's words and they echoed off the pink sandstone. "Thirty years . . . I'll make sure none of you are out for thirty years."

Expressionlessly Lieut. Rossetti handed him another, longer envelope. "I have here a list of the men who are accused of committing adultery with the Marchioness of Strummet. All the men concerned have been precognosed. I have asked Major Drob of the Judge Advocate General's office to take care of your legal rights, which as far as I am concerned are nil. . . ." He barked, "Regimental foot-major."

The regimental foot-major screamed, "All men who have been precognosed three paces forward MAAARRch."

As a man, the battalion slammed three paces forward, leaving behind a sprinkling of N.C.O.s, scattered over the parade ground. "Dismiss the N.C.O.s, regimental foot-major," Colonel Strachan ordered. "It's damned well seen they all came from the 1st Battalion."

The foot-sergeants, corporal-majors and lance-footmen pivoted right and marched off.

"Major Drob will now address you." Colonel Strachan moved to one side and allowed Drob to take the microphone.

Drob's legal voice emanated thinly from him, seeming to be drawn from the depths of his highly-polished brown boots, and spiralled upwards through his thin neck, corded with anxiety, and eventually making contact with the outer air in a squeaky resonance. He introduced himself and opened the envelope which Colonel Strachan passed to him and pulled out the closed record of the divorce. "*In causa* the most honourable Bodkin Stuquely Vane Strummet, Marquis of Strummet. . . ."

"Excuse me," Colonel Strachan said and pulled the microphone from the military lawyer. He shouted into the microphone, "If one word of this reaches the Press, I'll personally flay the man responsible. I'll lash the skin off his back. . . . If you've any questions when Major Drob has finished speaking, don't ask them. If any man dares to open his mouth, I'll give him eighty-four days for being idle on parade to start with."

Drob began again, "*In causa*. . . ."

As he spoke, the first green balloon-shaped object floated around the corner of Culloden block and hovered over the parade ground. Another and yet another of the green balloons, shaped like sausages and seemingly not quite inflated at one end, drifted around the end of the barrack block, and the prevailing wind carried them over the heads of Lady Jayne's Own. The ritual chant of the 2nd Battalion began. ". . . cha, cha, cha." A piper struck up

"The Battle of the Boyne" somewhere high in the block, and on the faint breeze, the voices of the Derry Mutineers sounded over the barracks:

"O my faither was a Derryman
  In the bygone days of yore,
  And hail or rain
  We're up our Jayne
  For she's a Papish whore. . . ."

There was an ominous swelling in the ranks as the contraceptives dyed green in a final insult to Roman Catholics and the Pope's continued ban on contraception, eddied over their heads, almost in time to the obscene singing. The sergeants were needling and hissing at the men, vainly attempting to instil order into the bulging ranks.

"That will be all." Colonel Strachan was enraged. "Dismiss them." He knew he would never be able to discover the identities of the men responsible. There was a ferocious scream from the regimental foot-major and the battalion moved off the parade ground and rounded the Culloden block. A grenade swept in a deadly parabola upwards and through the open window of the barrack room where the singing had begun.

The grenade, in a brown plastic casing, was fused for only four seconds, and as it rolled almost to the edge of a barracks bed it erupted, fragmenting through the air at waist-height like a horizontal hail of scalpels. Eight Derry Mutineers were seriously wounded, two in the groin.

The next morning, the 3rd Battalion was sent on a toughening exercise to Dunstrummet, alternately running and marching the seventeen miles, carrying laser-ray weapons and generators. They were exhausted by the time they had doubled back over the hilly lochside road, and stumbled to their barrack block. The first man to pull the chain in the third cubicle of the first-floor lavatory detonated another grenade. His trunk and head were blown through the washroom window. The remains of his body had to be flushed out with a hose. The Derry Mutineers' voices rose outside the washroom window in a different chant:

"He wasnae Sammy Hall, Sammy Hall.
He wasnae Sammy Hall, Sammy Hall.

Sammy Hall, he had wan ball:
This wan had nane at all.
He wasnae Sammy Hall, Sammy Hall."
Meanwhile the 2nd Battalion had also received their instructions about the divorce hearing.

"Is that you, Mr Digby?"

"Who's that?" Digby had come north to write preliminary articles on the divorce hearing.

"It's Big Bad Jock. Listen, I've got a great story for ye. I'll meet ye in the Portobello." McEntee named an exclusive restaurant in the centre of Glasgow. "It's like this," he said when he met Digby. "They've named every fucken wan of us in the divorce, see. Every man that's recruited to the new brigade."

"Is that all?"

"As God is my witness," said McEntee. He crossed himself. "What's it worth then? I'm on the run. I need the money bad."

"I know all about it. Nothing else to tell me?"

"They read us the Official Secrets Act and said we'd get thirty years if we tellt the Press. What a fucken laugh."

"The crafty swine," said Digby. "So that's how they're going to do it? It isn't you they're after. It's us. They'll have a D-notice out tomorrow."

"Whatdyamean? A dee notice? Whatsathen?"

"It's what the Government uses to keep the newspaper boys quiet. If they issue a D-notice on the Strummet Foot, it means we can't print anything about them because the regiment's gone on the secret list. . . . And the bloody divorce is gonty start next week. . . ." Digby, to his embarrassment, found himself slipping into Glasgow speech patterns to make his meaning clearer. ". . . It's like a censor, see?"

"A censer?" McEntee brightened as the opportunity presented itself to reveal his sophisticated humour. "A ken whit a censer is. It's whit a homosexual priest carries instead o' a handbag. Haw, haw. Get it? Get it like?"

The mock-Georgian room was cleared for the confidential report from Horton Pond, given by the director, a cavernous-faced man who was tall and had a haunted look. "I shall try to speak as non-scientifically as possible."

Tony Pleasance said pontifically, "I think you will find that Mr Makebelieve and myself are capable of understanding anything you say. Go through it first, then we'll put questions to you on the military and policy aspects."

To Pleasance's horror, the scientist then took out a series of black and white orbs from a long wooden box and began to assemble them into the three-dimensional shape of a molecule of deoxyribonucleic acid. "These will serve to demonstrate what I mean," said Dr Dregs, as he deftly pushed the helices into shape. "As you know much work has been done on unravelling the genetic code which is carried on the genes, themselves carried on the chromosomes. We have progressed to the state where we understand the code but we don't know what it is saying." Basil Makebelieve winced and floated a little grated nutmeg on to his warm milk. He sipped it, added a sprinkling more of the hallucinogenic powder and returned his silver nutmeg grater to his green velvet waistcoat. "What we do know now is that the key to 5-hydroxytryptamine production, and thus depression, is carried on chromosome twenty-one, which is of course an autosome, quite distinct from the sex chromosomes. We discovered this astounding—and I use the word as a scientist who is the only person possibly capable of comprehending the full implication of the word— astounding fact due to studying the effects of nerve gas OZ3 on mice and rats, and later, dogs and horses. At first we thought the gas had a similar effect to nitrous oxide or laughing gas, as the lay public have familiarly called it for some years, in that the experimental animals became contented and incapable of being irritated. We first tried to irritate them using normal methods like thirty continual hours on the treadmill and so on, giving electric shock in the case of failure. Later we introduced physical sensation by stimulating them with laboratory tools. . . ."

"Such as?" asked Basil Makebelieve, sipping his milk.

"First, we dropped varying strengths of acid on exposed skin, squeezing limbs in tweezers, the usual sort of thing . . . does that answer your query? Further examination by microscopy—through a microscope, you know—revealed subtle differences between them and control animals, or those that were left, and we discovered that a highly powerful piece of molecular engineering had been achieved and, shall I say, accomplished." He proudly touched the helices at two points. "These become transposed and the ribonucleic acid which is released is mutated. We are very excited about this. In simple terms, we have achieved a breakthrough."

Tony Pleasance said, "I don't understand a bloody word you've gabbled. How can you understand a code when you don't know what it means? I did get the bit about torturing animals though." He rifled through his papers, and looked across the table to Basil Makebelieve for support.

The Minister for Redeployment looked bland. "At the risk of sounding unfeeling and pompous, Tony, it's crystal clear. Dr Dregs has given a most lucid account of his work." His voice was serpent-smooth. "He is saying they have found a means of making sad rats happy."

"Rats? Happy? God in heaven I'm looking for a weapon to subdue about a hundred million Mongolians, not cheer up a few rats."

"Perhaps I have not proceeded far enough with my explanation, Minister." Dr Dregs opened his briefcase and brought out an aerosol can, no larger than a tin of hair lacquer. "If you sprayed this over a battalion of troops, the contents would instantly remove their aggression *in toto*, they would fall into a deep sleep, and when they awoke, they would be incapable of fighting. According to our work on experimental animals and fishes, which can be extremely savage, they would find the idea of aggression ludicrous. They would simply laugh at the prospect of attacking an enemy."

"You mentioned fish." Makebelieve made a thoughtful bow of his mouth. "Could this be used in water supplies?"

"If you bombed, if that is the correct word, the water supplies of an enemy nation, achieving a concentration of one part per billion billion—British billions, of course—you would be given a hero's welcome when you marched in. They would . . ." Dr Dregs coughed and an uneasy flush drifted into the caverns of his face "embrace you."

"But you can't be sure of this?"

"Not until we have tested it on experimental humans. This is where we need your official blessing."

"But why should depression be the key condition?"

"Depression and aggression are inextricably linked. This is the latest theory."

Pleasance and Makebelieve stared at each other for a few seconds. As usual the Minister of Redeployment was first. "I think that will be all, Dr Dregs. Please leave your models. I would like to study them at greater length."

The scientist was led out. Pleasance wet his lips and they glowed crimson. "The Strummet Foot," he murmured. "We wouldn't want the Strummet Foot any longer . . . or ever again." He removed his hand from his jacket pocket.

Basil tinkled with laughter. "And how, pray, are you going to disband them without looking a total fool? Or do I need ask?"

The Minister of Aggression knitted his fingers together and sighted down the notch made by his knuckles. He knew he was perfectly safe. His micro-engineers had tested the room for listening devices that afternoon. No indiscretions could possibly be recorded and used elsewhere. "Bang, bang," he said, getting Basil Makebelieve in his sights. "Bang, bang, you're dead."

Mr Duncan Habib Strumpet sat in the office of Sir Toby Braxfield, the genealogist, who was a descendant of the 18th century judge, Lord Braxfield. Sir Toby was attempting to explain the laws of inheritance in Scotland to the new clan chief.

"It is very complex. I suppose I am in a way fitted to advise you about this incredibly technical poser because my ancestor was a famous judge, you know. A man of unimpeachable moral and physical qualities. He left his mark on the Scottish bench; his resoluteness in putting down crime was a joy to behold. We could do with more of it nowadays. There was a fellow appeared before him for stealing a sheep or something like that and had the infernal impertinence to talk back. 'Ye wad be nane the waur o' a guid hanging,' said my ancestor. 'So ye'll be hangit.'"

He noticed Mr Habib Strumpet's blank stare and translated. "He said the felon would be none the worse of a good hanging so he would be hanged. . . . It became quite a byword in the courts. Life was cheap in those days, thank God. In those days the judges could drink hard, too. They used to sit with a decanter of port on the Bench, as they dealt with the criminals. The sessions went on so long on one occasion the decanter had to be refilled four times. Wonder they could see by the time the court rose, it was so dark."

He continued reflectively, "There are uninformed people nowadays who say that Braxfield was too stern; even try to make the monstrous suggestion that he was corrupt, but the way he dealt with the treason trials would have gladdened the heart of any man with his heart in the right place. The Jeffreys of Scotland he was called. He was a contemporary of Henry Dundas, you know, possibly the finest man to emerge from Scotland. He was the man who put into effect the policies of Pitt and really helped to make Scotland a part of Britain, by taking the rough edges off our national character and moulding us closer to the English desire. His stamp is alive on the Scottish bench today. Dundas was Pitt's man in Scotland as Lord Advocate, you know, and controlled the Bench by nominating the men he thought most suitable for the job. Still does, as a matter of fact."

Duncan Habib Strumpet was mystified. "What about judicial qualities? Aren't they the attributes which most fit a man for the Bench?"

"Are you daring to murmur a judge? It's a serious offence in Scotland, I'll have you know. Our judiciary are the finest in the world. Not, for example, like the tawdry American system, where they elect their judges in a piece of blatant political opportunism. Ours, as I say, are appointed by the Lord Advocate, who is appointed by the Government of the day, and a damned good system it is.

"When one party is in power, they appoint their nominee: when the Opposition gets into power, they elect their man. All the men who have been of political service to the party are considered; lawyers who have fought election campaigns and even got into the House, although there are very few who are actually elected, oddly enough. For some reason the electorate can't seem to appreciate their qualities."

Mr Habib Strumpet said, "Does this mean that, say, an MP who was a lawyer could be made a judge for political services?"

"Certainly. But they assuredly do not elect politicians to undertake judicial duties."

"But how is your system different from the American system?"

"As I say, over here, they are not elected. They are appointed and this is done in a civilised and refined manner, apart and away from the hurly-burly. Most of the time the Lord Advocate appoints himself. . . . It causes less bickering that way, you know. And they can't be got out again, not without a great deal of fuss and bother. That's what makes it so democratic. We have an equal balance of parties on the Bench. Except for the Scottish Nationalists, of course. No one could contemplate one of those in a position of authority."

"You aren't on the Pill, my dear?" Knapbone drew back in horror, his Adam's apple rising and falling furiously in an index of alarm. "Don't you know what it does to you?"

Angela Proof looked sceptical. "I know all that stuff about thrombosis and so on. The possibility of an accident is so rare that it's almost non-existent."

"It isn't that," said Knapbone in anguish. "It isn't that at all. It's one of Nature's biggest practical jokes. Tests on monkeys, fleas and humans have shown that it causes excessive production of mono-amine oxidase in the female, leading to clinical depression and loss of libido."

Angela Proof said, "I'm afraid I don't understand what you're talking about, professor. I've already told you Mr Gerontian-ffylde is still in Scotland. And I think your questions are more than somewhat personal, I may add."

"Please, please," begged Professor Knapbone, "understand me. The pill that was to prevent the effects of copulation actually removes the urge to copulate. Eventually you wouldn't need to take the pill because there would be no need to. It makes you frigid."

McPhuig asked the marquis, "Did you bring back the negatives all right? I take it you've also got the names and addresses of the witnesses?"

"I've got them in my notebook." The marquis produced a diary, with a gold, locking clasp. To make conversation, he added, "I saw that fellow Gerontian-ffylde out there, you know. I used to be friendly with his second cousin Bertie."

"You what?" McPhuig and Odhar snapped at him in unison.

"I was friendly with his cousin. . . ."

"Never mind him. What was this fellow Gerontian-ffylde doing there? He wasn't staying in the same hotel as your wife, was he?"

"He was, I suppose. Come to think of it, he must have been staying in the next room until that girl came to take him away."

"What girl?" The marquis explained as far as he was capable. "I don't see why you're so worried about him. He didn't have time to do anything."

They looked at him pityingly. "You leave it to us," said Lorimer, as if he was speaking to a mental defective. "Just you leave it to us."

Next day he appeared in front of the bench. "Permission to open the record, my lord."

"What again? You've been into this record so often you'd think it was a lucky dip."

Gerontian-ffylde's copy of the closed record was served on him by two messengers-at-arms. Pasted on the back was a printed notice which read:

Form of intimation to alleged adulterer (not being a co-defender) in action of divorce or separation.

To Alain Seymour Grant Gerontian-ffylde, of Breacogle Castle, Scotland: Take notice that in an action, a copy of the amended closed record in which is prefixed hereto, you are alleged to have committed adultery with the defender on the occasions therein specified, and that, if advised, you may, within fourteen days from the date of service hereof, apply to the Court for leave to appear as a party in order to dispute the truth of the averments made against you.

Details were added about staying in the next room to the marchioness in Kushta.

Gerontian-ffylde thought it was a lot of dangerous rubbish. He showed it to Digby and asked his advice. The reporter looked drawn. "I think you should see the marchioness's lawyers," he said.

10

A brilliant blare of E flat trumpets preceded Lord Divot to the bench, and the radiant, if piercing, sound soared over the heads of the spectators jammed into the public seats of No. 1 Court in the scabrous High Court buildings in Glasgow, and shattered on the walls, dappled with starling droppings.

Lord Divot was angry. He had just received a ruling from the Secretary of State for Scottish Affairs about his position in the hierarchy of the Scottish judges. His was a new appointment: the first Divorce Court judge appointed in Scotland, and his selection was even a departure from the traditional method of selecting judges, in that the Establishment had yielded to the constant and noisy harangue from solicitors to elect one of their professional brothers to the Bench, instead of drawing on the pool of advocates who had performed high and unusual political service to the country. He had also fought a by-election, losing what had been formerly a safe Government seat by 8,340 votes to 45,753.

The fanfare, played by two Co-operative milkmen especially brought from Edinburgh for the ritual occasion, died completely away and Lord Divot scowled at the stream of pink-faced advocates filing in front of him, papers quivering in their hands, and mouthing their lines about clients they had never met and hoped they never would, opening and closing records, inserting pleadings and inter-locutors and other pathological acts in the pantomime of law.

Lord Divot tapped his fingers impatiently on the mahogany bench. The communication had informed him that, in precedence, he was to walk behind even the First Division judges in the processions to and from the law courts in the capital, who in turn walked behind the Second Division judges, who in their turn were forced to walk behind the Land Court judge, a hierarchical arrangement which had caused much resentment and even grief in the past.

He hunched his peach silken robes, embroidered with a crimson double cross, around his massive shoulders, and glowered. Lord Divot, who had taken his title from his name, in the common practice of Scottish law lords, curiously resembled the object to which the ancient Doric word referred: sod. He ·was a hairy man, with root-like tendrils appearing all over his face, and had often been mistaken for a market gardener, although not in court. He was also a realist, brought about by years of association, in his Sheriff Court practice, with criminals and hoodlums, with whom the lawyers had come to live in a form of symbiosis since the passing of the Legal Aid Act. Even when a local newspaper had unfortunately put out a street bill on his appointment which had unhappily read, "Reason for Divorced Judge", he had applied realism to his predicament.

Legal wits had recalled the drunken law lord who had been asked in the court lavatory if he intended to take action against a vulgar newspaper which had greeted his appointment with a bill stating, "New Sottish Judge". The new law lord had buttoned up his fly and replied, "I think I'll just sit tight."

When Lord Divot, who, like so many of his legal colleagues, had some pretensions as a rhymester, had been asked what his action would be, he had replied well up to standard, if mysteriously,

"Sticks and stones
   May break my bones
   But broken homes
   Will feed me."

Now his fingers were curled around the closed record of the Strummet case, of which he had dreamed for several months. He was also engaged in writing a pamphlet with the leader of the Right Wing renascent Tory Party in the city, intending to expose the malefaction of government, coupled with the corruption of the aristocratic classes, setting out the thesis that only rigid personal conduct and morals could save the country, which would be better under even the Labour Party, than the present decadent lot, but better still under the puritanical New Conservatives.

Dimly he heard the clerk, in his batwing black cloak and horsehair wig, call the case. Boxes and bales of legal papers and documents overflowed from the table in the court well on to the floor between the advocates' feet as they primped and preened their wigs and chattered vivaciously before their audience.

Then the usher's shout echoed into the corridor and was taken up by other booming voices, and the public address system: "Call the Marquis of Str . . . u . . . mm . . et." It was the first time the marquis had appeared as the pursuer in a divorce case, although he had already been through one divorce and had a vague idea of the form. He took the oath and stood in the glass-fronted witness box.

"Are you the Marquis of Strummet?" McPhuig was grave. The marquis stared back at him in bewilderment.

"Of course I am." The bizarre legal formula groped forward and ascertained that the marquis had been born in Scotland and lived there, had married there and was entitled to seek a divorce there.

"You have lived with your wife for the past three years?"

"Until I put her out," corrected the marquis.

"Answer yes or no please."

"How can I answer yes or no to that question?"

"My lord, this is the form we request our answers in."

"But I'd commit perjury if I answered yes or no to that question. We've been over that before."

McPhuig was scandalised. Lord Divot craned forward and appeared to have heard. "Are you suggesting you have arranged your evidence with my learned friend?"

McPhuig was signalling mutely, his eyes straining from his head, pleading for a denial.

The marquis said, "No, I do not."

"My lord," prompted Lord Divot.

"Yes. What is it?"

"I mean you address me as my lord when you speak to me." Lord Divot's temper grew worse. He rocked on his chair, furiously, back and forth.

McPhuig asked, "Did you notice anything strange about your wife's behaviour?"

"Yes, she was a nymphomaniac."

The court stirred as Lady Jayne's senior counsel, Mr Crook, flung himself to his feet, protesting.

The judge's fingers twitched. "Objection sustained," he intoned.

"Did you notice any specific instance, any specific behaviour which puzzled you?"

"Yes, she fainted. She used to faint."

"When did this take place?"

"Whenever she saw a man's private parts, provided they were big enough."

"How do you know this?"

"She saw mine, you know." Lord Divot smiled grimly behind his hand.

"But you implied plural parts. More than one man I take it, unless . . ?" McPhuig paused proudly for his first big laugh. The court laughed.

"She spoke about events before we were married."

"Explain what happened to the court."

"She used to tell me, 'I've never seen such a big one in my life. It was so big I fainted.'"

"What happened next?"

"She claimed that when she was unconscious, or had swooned, as she put it, the man took advantage of her and had intercourse with her."

"Did you find this true in your personal experience?"

"Only in part. She fainted but she came to in a bit of a hurry."

"Why was this?"

"I gathered she was enjoying it."

Laughter burst over the court. Lord Divot rapped his hammer on the bench. The clerk and the usher shouted for silence. Two Italian reporters and one American feature writer walked out and went to telephone from the basement Press room.

"So the faint was merely a front on her part?"

"Undoubtedly. She knew perfectly well what she was doing. She used to wriggle."

"When next did she faint to your knowledge?"

"After we were married."

McPhuig hurried on. "Tell the court, please."

"She told me that she had met a television scriptwriter. She said that he was getting on and that she took pity on him."

"Getting on?"

"I mean in years."

"What did you infer from this behaviour?"

"I inferred nothing. She said that out of pity she told him he had the biggest penis she had ever seen, and pretended to faint."

"And they had sexual intercourse?"

"Yes, as far as he was capable."

"What happened next?"

"She told me it was a temporary and single aberration when she had been drunk, and I forgave her."

"You have a forgiving nature?"

"I think so, yes."

"When next did you notice anything curious about her behaviour?"

"When she was adopted as the mascot for my regiment."

"Tell the court what transpired."

"I told her that if she brought disgrace on the family name I would divorce her."

"What was the cause of this scene?"

"When I saw her photograph in the paper with . . ."

McPhuig realised he had been asking about the wrong photograph. Instantly he snapped, "This was after she had started the recruiting campaign?"

The marquis was puzzled at first. "Yes. . . ." Then he remembered the agreement about Basil Makebelieve. ". . . ah, yes. When she took part in that dreadful riot in Glasgow."

"What did you find out?"

"According to the newspaper she had suffered from a

series of fainting fits during the recruiting campaign."

McPhuig turned to Lord Divot and said, "Number one thousand and forty-one in the process, my lord." The usher shuffled forward and handed a copy of the *Sunday Tentacle* up to the judge. McPhuig asked the marquis, "What did you do?"

"I immediately contacted my lawyers."

"Why?"

"I knew that she had been committing adultery with whoever was present when she had fainted."

"Who were these people?"

"Every man she recruited to my regiment, dammit."

"Was this confirmed?"

"My lawyers told me every man admitted . . ." Mr Crook was on his feet, gesticulating.

Lord Divot droned, "Objection sustained."

McPhuig went on in triumph. "Have you ever seen your wife since this episode?"

"Yes, I saw her in a hotel at Kushta."

"Why did you go there?"

"I heard she was there and I flew out to plead with her to abandon her habits and agree to a quiet divorce for the good of the family name."

"What was her reaction?"

"She threw me out of her room."

"Have you seen her since?"

"Not until she appeared in the courtroom today." He bared his teeth at Lady Jayne, who sat on the bench behind her counsel and lawyers.

"That is all, my lord."

Mr Sholto Crook, QC, senior counsel for the marchioness, got to his feet and stared at the marquis for several moments. Despite his immense knowledge of law, Mr Crook had an undistinguished appearance, apart from a long, pocked nose which resembled a wedge of lung tissue. He paced towards the marquis, his black gown like an approaching limp banner of doom, until his nose was within a few inches of the marquis's face. He squinted at him.

"Do you drink heavily?" he suddenly asked.

"No, I do not."

"Never suffer from alcoholic hallucinations?"

"How dare you."

"Answer yes or no."

"No."

"Are you fond of gardening?"

This sudden switch in questioning, accompanied by the hypnotic fear evoked by his nose, was extremely disconcerting, and a device which he invariably used.

The marquis was quite off balance. "Moderately," he mumbled.

"Have you ever gardened at midnight?"

"At midnight?"   ·

"With a felling axe?" Crook's voice rose to a clarion shout, determined to prove that the marquis's aristocratic background did not intimidate him. "Gardening amidst the rhododendrons at midnight with a felling axe while the ancient retainer holds up a lanthorn?" He paused, then shouted triumphantly, "Well, did you?"

The marquis stared back at him, mottle-faced.

"Well, your lordship? Well? Come man, answer me." Crook's revolting nose was almost pressed against the marquis's face.

Again the marquis recovered himself. "I don't quite understand the relevancy of the question."

"Do you still insist you don't drink heavily? Perhaps you can't remember?"

"I have a perfect memory."

"When you first discovered my client's unfortunate affliction of fainting I think you said you were not married to her at the time?"

"I was not."

"Were you married at the time?"

"Yes."

"But not to my client?"

"No."

"So you committed adultery with her?"

"If you care to put it like that."

"So you stand there as a self-confessed person of low morals? An adulterer?"

"If you care to put it like that."

"How else can I put it?"

"She was committing adultery too, you know." The spectators tittered.

"Has your wife ever made love to anyone else with your consent and connivance?"

"Certainly not."

"Yet you admitted she had made love to a television scriptwriter with your consent."

"I certainly did not."

"You gave consent?"

"I did not assent."

"But you approved of it. You told my learned friend that you approved of her behaviour."

"I said I forgave her."

"So you condoned her behaviour. Have you ever given your approval to other men having affairs with your wife?"

"I have never given my wife approval."

"Have you ever heard of a man called Gerontian-ffylde?"

"Yes."

"Did you make a certain suggestion to him in a night club in Kushta?"

"I did not."

"Did you mention buggery to him?"

"Certainly not."

"Did you indicate that you were . . . how can I put it . . . not averse to such behaviour?"

"I did not."

"Were you drunk at the time?"

"I had been drinking, but I was not drunk."

"Celebrating?" Crook's voice was inconsequential.

"In a way, I suppose." The marquis was glad of the human respite.

"You mean you were celebrating being thrown out of your wife's room after you had flown thousands of miles to implore her to accede to a quiet divorce?" His voice rose. "You were celebrating?"

"No, I. . . ."

"Perhaps you can't remember again."

"I can." The marquis's face was suffused. His heart was racing alarmingly. He knew that the question of which he had been warned was due at any time.

"What took place in your wife's room?"

"I felt sleepy so I lay down on the bed beside her."

"Did she protest?"

"She was asleep."

"Had she fainted by any chance?"

"I, uh. . . ."

"What happened next?"

"I ordered champagne to be sent up to her room. Two waiters arrived with it."

"Did they find you in bed together?"

"Yes, I suppose they did?"

"I put it to you: you had intercourse with your wife on that night in Kushta."

"I did not." The marquis's blood pressure began to go down and his face developed an expression of injured innocence. "I promise you I did not."

"I put it to you that you further encouraged your wife to consort with other men for reasons best known to yourself."

"I have not. I emphatically deny that."

Crook's nose was upturned and probing. In the Press bench Digby thought he could even see a faint blob of moisture hanging from a gaping nostril. "I put it to you that you have adopted a policy of encouraging your wife to sleep with other men while you busied yourself with your own pursuits."

McPhuig shouted across the well of the court, "Don't answer that question. I protest most strongly. I must ask you to order counsel for the defender to refrain from these questions and statements."

High above the court, Lord Divot grunted in assent.

In a flurry of black robes, Crook wheeled round to the judge. "I have no more questions," he said contemptuously. He moved across to his bench and sat beside Whimbrel, his junior. "Always give that dramatic effect, my boy, when ending your examination in Glasgow. It's the sort of law these people appreciate. What a pity we weren't appearing before a jury." He made it sound like an act in a vaudeville show.

McPhuig had begun the delicate task of re-examining his client, in the legal fiction that he could prop up the wreckage of his character, ruined deliberately by Crook.

"Have you ever at any time made an indecent suggestion

to Mr Gerontian-ffylde in a night club in Kushta?"

"Never." The marquis's voice was firm. He breathed out. At least McPhuig had the wit to realise the remark had not been made in a night club. He was being perfectly truthful.

"Are you a keen amateur botanist?" McPhuig began to probe skilfully.

"Yes, I am."

"What do you specialise in?"

"Rhododendrons."

"Have you ever invited fellow botanists to stay?"

"Yes."

"Have you ever perhaps tried to cut a rare rhododendron bloom to show a fellow botanist late in the evening?"

"Yes, I have."

"What cutting instrument did you use?"

"The only instrument I could find was an axe," replied the marquis gratefully. "Everything else was locked up, and we were in the midst of a technical discussion about the dehiscent fruits which formed part of the polycarp . . ."

"Yes, yes . . . ," McPhuig soothed the marquis. "Have you at any time indicated to your wife that she should have physical contact with anyone else?"

"Never," said the marquis in a loud and fearless voice, as previously instructed. "Never on my honour as a gentleman."

The next witness was Col. Strachan.

"You accompanied the defender on a recruiting campaign in the West of Scotland?"

"I did."

"Did you discover anything strange had been happening?"

"Yes, the marchioness had been having fainting fits."

"Did you discover any reason for this?"

"The faints seemed to coincide with the number of recruits she obtained for the regiment."

"How did she interview these recruits?"

"In a closed tent. She insisted on privacy."

"What was her function?"

"She was to give a kiss to every man who joined the regiment."

"In privacy? Didn't you think the insistence on privacy was strange?"

"I am a soldier. I do not think about things like that."

"When the men appeared after she had fainted, how did they look?"

"Hot and bothered would describe it."

"Did you ever look inside the tent when she was inside with the privates . . . ?" McPhuig slurred the final word. He looked prurient.

"How dare you make such an insinuation." Colonel Strachan's face was creased in anger.

"Do not raise your voice to me. Answer the question."

"I am not in the habit of peering into women's quarters. Nor of answering obscene questions."

"I am merely testing your veracity as a witness."

"Nonsense. You are being obscene."

McPhuig turned to Lord Divot. "Really, my lord, this is too much. Would you be kind enough to instruct the witness?"

"You must answer counsel's questions," said Lord Divot. "There is undoubtedly a reason for them."

"But must I answer questions which are offensive, degrading, obscene and pointless?"

Lord Divot tapped on his bench. "Mr McPhuig, I repeat, has his reasons, and they are undoubtedly clear to the legal mind. Please do not cause offence in this court or I shall hold you in contempt."

"No more questions," said Mr McPhuig, and sat down.

In a reciprocal movement, Mr Crook rose.

"Did you ever have reason to believe that my client acted in anything but a correct way with your recruits?"

"No, sir."

"What did you put these fainting fits down to?"

"I did mention the possibility of her tent needing more ventilation."

"How long was each recruit in the tent?"

"A minute or so. A very few minutes at most."

"Why should the recruits have looked, I think you said, hot and bothered?"

"I think most men would feel acutely uncomfortable if a titled lady fainted in a tent beside them . . ."

There was a stir as the usher took a folded document from the doorkeeper of the court. Crook halted his questions. The usher walked across the well of the court and handed the document to the clerk. Counsel and spectators watched intently as the clerk unfolded the document and passed it up to Lord Divot. He read it and scribbled a short message and pushed it back to the clerk, who handed it back to the usher. Gravely the usher crossed the court. Spectators craned forward. Lord Divot sat stone-faced. The usher whispered in the doorkeeper's ear, "Woodentop wants egg and chips for his dinner." He handed the menu back to the doorman, who disappeared.

"No more questions," said Crook.

"Dominic Ignatius Eugene Gregory Knapbone, raise your right hand."

"I wish to affirm to telling the truth, my lord. I do not wish to take the oath on the Bible. I am no longer a Christian." Professor Knapbone was permitted to say that he would tell the truth.

"You are a sociologist?"

"Yes."

"But you have other qualifications. State them, please."

"I am medically qualified and I also have a doctorate of medicine."

"Would you explain the difference?"

"I scarcely see the relevance but the word 'doctor' is a courtesy title in most cases, and most doctors aren't doctors. They rarely hold the qualification which entitles them to be called doctor."

"What would you call them?"

"I would call most of them a . . ." Knapbone halted and peered at the counsel. "Physicians," he said tartly.

"So you are well qualified?"

"Yes, I suppose I am."

"But you are a sociologist?"

"Yes, I found it a more fruitful field, especially in giving social diagnoses on my colleagues."

"How many degrees do you hold?"

"M.B., Ch.B., Doctor of Medicine, Diploma in Psychological Medicine, Doctor of Philosophy for my thesis on psychological manifestations of anti-social traits in psychiatrists."

"Yes, yes . . . You are licensed to practise medicine?"

"Yes, I am."

"Were you at any time asked to examine the defender?"

"I was."

"What was the result of your examination?"

"I cannot tell you."

"But you must tell me."

"But I can not."

Lord Divot leaned forward. "I require you to tell the court. You can not shelter behind this ridiculous doctor-patient relationship you claim exists."

"How can I tell you if I did not perform an examination?" Professor Knapbone was firm, as if speaking to a child. "She refused a physical examination, or an electrocephalograph, and I was unable to take a blood sample for our latest psychiatric assay tests."

McPhuig, still flushed, was cautious. "Did you come to any conclusion regarding the defender?"

"Yes, of course. Why didn't you ask sooner? I came to the conclusion after observing her behaviour intimately over a period that she was suffering from a transient fugue state, even global amnesia, further complicated by an overlay of mild nymphomania of some standing, which itself was further overlaid by feelings of inadequacy and guilt."

McPhuig was visibly shaken. Professor Knapbone *was* a witness for the marquis. He began to worry about the consequent legal implications. "I trust you are not saying she was insane?"

"Oh no, she was as normal as you are."

McPhuig looked discomfited. He plucked the lapels of his gown and held them rigid over his heavy-set belly. "How could these symptoms manifest themselves?"

"She might want sexual intercourse and be unable to remember it. Alternatively she might give the appearance of fainting and then having sexual intercourse without appearing to notice."

"Would you say that, if she was reported to have fainted, she might have been having sexual intercourse with the person she was with when she fainted?"

"You shouldn't ask me that question." Knapbone's mouth snapped shut in disapproval. His shoulders were set aggressively forward.

"I shouldn't?"

"Certainly not. I am a professional man. I can not answer a question like that."

"But I must ask you that question." McPhuig was taken aback and nervous. What was Knapbone up to this time? He was afraid of making a fool of himself again, knowing that the doctor in his turn could bully him by speaking above his head and making him look stupid. He took refuge in servility. "Perhaps I have phrased it badly?"

"Indeed you have," said Knapbone. "If you had asked me if sexual intercourse could be accompanied by fainting in the marchioness's case, I could quite easily answer."

"What would be the answer?"

"To what question?" Professor Knapbone was growing impatient. He wagged his right forefinger at McPhuig. "You must ask me a direct question before I can give you an answer, surely. This is the principle of scientific, forensic and presumably legal research. Always answer one question before moving on to the next."

McPhuig swallowed. The Press bench laughed. "Could sexual intercourse be accompanied by fainting in the marchioness's case?" shouted the counsel.

"Yes."

"If the marchioness had fainted in the presence of a male, could she have had sexual intercourse with him?"

"Certainly."

"Why then did you refuse to answer my first question?"

"Because you asked for an opinion, which I could not professionally give on the evidence. My second answer was a prognosis based on the known factors of the case. It is quite simple if laymen could only understand the fundamental questions of . . ."

"No more questions," said McPhuig. He hurriedly sat down.

"By the same token," said Crook, "the marchioness could also be a virgin, could she not?" His manner was deferential.

"But of course." Professor Knapbone seemed delighted to be confronted by a man of his own intelligence. "Fainting and sexual intercourse need not necessarily be interlinked. Extensive work carried out at the University of St Louis has shown that . . ."

"Quite," Crook said to halt him.

Lord Divot scowled downwards from his bench and drummed his fingers on the mahogany surface. He was clearly displeased.

"And sexual intercourse need not necessarily be accompanied by nymphomania?"

"Of . . ." Professor Knapbone took off his spectacles and carefully bit the left leg. He considered the implication of the question. "No, of course not."

"Did the marchioness confess to nymphomania to you?"

"No."

"It is quite possible through a great effort of will power that she was quite capable of withstanding the pressure of this affliction which you claim she laboured under?"

"Laboured under?" Knapbone smiled faintly as if he was going to make a joke. Lord Divot was still frowning at him. "Quite possible."

"So we have here a lady who is quite normal, as normal as my learned friend, but suffering from several minor neuroses which could be encountered in anyone today, like my learned friend, as you say, or even yourself, Professor?"

"Yes, I fear so. The sword of modernity leaves its scars on many a psyche."

"Are you a male nymphomaniac?"

"Certainly not."

"That will be all, Professor."

"Wait a minute." Lord Divot grunted at Knapbone. "Wait . . . what was that reference you made to St Louis?"

"Dr Masters has done a great deal of research into orgasm under laboratory conditions at St Louis and has proved many hitherto unaccepted facets of sexual relationships and emotion."

"You mean he has actually studied couples having sexual intercourse in his laboratory?" Lord Divot's hairy face shone.

"Oh, and masturbating," said Professor Knapbone. "His results have all been published."

"Masters, you say," mumbled Lord Divot, busily writing. "Masters . . . that will be all. You may step down."

Lieut. Smith, his immense brogues brown and gleaming, entered the witness box. McPhuig looked at him, as if he did not believe such a person could exist.

"Lieut. Smith, have you ever had sexual intercourse with the Marchioness of Strummet?"

"No, sir."

"Have you ever been alone with the marchioness?"

"Rarely, sir."

"In a tent, perhaps, at the Strummet Highland Gathering, earlier this year?"

"Only for a few seconds, sir."

"And if your activities had been overheard, you would not have worried?"

"I should not have worried, sir."

McPhuig rounded on him. "Did she faint?" he spat.

"Oh . . . uh . . . momentarily, sir."

"Before or after you had sexual intercourse?" McPhuig no longer appeared to care about the niceties. He stared scathingly at the two pips on Smith's shoulders.

"I did not have sexual intercourse." Smith's heavy face was twisted in an effort to concentrate on what McPhuig was saying.

"Such a junior officer," added McPhuig. "I suggest that you did."

"I was alone with her for only a few seconds, minutes at the most."

McPhuig spread his robes apart and put his hands on his hips. He stared at Smith with an air of benevolence, his face round and gloating, and his faint fair moustache bristling, like a walrus newly fed in a zoo.

"Come now, Smith," he said. He dropped all pretence of courtesy. His voice rose. "Come now, Smith." He repeated the name insultingly: "Smith."

For the first time, Gerontian-ffylde, seated on the second row of benches, felt sympathy for Smith. Even for an advocate, McPhuig's behaviour seemed intolerable.

"Would it surprise you to know that you had been listened in to?"

Gerontian-ffylde felt the merest prickle of apprehension in his stomach muscles. Colonel Strachan's face was betraying only a minor tic which rippled at the outside corner of his right eye.

"Supposing I was to repeat the conversation, Smith. Supposing I was to say . . . ." He mimicked a woman's voice, "Me Jayne, you Tarzan . . . What would you say then . . . Smith?"

Smith could not look McPhuig in the face. The marquis's counsel stood before him, smiling and winking in excitement. "Tarzan," he repeated salaciously. "Tarzan . . ."

Smith still did not answer.

McPhuig said in a loud and manufactured voice, "Did you commit adultery with the Marchioness of Strummet?"

There was still no answer. Crook looked at Smith's bowed head in disgust, then at McPhuig, and shook his head. Smith stumbled down the steps of the witness box, his heavy brown shoes, which he thought had looked so smart and military, seeming to mock him.

As if a signal had been given, McPhuig and Crook approached the bench. Earnestly their heads were raised towards Lord Divot, who craned down. "Condonation . . . waste of time . . . admissions . . ." The counsel walked back to their seats. The Press box was humming like disturbed bees. Spectators raised their heads, as alarmed as flushed bustards in long grass, weaving and bobbing in the sea of faces.

Lord Divot rapped on the dark-brown tablet beside him. He cleared his throat and poured a glass of water, which he drained. "A most unusual agreement has been reached for the public good between counsel for the pursuer and the defender in this difficult case, and I must thank and congratulate them. To avoid troubling the court unnecessarily with examining the other co-defenders in the witness box and thus taking up weeks of the court's valuable and irreplaceable time, counsel for the defender is willing to make an admission on behalf of his client that she committed some measure of misconduct with the men named in the closed record. In his turn, counsel for the pursuer has gracefully assented to admit condonation on the part of the complainer of this misconduct by the marquis's conduct in the St Andrews Hotel, Kushta, where he has now admitted that he had marital relations with his wife. In turn the marchioness has also admitted that marital relations took place in the same hotel, thus condoning certain allegations which she had made in her counter-suit for divorce against the marquis and which is now withdrawn . . ."

An American reporter said to Digby, "What's that gooky old bastard trying to say now?"

"It's simple. The marchioness admits misconduct which the marquis condoned by screwing her in Kushta. Because she has to admit being screwed, it means she has condoned whatever he was up to, and she's had to drop her own suit for divorce."

Lord Divot was droning on. "In this event the co-defenders and witnesses already heard can be released by the court and may return to their duties, with the exception of the witnesses still to be heard and the party minuter . . . if he wishes to give evidence."

He turned to the Press box, where reporters were already rising to their feet, and said sternly, "I take it that the Press understands the legal position. Although this is a submission, it relates to evidence which has already been heard, and nothing must be published at this stage which may indicate any of this evidence. I also understand that another Act has been brought to your attention to ensure that this case has the privacy which it fully deserves and to avoid undue sensationalism in the Press. I, therefore, warn you that the court will take the gravest exception to any of today's pro-ceedings except those which may be covered by the 1926 Act* and which can not be mentioned in any event. I shall sit again next Wednesday at 9.30 a.m."

"Co . . . . o . . . . o . . . . ou . . . . rt," shouted the usher. Lord Divot went home for the weekend.

"Well, I'll be ruptured," said Gerontian-ffylde. The marchioness's junior counsel overheard and leaned back-wards towards him. "I'll say," he said sympathetically. He thought it discreet not to elaborate.

The court resumed on the following Wednesday. The first person into the witness box was the Persian floor waiter who had taken champagne to the marchioness's room. Had the adjoining room to the marchioness been occupied? Yes, by Mr Gershwin-feel. Could he be identified? Yes, that was the *mesqin* gentleman sitting there. Yes, there. Had his bed been

---

*Judicial Proceedings (Regulation of Reports) Act, 1926.

slept in? Assuredly not. Where did Mr Gerontian-ffylde in fact sleep? That he could not say, sir, but his bed had not been slept in.

The *suffragi* on the same floor confirmed his evidence, through an interpreter brought from the docks. Gershwin-foul Effendi had not slept in his bed. It had been the tenth day of Ramadan and he had taken particular note, because he had been so exhausted after staying up all night feasting and drinking to compensate for the next day's fasting and thirsting that he had been forced to sleep in the bed of Gershwin-feeler Effendi which had not been previously disturbed.

"Bit strange of advocates not going out to Kushta to take evidence on commission instead of bringing a couple of wogs all this way?" Digby went on drinking coffee in the court snack bar and pretended to pay no attention to the gossiping solicitor. "Mean old bastard, the marquis," said the solicitor. "He reckoned the wogs would cost less to put up in Glasgow than three advocates in Kushta."
"He didn't refuse them permission to go out?"
"He certainly did."
"How much did it save him?"
"You must be joking . . ."

The marchioness's counsel conferred with her lawyer and realised they dared not put her into the witness box. Gerontian-ffylde was the final witness. He was dressed in a dark lounge suit, with a pale pink shirt and stiff white collar. He had decided against school or University colours. He wore a discreet blue tie, with a faint thread of red, and twin golden specks. His only concession was to pin a sprig of lucky white heather behind his lapel, to please Angela Proof, who had sent the heather from London with a good luck note. He went through the tedious rigmarole with Crook of establishing his identity, address, occupation and association with the marchioness. The only thing he did not admit was the scene at his bedroom door in Kushta, or where he had stayed the night, and he denied committing adultery with the marchioness.

"It was your idea to expose the marchioness to the attentions of these recruits?" McPhuig was at his best.

"I put the suggestion forward to my superiors who acted on it."

"But you thought you might be around for a few crumbs from the cake?"

"I did not." Gerontian-ffylde was determined not to be provoked.

"You met her on many occasions subsequently?"

"On several occasions in connection with my duties."

"You manoeuvred it so that you were available whenever she was alone?"

"I did not. I merely carried out my official Ministry duties."

"And did these duties include squiring the marchioness to Kushta?"

"I was asked officially at high level to accompany her ladyship to Kushta."

"And you booked adjoining rooms?"

"I did not book adjoining rooms."

"But you occupied adjoining rooms?"

"I discovered that the marchioness had booked a suite and I was allocated a bedroom in it."

"And you took advantage of this, didn't you." There was no longer an attempt at questioning. McPhuig's voice had become bullying and hectoring; his sentences had become statements.

"I do not understand your question."

"You are hardly going to deny that you did not spend the night with the marchioness?"

"I did not spend the night with the marchioness."

"But your bed was not slept in."

"I did not sleep in the hotel."

McPhuig halted in mid-flow. Digby was staring intent and white-faced from the Press box. The silly, stupid, gentlemanly bastard was going to throw it all away. Gerontian-ffylde stared steadily back at McPhuig.

"You did not sleep in the hotel? A likely story."

Gerontian-ffylde said obstinately, "I did not sleep in the hotel."

"You flew to Kushta on an assignment—or should that

be assignation?—with the marchioness. You took a bedroom in her suite. Your bed was not slept in. You undoubtedly admit to flying back to this country with her. But you claim . . ."—McPhuig made the word sound as if it was the production of a pathological liar—". . . you claim you did not sleep with the marchioness." He demanded, "Where were you then? Where did you sleep?"

Gerontian-ffylde repeated, "I did not sleep at the hotel. I stayed with a friend on the night in question." He was aware that Digby's dark and glaring eyes were fixed on him. He could see the court sharp and receding away from him, the figures shrinking in dense blues and purples into the distance with perfect clarity. It was as if he was staring at the court through the wrong end of a telescope. His mind was as clear as water. Digby was still glaring at him. Damn him: damn all of them. Why should he be forced to drag Angela Proof into it? The truth must be evident from his face alone. Why should he be made to trail another innocent life through the ordure which the advocates had spread so well. Tainting themselves as much as the people they were libelling. McPhuig was smiling and expansive again. Angela Proof was the only person who had been loyal to him in his life. Why should he be disloyal to her now? There was no need to, surely? They couldn't have bribed witnesses to say he had been to bed with the marchioness? There was nothing else he could be accused of? He said again, his voice steady, "I did not sleep with the Marchioness of Strummet, then or at any other time."

McPhuig sneered, "You expect us to believe that?"

"I do."

McPhuig walked away, his back exuding confidence, disbelief and arrogance. As he sat down, he said contemptuously over his shoulder, without even looking at Gerontian-ffylde, "I have no more questions to ask this man."

In his mind Lord Divot was formulating the reply to the Secretary of State, demanding parity in judicial processions with the Land Court judge, and if not, at least with judges of the Second Division. The sudden cessation of noise and of McPhuig's bullying voice startled him. He looked up in a practised way from behind his hand. It was apparent that evidence had been concluded. "I'll hear closing speeches tomorrow," he said, his voice as rough as broken stone.

The lonely, tormented cry of the court officer echoed like a sick dog through the court, and everyone stood as Lord Divot scrabbled his papers together and walked stiffly out.

Digby said, "He'll probably hear the speeches in the morning, and give the judgement in the afternoon. It looks an open and shut case to me."

"How did I do?" Gerontian-ffylde took the treble brandy which Digby had ordered, and swallowed it.

"Don't you know?" Digby's voice was surprisingly soft. He bought him another triple brandy. "Unless you'd like some white lightning. It's a local amnesic. Juice of the crushed and fermented grape pulp mixed with rough cider. It helps to dull your feelings about Scots justice."

Lord Divot did not give a spoken judgement the next day. Instead he heard the closing speeches, rambling and wordy, all morning and retired for the afternoon. The day afterwards he issued a written judgement, and it was sent to the parties concerned, and a copy was sent downstairs to the Press room in the High Court buildings. One reporter dictated it to another reporter who typed out a dozen blacks, or carbon copies, and distributed them to reporters from other papers. It was not a long judgement. After Press criticism of divorce judgements which had been so long and detailed that the public had been given a clear idea of the evidence, expressly forbidden by Act of Parliament, the statement produced by Lord Divot was a model of conciseness, allowing for the incoherences which bespatter every legal document. One of the copies was sent to the hotel where Digby and Gerontian-ffylde were staying, in a glen about twelve miles north of Glasgow.

Digby read the copy over to Gerontian-ffylde. He knew his anger was pointless. He said, "I wonder what I should slug this rubbish." The fawn copy paper was quivering in his fingers. He knew he would scream if he let his control go for a second.

"Slug it?" Gerontian-ffylde gazed blankly at him.

"I'm sorry. Every newspaper story has a word typed on the top called the catch-line or the slug. Instead of numbering your sheets one, two and three, you number them 'speech one', 'speech two', 'speech three'. It's for identification purposes. These sheets are called takes." He knew he was gabbling but he did not care. "All the lines of lead and the headlines and the page plans are slugged with this single word which usually indicates what it's all about."

"Why don't you slug it epitaph?" demanded Gerontian-ffylde in a sudden fury. "That bun-faced old fool sitting up there and those disgusting hooligans in their stupid horsehair wigs and antique cloaks. It's a measure of their truth that I'm the only man who never touched her, yet I am to be the scapegoat for all these seamy lawyers. All they're concerned with is trapping people in the law, or getting them off the law. It's a device: it isn't the truth any more."

Digby said, "Why should the truth affect them? Edinburgh was never very much noted for the truth. It's where they all come from."

Gerontian-ffylde was so angry he was drumming on the table with both fists, clenched and booming. "Three-generation gentlemen, all of them. And because I act like a gentleman and protect a lady's name and reputation, what have they done to me? They've branded me a cad." He rubbed his hand over his eyes. "It might seem funny to you, Digby. It might make you laugh to know it was one of the things that mattered to me: to be a gentleman. Nobody cares nowadays, but I do. All my life I tried to be a gentleman. And these creatures have brought me down to their level and taken it away from me."

"I'm sorry, Puff," said Digby. He felt helpless and too inadequate to deal with Gerontian-ffylde's grief. It *was* grief, he realised. He began to type:

The Marquis of Strummet has been granted a divorce from his wife on the grounds of her adultery with an Army liaison officer.

The judgement was given by Lord Divot at the Glasgow Divorce Court yesterday after an action which has lasted eight days and is reputed to have cost £60,000.

The judge found that the Army liaison officer, Mr Alain Seymour Grant Gerontian-ffylde, had committed adultery with the marchioness in a hotel in Kushta, "that sordid city of sin and sex mania by the sea."

Although Mr Gerontian-ffylde, described as party minuter in the action, had denied adultery, there was "little doubt" in the judge's mind that misconduct had occurred. They had stayed in adjoining rooms and the party minuter's bed had not been slept in on the night in question.

Earlier evidence had shown that the marchioness, "a typical example of lascivious morals and uninhibited living in the aristocracy, was a woman of loose moral character." Anyone found living under the same roof as her at night as the party minuter was, for "only a minute or even less", was bound to have committed adultery. "In my long experience I have discovered that the act of adultery takes but a few seconds to complete."

The party minuter had been unable to give a convincing account of his movements on the night in question and was a dubious witness. "This sprig of the aristocracy, who had found himself in close proximity to the marchioness, had undoubtedly taken advantage of his privileged position to force his attentions on the marchioness, who eagerly accepted them.

"A measure of condonation had been provided by the marquis prior to the seduction by the party minuter. His evidence, while not totally worthless, was suspect, but had been supported by two servants who had supplied the necessary corroboration in law."

Digby closed the quotation marks at the end of the paragraph and asked Gerontian-ffylde if he wanted to comment. He tried to say it lightly, as a joke.

Gerontian-ffylde's tumbler cracked in his fingers, the slivers of glass cutting petal-shaped into his fingers, so that the blood ran down his inner wrist in tendrils. He raised his wrist and licked it. He said, "Tell them they are vulgarians."

Digby sighed and typed, "At his hotel near Glasgow last night, Mr Gerontian-ffylde said, 'I am glad that it is all over. There seems little more that I can add.' "

11

"Government by newspapers . . . We can't have that sort of thing, Lorimer."

"But it's the public. They seem to be genuinely distressed and upset by the marchioness taking the salute at the Gathering."

"I don't think so. I think it's only the newspapers. They don't genuinely reflect what the public feels, you know. They only claim to do so to make the situation look worse and cause us more trouble. Of course the cermonial parade must go on, to show what stuff the Strummet Foot are made of." His voice was opaque. "We can't be dictated to by Acarid and his tribe of hooligans."

Lorimer said intently, "We're not even too sure of how the regiment will behave. Some of them seem to have got hold of the idea that it has been turned into a suicide brigade. I don't know how the idea got around. I rather gather they think they're being conned."

"Conned?" Tony Pleasance stared at him in affected distaste. "Conned? I appreciate you come from Glasgow, but do you have to use these expressions in my Ministry?"

"They appear to feel they have been duped. According to our latest information, they are on the point of mutiny. Our consultant sociologist pointed out to me only yesterday that if an emotional trigger situation presents itself, it may be impossible to restrain them. There may be a case for calling off the parade altogether."

"I think everything will be all right, Lorimer." Under Pleasance's strong and manly stare, the Minister for Internal Security, Scotland, reluctantly rose. "I think you'll find we may have something up our sleeve . . . and forget the newspapers, my boy. We're in charge, you know; we govern. We're the people who are firmly in control."

Like a puppet, Lorimer walked to the far end of the long mock-Georgian room and vanished through the arched doorway. Pleasance lifted the telephone and asked for Basil Makebelieve.

He switched on the tape recorder. "I think your plan may have been successful, Basil." His compromise was meticulous. "I've just had that fellow Lorimer in here complaining the regiment was almost out of control . . . I take it your men must have had the situation firmly in hand."

Basil Makebelieve's reedy voice filled the ear-piece. "Absolutely, Tony. I must compliment you on your foresight." Audibly and in anger, Pleasance snapped off the tape recorder switch. "I think we can expect suitable action on Saturday . . . There is one thing, though."

"Anything within reason."

"We couldn't arrange for a few of these football temples to be knocked off? They seem to be the focal point of this love-hate religion they have up there. Heathen gods and all that . . . If we got them out of the way, we could really drag the bloody Scots into this century." His voice shattered into icy tinkles of laughter.

"What's so amusing?"

"I think it's so exciting, bringing civilisation to the Scots at this late date. I feel like a missionary."

"Up to you entirely," said Pleasance, intent on revenge. "But don't land up in the police court, ha ha."

He slammed down the receiver and moved to the scrambler telephone which linked him with Horton Pond. "I think we may have found some experimental material for you . . . no, only Scots. I suppose they *are* suitable for experimental use? In that case, hold yourself in readiness for the week-end, but remember . . ." His voice blunted and his heavy North Country vowels intruded. "I don't want another political scandal. You must guarantee this won't kill; at least, more than one or two. We merely want to disable them . . . Splendid; keep in a state of constant readiness."

It was a crisp October day, with a faint, thin breeze blowing down, in the sharp sunlight, from the first snow whitening the summit of Ben Odhar (the local guidebook admits the difficulty of translating the Gaelic name into English, but suggests it can be approximately rendered as Blotchface Peak or Mudface Mountain) and etching patterns of radiant diamonds on the waters of the Sound of Strummet. The streets of the village were choked with clansmen and clanswomen, gathered loyally from all over the Commonwealth and America, cameras and tartans and cromachs, all tangled in the main street and overflowing into the lanes and alleys. Middle-aged men in paunchy black and yellow kilts pushed shoulder to shoulder with lissom girls in tartan skirts and boys in trews and bodices. Street salesmen from Glasgow were hawking Strummet tartan balloons, filled with helium and depicting the marquis's face, all winging off into the autumn sky, bearing goodwill messages to clansmen overseas, amidst the clamour of voices. "Send a lucky message to loved ones abroad," they shouted. And overlaying and obscuring their huckster voices was the continual moaning of bagpipes as pipers dotted through the nooks of Dunstrummet vainly tried to tune their soaking reeds. Both bars were heavy with drunks, the doors standing open to the outside air, contravening the drinking laws, and people milled out on to the pavement with forbidden glasses and mugs of beer and whisky. The hotels were acreak with visitors, but reserved only for personal friends of the marquis, who were able to produce embossed invitation cards: others ate from mobile canteens and fish and chip vans, belching smoke and burning fat fumes, in the jammed car parks. Jangling bells assaulted old men with hearing aids. Kipper salesmen cried from street booths. Ornamental mussel shells sold for ten pence each. Strummet rock went for thirty. Genuine Strummet stag horn buttons two pounds a dozen. Dazed with power, the vendors cleared their stock to souvenir-hungry tourists.

Digby sat in the window of his room in the Strummet Cave and gazed glazedly down at the clansfolk. "Do you think they're real? Do you think they really exist? Are these people, people, or are they conjuring tricks?" He was drunk. He handed his bottle to Gerontian-ffylde who took a thoughtful nip. "Perhaps I've written them into being. We've created the popular imagery of the mighty Strummet, with the aid of a few unkempt and dishonest history books, and here they all come to savour the beauties and realities and delights of belonging . . ." He threw the window open. "You belong; you all belong," he shouted to the people in the street. "You belong. I've made you belong." His voice was lost in the hubbub of the clanking, chattering, ringing, noisome crowd. Gerontian-ffylde pulled him back and secured the window. "You're talking too much, Digby. I don't know what's gone wrong with you since the divorce. You'd think it was you that got it in the neck and not me."

Digby mumbled, "Perhaps I have . . . or perhaps it's part of the great symbiosis between the reporter and the reportee. We can not live together: we can not exist apart. It's love and hate and boredom and horror . . ." He swigged from his bottle again. "It only happens to you once or twice in your lifetime, but it happens to me all the time." Digby lurched towards Gerontian-ffylde, knocking over the small table, the glasses and water jug shattering on the floor. "Give me my bloody bottle, mate. I'm going to kill it and me and every fucking one of you. I've had it. I'm dead before it happens and I know what's going to happen." He realised he still held the bottle in his own hand. He drained it and it slipped from his fingers and fell beside the broken glass. "Let's go up and watch the riot."

"The riot? What the hell are you talking about?"

"Let's go and watch the race riot . . ." They fought their way downstairs and left by the back door. Digby, so drunk he could scarcely stand, directed Gerontian-ffylde by flourishes of his arms, weaving through a series of lanes, the Michaelmas daisies still purple and blooming in the sheltered air. They arrived at a gate in the high wall of the castle grounds. "The entrance to my treasure house of wishes," he mumbled. "Come on. Show your Press pass, darling, and walk through." He took a key from his pocket and managed to turn it in the lock. Digby fell through the gate, dragging Gerontian-ffylde with him.

They were at the wooded end of the games field, with its familiar wooden platforms, now transformed into a saluting base, and the field was dark with soldiery and tourists. Hundreds upon hundreds of spectators filled the far side of the field and almost hid the three battalions of the Strummet Foot, drawn up in a hollow square, between the saluting base and the castle walls.

The First Battalion were in the ceremonial place of honour, facing the base, with their backs to the castle wall. Uphill, on their right, were the Third Battalion, their green hackles a cacophonous break in the sea of black and yellow tartan, while the Second Battalion, its white horse standing proud of them, were drawn up with their backs to the great ditch and the water gate.

Brigadier Strachan was assisting Jayne, Marchioness of Strummet, who had assumed the dowager title, on to the saluting base, where the official party were assembling after inspecting rank upon rank of the regiment. Behind the marchioness was the lord lieutenant of the county and the general officer commanding, all in red and peacock blue, but outshone by the magnificence of the Marquis of Strummet in his kilt and plum-coloured doublet, with silver buttons and foaming lace, his cromach high and his eagles' feathers stabbed in his bonnet.

The First Battalion was ready to march off in review order, across the hollow square in three ranks of 100 men, aimed directly at the saluting base, where they were to wheel and be followed by their junior battalions. The drum major's mace was poised, its silver chains and tassels faintly chinking as his nerves caught him. The regimental foot-major's mouth was opened in a dreadful arc; the pipers' right arms were rigid as they readied themselves to throw their drones on to their left shoulders.

Into the great echoing silence marched a solitary dark and upright figure in a Strummet kilt, carrying a loudhailer. A few yards behind him, were eight graceful young people, followed by a trail of elderly and embarrassed men in longer kilts. From the corner of his bloodshot eye, the regimental foot-major could disbelievingly see the straggling party make its way down the corridor in the field, their feet kicking up the tufts of nardus grass, yellow and sere from the first frosts, and take up its position between him and the official party, agog on the platform.

The foot-major's face was frozen into a purple block. Horrified and fascinated he watched the loudhailer come up, and unable to speak, unable to move, unable to break the doll-like tableau with the single word which would snap it back to reality, stood like a marionette.

Duncan Habib-Strumpet switched the loudhailer to full volume, and his voice bellowed across the field, "My clansmen, my soldiers, my people. I have travelled many thousands of miles to be with you on this precious day; so precious to me, but what must also be so precious to you. . . ." The marquis was gibbering, "Shut him up. I know all about the wog bastard. Shut him up." But the platform party was struck equally dumb and ignored him.

"I stand here before you. . . ." The loudhailer voice buffeted off the weathered sandstone walls of the castle, ". . . as my great ancestors did in time of impending insurrection and danger to the clan, to rally you with words of wisdom and war. Now it is my privilege to take my place as your rightful leader. . . ." He bowed ceremonially; behind him, his children inclined their heads, ". . . as the rightful chief of Clan Strummet, the rightful Earl of Pumphrey and Marquis of Strummet, colonel-in-chief of my regiment."

There was a roar from the ranks of the Derry Mutineers, "Where's your busman's hat, yu Pakistani bastard. . . ." In the tumult, cries of "Pape", "Your father was a spear-chucker," "Lady Jayne's a nigger-fucker," creased the air. In revenge Private McEntee threw a string of thunderflashes right across the hollow square and it started to explode through the ranks of the Derry Mutineers like a leaping carronade, burning naked knees and shredding kilts and singeing body hair. The battalions broke in a swaying bulge of hatred and met like a monstrous gong being hammered. The shock of meeting threw the ranks temporarily back, then they were sucked together again, machine pistol butts flailing, winkle-picker bayonets darting like lizards' tongues into bloody sides and faces. Gouging and stabbing the 3rd Battalion drove their hated Protestant opponents down the hill. Spectators were caught in the horror, transfixed as the black and yellow fury spun and eddied on the field. "Launchers . . . launchers . . . launchers." The shrieks were rising. McEntee had assumed command of his platoon. They were up and along the side of the castle wall, running like crazy men, to their troop carriers and heavy weapons. Behind them men were shrilly whistling in a pre-arranged plan. The green cockades suddenly flattened to the ground as the first unarmed rocket streaked at head-height through the 2nd Battalion and slammed into the ancient stronghold, driving a deep concavity into the stonework. "It'll fucken strike this time," spat McEntee, adjusting the micro-screw of the infra-red homing device. A dreadful scream came from the 2nd Battalion's white horse, as the rocket passed through its belly, splashing its entrails into the great ditch behind the water gate. A haunted face locked through the bars in the door and started to gurgle in pleasure as the blood ran down on to its lips. Torquil Strummet, standing on the battlements, saw the face and turned away to be sick. The air was alive with rockets, swishing and curving.

The 2nd Battalion were scattered, defeated by the slope, moaning and bleeding on the banks of the great ditch. They began to rally but it was too late. The Lady Jayne's Own were into their battalion transport, their faces reddened, swollen and flushed with battle, and their blood lust up. "Burn them," a soldier chanted. No one had seen him before. "Burn them, burn them." The chant was taken up into a hellish refrain of three centuries of bigotry and duped violence. "Burn them, burn them . . . burn the Orange bastards."

Standing fast on the castle side of the hollow square, the 1st Battalion watched with apparent disinterest. Their sergeants and corporal-majors were invoking them in mighty whispers. "Steady, men . . . stand steady . . . stand steady . . . steady, men; steady. . . ." The regimental foot-major was still rivetted to his ceremonial position. Then the Derry Mutineers were after their enemies, up the stained grass, into their eight-wheeled trucks and were hurtling down the long driveway.

Tony Pleasance excused himself from the platform party and walked through the debris of bloody bodies and discarded equipment. He nodded to the foot-major, apparently stunned with shock, and entered the castle by the wicket gate. He found a telephone and gave the code name and number of the war emergency exchange. "Tell Horton Pond to begin phase one. Tell them it's all as expected. Probable destination Glasgow. Yes, full alert, but under no circumstances disturb them on the way. They'll probably only want to attack each other at this stage. Yes, it looks like that. Treacherous bunch, the Scots." He put the phone back and walked whistling through to the study and poured himself a large glass of the marquis's whisky. Exquisite, he thought.

The troop carriers shrieked into the afternoon, looping and wheeling over the lonely roads, heading south to the ugly mass of Glasgow. The soldier who started shouting "Burn them," crawled up beside McEntee. "Let's burn Ibrox. Let's show these bluenoses who's boss." Police watched the carriers vanish through the main streets of grey villages, and radioed ahead to other forces. The 3rd Battalion retained their lead. They were on the worn and sagging motorways, their wheels lurching in the potholes. They forced their way through the jammed streets of Stirling, scattering the queues of traffic, and almost squashing a road surveying team into the ground, and sped into their own territory. Slag heaps rose up. The squalid wastes of Coatbridge and Airdrie were on their left. Through Stepps they went, and a tumultuous cheer went up as they passed Barlinnie Prison.

The 2nd Battalion began to sing their obscene and familiar song. The radio operator, attached to the Derry Mutineers only three days previously, shouted, "They're gaun to burn Ibrox. They're gaun to burn it. I've picked up their signals." He ripped off his headphones. "Parkhead," he screamed. "Let's burn Paradise. Burn the papish rats to the ground."

Dusk was well down and a stinking mist rose from the River Clyde as the Lady Jayne's Own roared over Kingston Bridge and skidded right along the dockside road. The chanting was higher now, hypnotic and more intense and hysterical. "Burn them . . . burn them . . . burn them."

McEntee's armoured carrier was first—smashing through

the double doors of Ibrox Park and gouging up the tawdry marble staircase. Screaming, the men flooded from their transport and laid waste to the stadium, their eyes glistering, intense and fixed. A pinpoint of flame spread from the south-west corner of the stand. The prevailing wind caught it and flared it. The steady thud of plastic explosives in the offices shook the wooden flooring and bench seats. Shooting into the air, a funnel of blinding flame and scarlet heat burst upwards.

"Hampden," screamed the small unknown man. "Burn it . . . burn it." Behind them, the 2nd Battalion had blown up the main stand at Celtic Park, which the natives called Paradise, and threw phosphorus bombs into the wreckage. Tracers whipped into the debris and flame mushroomed out. A fat, jowly man, his arms wide and obviously crazy, ran towards them, ordering them to stop in the good name of Celtic. Bullets zipped through his trousers and he fled, clutching his enormous buttocks. Gouts of flame were everywhere. The same fear gripped them. "They're burning Hampden," shouted the radio operator, who omitted to tell them he had turned off his wireless twenty minutes previously. "They're burning Hampden to the ground."

In a frenzy the Derry Mutineers ran back to their trucks and wheeled through Bridgeton Cross and down the Gallowgate and over the river. The Lady Jayne's Own were forcing their way through the traffic, demoniacally and obliquely crossing the city on the south side of the river. Tiring and slowing, the forces burst into Hampden from opposing ends, the darkness dispelled only by the gleam of the troop carriers which had trundled to the top of the terracing.

Suddenly the pitch was filled with foot soldiers, their faces grey with fear as they realised this was the final cold confrontation. They were shivering. Men clutched their trousers suddenly. Others knelt.

In a white blinding glare, the overhead lights flashed on over the men. The incandescence forced their elbows over their faces in a reflex action, and their faces turned up. A soft, clinging, pearly pink miasma seemed to hover in the air, then evanesced in fewer than fifteen seconds. Wave after wave of men went down, the strongest men from both battalions surviving a few seconds longer, but they, too, slid to the muddy grass, completely unconscious.

High in the directors' box, the two men in the gas suits packed their aerosol cans and stripped off their protective clothing.

The leader said abruptly, "I think you were wrong, damnably wrong. You switched on the gas too soon."

"Why's that?" The other man was disinterested.

"If you hadn't gone off reprehensibly at half-cock, some of these bastards might have killed each other, or maimed each other at least. We don't know for sure how long the effects will last in humans."

"Didn't you notice?" The other man was jeering.

"Notice what?"

"When it came to fighting on a cold stomach they were chicken. I told you they were psychopaths. Didn't I tell you that?"

McEntee woke first and found himself lying over the body of a gigantic Orangeman, whose face had relaxed into a baby-like simper. "Are ye a'right, son?" asked McEntee. He shook him gently. "Awdearyfuckenme... have I hurt ye, son?" Tears were streaming down his face. "Oh, ma wee son, ye'll be a'right. There, there, there. I'll look after ye, son."

A British spy plane flew over Lake Oz Baikal at a height of 40,000 feet and dropped three water-soluble cachets into the water. Three days later spontaneous dancing broke out in the streets of Irkutsk.

12

Torquil Strummet lay back in the natal cup of the black basalt rock called the Earl's Chair, sheltered from the west wind, and allowed his eyes to merge with the translucent greyness of the Sound of Strummet, where the sea had drifted into the pearl-grey sky, and the horizon had vanished, and miles out the distant speck of a fishing boat hovered, apparently suspended in the curved eternity of space. It was as if the world ended there. His sister, Sheila, perched on the lip of the rock, said, "Don't gloom so, Torquil. I'm sure there's a way out. Digby told me he had thought of something."

"But Sheila." His lips were stiff and scarcely moved. "How can Digby help? He's only a reporter. All these doctors have been here and none of them have helped . . . I hate it so much I would rather be dead than go on like this. To go on through all these bloody years, surrounded by all this greyness. . . . Out there, that's my mind, all in a grey cloud, with no beginning or no ending, moving farther and farther from reality and getting more and more useless and even fatter." He was acutely conscious of the fact that he had put on almost seven pounds in weight since the summer. "I don't even want to move these days, can't even seem to sweat. All I want to do is lie here. I can't do anything. I can't even remember the beginning of the sentence I'm speaking when I'm halfway through it and I wonder if it will vanish before it's finished and I just have to go on speaking, hoping it makes sense. I thought I found myself smiling the other day for the first time since mother died and I caught sight of my face in a mirror and discovered that I wasn't smiling at all, although I could feel it inside. My face was frozen and my mouth was like a clamp and I didn't even know it. My smile never reached my face." He was dry-eyed and staring. "I used to be such a happy child, Sheil, didn't I?" His voice had become imploring.

"Yes, darling." His sister squeezed his arm, then half-punched him. "But never mind. You've got your own back on the old man. He'll lose the title and everything, the chiefship, the castle . . . Duncan Strumpet's coming up this afternoon with the girls to discuss future arrangements."

"It's funny to think we've got Indian cousins: well, Pakistani cousins." Torquil tore a frond of dried seaweed from the rock and popped the brittle air bubbles, the staccato cracks riving the pure grey silence. "I like them actually. If you really want to know, I think Emerald is very beautiful."

"Look," said Sheila. "Here comes Digby." Digby was walking towards them through the quietness with Angela Proof and Gerontian-ffylde. In the still air she could hear the remote brushing of their feet, feathering up the fine particles of sand.

Torquil lay outstretched in the rock chair and did not turn his head. "Why is it that Digby always knows to arrive when something is going to happen?"

She said unexpectedly, "Because I always phone him." She laughed out loud, the sound flying out in sharp waves to the sky. "It's all been for you, actually. They pay what they call tip-off money, provided it isn't to criminals, and I arranged with Digby to keep it all for you, for your running away fund. There's enough for you to go away at any time if you still want to. He's managed to get almost a thousand quid for you."

He remained perfectly still. A single tear ran from the outside corner of his right eye, away from her, and she did not see it. "Do you mean you've been trying to find a way to help me and keeping it as a surprise for me?"

"We have, actually. Digby liked you. He seems to have taken rather a shine to you. He's very loyal to people he likes."

"Hello," said Digby. "I've brought some friends." He introduced Angela Proof. "You both know Mr Gerontian-ffylde." He added, "They've come up here to get married."

"Here in Dunstrummet?" Sheila clapped her hands. "How perfect."

"Quite frankly we hoped it would embarrass that sordid old bastard," said Angela Proof.

Gerontian-ffylde sat between Torquil and Digby. "He's going to be best man," he said and nodded at the reporter.

"How super," said Sheila. "Can I be best maid? I think I'd like to join the protest."

"I think I'd like to shoot the sadist," said Torquil. "There's something horrible going on up there again. He's got about forty Laotian refugees coming, and he's very excited."

"I see she got a D.B.E. for services to the nation."

"Being served by the Strummet Foot more like it."

"The late Strummet Foot, don't you mean?" said Gerontian-ffylde. "They've gone the same way as the Connaught Rangers. The British Army never would stand for mutiny. Still, I suppose the only thing they could do was disband them."

"There's one good thing. Crime seems to have vanished in Glasgow."

"Do you mean to say only a few hundred men were holding the city to ransom?"

"Yes, of course, I do. I hinted that to you before. Once the ordinary people began to realise they could live without fear of attack, they began to be human again and stopped attacking each other." Digby turned to the boy. "How's things?"

"Have you really been trying to help me?"

"Yes, I suppose I have."

"But why? Why me? You hardly know me."

"Perhaps I thought you could do with a little cheering up, I suppose. We could all do with being cheered up from time to time. Perhaps you represent my cheering up campaign."

Torquil tore off another strand of seaweed and threw it on to the fine white sand beneath the rocks. "I was saying to Sheila as you came up that I used to be a happy child, didn't I, Sheil?"

"Yes, darling. You were great fun." She turned to Angela. "Don't you have to be a virgin to be best maid or something?"

Digby said to Gerontian-ffylde so that Torquil could not hear him, "There is a way we can help him: a traditional way."

"What is it?" asked Gerontian-ffylde softly.

"We'll need some rope and that boat over there . . . I hope the outboard's working."

Just above the sea-wrack that marked high water, a castle dinghy lay careened on its side, the outboard tilted up so that it had been out of the water when the boat had been anchored. The anchor rope had coiled itself over the flukes as the sea had gone down and allowed the dinghy to sink on to the sand.

"Get Angela and Sheila to suggest a trip round the bay. You get the rope round to the stern of the boat."

There was a little whispering, and Sheila said, "Come on, Torquil. Let's go for a roar round the loch." She pulled him by the arm. "Like we used to."

"Do I have to?" asked Torquil. "I don't want to move. Why don't you let me sit here? I'll be much happier staying here and not moving."

Digby already had the dinghy down and into the clear water. He lowered the outboard, coiled the starting rope round the flywheel and pulled the toggle. The engine caught and spluttered and rocked into life. Deviously Gerontian-ffylde picked up the anchor, while the two girls jumped over the thwarts. In a sudden movement the rope somehow snaked around Torquil's leg and the outboard engaged. In a creaming swirl of water the dinghy surged away from the shore, dragging Torquil by the leg, so that he skated, shrieking in fear and horror, over the surface of the loch.

The dinghy roared onwards in a vast clockwise arc, and alternately shrilling and bellowing, Torquil creased into an arrowhead of foam, his leg rigid and his spine skidding and keeling over the water. The girls were shouting to Digby to stop but his hand was taut on the tiller and his teeth were bared in a strained and unearthly grin. Gerontian-ffylde was pulling at him shouting, "I didn't think you'd go as far as this," but Digby shook him off. The parabola was almost complete. In front of the prow, the white sand was coming up to meet the dinghy and they grouted ashore in a long searing shudder.

In a flash Digby cut the engine and leaped over the stern to support Torquil just as his head began to sink. He freed the rope from his ankle and carried him to the *machair* and laid him down on the wiry grass like a baby.

It was as if Torquil was in a state of shock. His face was soaked, not only with sea water and spray but with sweat, thickly curdling from his brow and cheeks. His body shook once or twice, then he screamed at Digby, "You tried to drown me."

He was on his feet, his chest heaving and his face alight with rage. The heavy dullness had cleared. His eyes were bright with anger. He suddenly became aware of himself. "You. . . ." His hand ran over his face: he realised emotion had returned to him. He traced an attempted smile with his fingers. It was *there*. Delight swept over him.

He threw his head back. "I'm free. . . . You've freed me." He started dancing a jig and the girls joined in, prancing and falling over the sand in joy. Above them sea birds wheeled, screaming in the pale light.

In amazement, Gerontian-ffylde demanded, "What exactly have you done to him?"

Digby looked at him in a strange and almost fey way. "Sometimes the old ways are best if they're tempered with modernity."

"Are you being clever again?" Gerontian-ffylde began to move threateningly towards Digby. "I don't think I could stand you being remote and superior and smart again. I think I'm going to kill you unless you tell me what you've done."

Digby smiled in an odd humourless way. "I'm not superior, Alain." Gerontian-ffylde stopped abruptly. "That's the first time you've ever used my Christian name," he said.

"Perhaps it's the first time an outboard was ever used to

cure depression. Didn't I ever tell you that depression was what Torquil was suffering from? It's an illness just as grave as, say, TB, and much harder to bear. These bloody doctors were so smart they couldn't see it staring them in the face."

Gerontian-ffylde said, "But what have you done?"

"The Greeks used to do it by putting the patient into the cave of Trophonius and terrifying him in the darkness. They used to say after the treatment, 'And laughter returned to him.' In the Hebrides, they found they could cure depression by towing a man feet-first *deiseil* round a loch and half-drowning him."

He saw Gerontian-ffylde's lack of comprehension at the use of the Gaelic word. "It means clockwise, with the sun. The ancients believe if you travelled sunwise you shook off the evil spirits and they could not follow you. I think myself it must be some primitive form of shock treatment. . . . It seems to work, doesn't it? I suppose it was discovered when some sad sailorman was caught in a rope's end and dragged through the sea."

Torquil was far up the field, running towards the castle. "I'd hate to be his father when he gets there," said Digby. "I'm going to have a drink now, and toast the ancients." He took out his whisky flask and offered it to Gerontian-ffylde. "Sit and be atavistic with me. Celebrate being in league with magic and the spirits around us. Celebrate going back to the roots of time." They sat together on the basalt rocks and Gerontian-ffylde accepted the flask, and said, "I don't think I'll ever get to know you, Digby. You're an odd character. You appear to know so much unrelated stuff which you never seem to put into practice. You never talk about yourself, or what makes you tick. You only suggest things by analogy and take our emotions away from us. . . . Don't you think you're being unfair?"

"What could I tell you that you wanted to hear?"

"Perhaps it's the things that we don't want to hear that you should tell us about. You always moan about the people who go away and leave. It's people like you who always go away and leave us nothing. You're even more to blame than we are."

"Not in Torquil's case."

"Torquil became a sort of symbol to you, didn't he. He became the epitome of what has happened up here. It's why you won't stay."

"But you musn't let a journalist tell you."

"O, stop sneering, Digby."

"Yes," said Sheila Strummet, approaching softly over the sand from behind him. She kicked him lightly in the back. "Tell us. We couldn't care less if you were a Chinese laundryman, or even a lawyer. Don't be so aggressively defensive about being a reporter." Angela Proof, beside her, nodded in agreement.

Digby appeared to be embarrassed. "I'll try if you really want me to, but I'm not used to speaking my thoughts any more. I'm too defensively flip. I've got out of the way of being serious in public . . . and if you must know, I'm even worse since my own divorce went through."

"Your divorce?" Gerontian-ffylde and the girls were astounded. "Your divorce? We never even knew you were married, far less divorced."

"I was rather ashamed of it, actually . . . I know it sounds pompous, but I'm afraid I married a lawyer. At least I revenged myself on that spiteful little toad, Odhar, over her."

He was aware of their puzzled expressions. "It's the best way to hurt a lawyer like that: through his pocket."

"You mean you managed to get money from him?"

"Perhaps I should explain from the start. When I moved to London to get away from her, she stayed in Scotland, working in a legal practice in the town where she lived, and doubling up as local prosecutor. She was defending local morals and all that, and even singing in the church choir. When I came up on this Strummet thing, I went to see her about arranging a divorce, and instead, found her in bed with some cheap little cut-price wine salesman, complete with beard, who was the choirmaster. She claimed my neglect had made her frigid, and she had to have sexual therapy to restore her libido. My fault again, apparently." He could not resist being malicious. "I rather gather the marchioness was as good in bed as she was."

"But how did you get your own back on Odhar?" Sheila Strummet discovered she was intrigued to the point of avidity.

"She asked me, obviously knowing what she was up to with her legal training, if I could put her in touch with a lawyer in Edinburgh to help reduce the costs. After you told me that Odhar was the person who schemed that petition into court, I asked him if he would handle my wife's divorce. Automatically he thought she was the aggrieved party. He thought he saw another chance of causing trouble for a journalist, and making money at the same time, and walked right into it. Stupidly he never thought of asking if she had an occupation." The grin of malice curved his mouth downwards, and he paused.

"So . . ?" Sheila Strummet's fingers hit him in the ribs. It was a gentle interrogation. "So? Don't be so secretive. Tell us what you mean."

"So, it was the biggest mistake he had ever made," Digby said. "Lawyers can't send bills to fellow-lawyers for personal services . . . Odhar had to pay the costs of my divorce."

Both girls rolled laughing on the sand. A swooping tern soared away in alarm, its coal-black pinion feathers raised like a fragile fan.

Gerontian-ffylde said, "I never knew, did I? Why do you never tell people of the things that affect you? Why must you always shut it up, your opinions, your fears, and presumably your doubts: that's if you ever have any behind that stone face of yours."

"I never think they're of interest to anyone. It never occurs to me that what has happened to me might be of value to anyone else, that my thoughts have validity, or even meaning any more . . . but I suppose I'm just as qualified as you to speak about divorce, now that I've joined the club."

Sheila Strummet asked, "Will you ever marry again, or has one failure frightened you off?"

The apparently irrelevant question seemed to worry Digby. "I don't know." He was hesitant. "I tell myself that I must be free, but then no-one is free. You always take your self with you and all its scars. I do know one thing. I never want to see or hear about divorce again, dragged through the toadying hands of those lawyers." His face flushed, a dull red spreading under the bold cheekbones.

"Do you honestly think that lawyers should be allowed to handle divorce cases in such a way? I was lucky because I could present a cut-and-dried case, and my legal wife was too scared of publicity to defend it, hoping it would slip through unnoticed by the Press. But do you honestly think it was the whole truth of what had happened to our so-called marriage? One cheap little act of adultery with an ageing choir-master? Do you honestly think the truth ever emerged in a court room? Do you think that two people in love know, or even care, they are entering a civil contract, or know its hideous implications, when they marry?

"All they want is to be together. . . . And don't you think these people should be protected from themselves, when their love has gone, from making vile accusations against each other, and being encouraged to, while the lawyers rub their salacious hands? And do you think these lawyers should unctuously be allowed to get away with saying, 'But we *are* protecting them from themselves' when all they are protecting are their inflated fees? Did you ever hear Lord Divot's doggerel?" He began to parody the judge's verse, hobbling about on the sand, raising his hands over his head and shoulders to protect himself from imaginary missiles.

" 'Sticks and stones
Will break my bones.
But broken homes
Will feed me. . . .' "

His voice, a faint curdling of his original Scots accent returning, boomed over the grey waters.

" '. . . and broken homes will feed me
. . . will feed me
. . . feed me.' "

He swung round, his arm a baleful, vindictive, accusatory prop, and levelled it at Gerontian-ffylde. "Look at him. There is the law in all its majesty, its truth and precise beauty.

"There is the guilty party in the Strummet divorce. There is the man found guilty of adultery while the other six hundred were let off. . . . Look at him: the only innocent man in court. The only man in the regiment who didn't lay her. The man who carried the sexual can for the law and all its comic organ-grinders."

He jumped on the black basalt rock and shouted, "It was the law and many divorce lawyers that should have been on trial, and laughed out of court . . . laughed at until they went away with their deplorable English and worse verse. Then we could have decent law and a civilised divorce to cloak the hurt of two people. The English were given it years ago, but still people in Scotland trade in human misery, squalor, salacity and legal trickery to keep their purses well-filled and their votes intact. Laugh at them, I say, till they burst in their unclean pomposity. Laugh at them till they vanish like a puff-ball hooted out of existence."

They began to clap. "Digby for Lord President." "Digby for King." "Marry me, Digby," said Sheila Strummet softly. She saw the look of disbelief on his face. "I was only joking, Digby," she whispered. "I was joking." She knew she was not.

Duncan Habib-Strumpet sat facing the marquis across the long library table, his face dark and furious. "I have observed the most scrupulous courtesy in dealing with you. I have ignored the rebuffs and the insults with which you have greeted my friendly salutations. Now I am tiring of your behaviour." On each side of him, his daughters sat erect, their backs parallel with the oak risers of the chairs, but not touching them. Emerald was on her father's right, in a soft green, clinging sari, which sheathed her almost like the leaves of a dusky crimson tulip.

The marquis hawked and spat in his handkerchief. "I've got more important things to do than sit in my own house and be insulted by a bloody coolie, even if you do happen to have some of my blood in you."

"How dare you," ejaculated Mr Habib-Strumpet. His daughters shrank at the insult and withdrew into their saris, their eyes tragic. "How many times do I have to tell you that it is not your castle. It is not your title. Nothing is yours. The trustees have bound up the estate. It belongs to the holder of the title, not to an individual. . . . If it were not for the disgrace attached to it, I would exercise my rights and have you thrown down the castle steps." Through the generations of calm Eastern blood there gleamed the original ruthless quality which had gained the estates for the family. He held up a document. "I have this letter, of which my lawyer has sent you a copy, proving beyond all doubt that I am the rightful head of this family." He flicked his fingers. "I could dispose of you like that. You forget, too, that I am descended from a royal house on the distaff side. In former days we would have baited traps with you."

"Oh, all right," shouted the marquis. "Let's have a wog clan chief. Let's see how that would go down in the council of clan chiefs."

"If by that, you mean coloured, we already have a coloured clan chief and I fear she is a much greater gentle person than you." He hesitated, apparently not sure of what his next move should be.

Because of his indecision, an expression of duplicity crept over the marquis's face. "What do we do then?" he demanded. "Do we appoint you chief and make the clan the laughing stock of the world?" Duncan Habib-Strumpet could scarcely hide his discomfort. The marquis pressed on. "Why shouldn't you? Throw me out on to the street and strip me of my honours, so you could justify your own obsession for power and your anti-white prejudices."

Duncan Habib-Strumpet stood up, quivering. "You really are the most repulsive man I have ever met. If this was another century I would call you out and kill you for that remark. Instead you have hardened my resolution. I am going to insist that the title goes to my eldest child. The succession permits it to go to heirs male or female of my body. If you insult me once more, I shall strip you of everything." He could not sustain his anger. "I don't especially want to stay here. At my age, I would be more comfortable at home in Lahore and I intend to leave as soon as things are settled to my satisfaction. But I intend them to be to my satisfaction and to see the true succession taking place."

"There is a way out," said the marquis swiftly. He knew he was not going to win. His words were tinged with obsequiousness. "We could effect a marriage between both sides of the family, if you like."

Duncan Habib-Strumpet relaxed. "You are being more reasonable. In my thoughts I had always hoped that somehow such a union would be possible. Who do you suggest from your side of the family?"

A terrified voice shouted in the corridor. "Get away from me. I only did what I did on instructions." The scream was dulled by the thick oak doors, which then began to open.

The marquis paid no attention. He was staring lasciviously and openly at the slender pale beauty of Emerald. "I'm a free man, you know." He began to salivate. "I'm divorced now. I could marry her. There's no reason why I couldn't marry her."

Emerald swooned, her dark head lolling against her father's shoulder. The double oak doors burst apart. Torquil stood for an instant, framed in the doorway, his face shrunken with hatred. Behind him the Master of the Chamberpot was sprawled on the flagstones.

Torquil walked forward into the library, his right arm going up the wall to wrench a dirk from a ceremonial sheath, never once taking his eyes from his father's face. "I heard what you said," he whispered. His voice was so intense that it carried the length of the room. "I heard you. If you lay one finger on Emerald, I'm going to castrate you." He was still walking towards his father, his elbows flared out, the hair visibly and primitively rising on his wrists and on the rear of his neck. His steps were jerky and his toes were pointed slightly inwards. "In fact, I wish you had been castrated before you met my mother. I wish I was never born of your spawn." He was making the dirk sway in front of him, the sharp edge upwards.

In terror the marquis shouted, "Don't, I beg of you, don't. Don't touch me. I won't harm her. I won't go near her. . . ."

A faint moan came from Emerald and she stirred against her father who had put his arm round her. Torquil dropped the dirk and swept towards her. "Is she all right? Will she. . . ." In confusion he said to Duncan Habib-Strumpet, "I'm afraid I don't know how to address you."

Emerald opened her eyes and gazed fully at Torquil. It was as if he was staring into the deepest pool in Strummet Water. He shook himself. He blushed and said, "I really should find out how to address you, sir?" In a rush of words he said, "If anyone's going to marry Emerald, it's going to be me."

Duncan Habib-Strumpet was dazed with pleasure. "You mean . . . you mean you want to marry Emerald? You would care for her?" He had to sit down. "Excuse me, my heart. . . ."

Torquil put his hand under Emerald's elbow. He said contemptuously to his father, "I'll leave you to arrange the details with my future father-in-law. I suppose you should keep the title till your death to avoid any more scandal." He steadily added, thinking of his investigation the day after the riot, "But if the agreement isn't to my pleasure or satisfaction, I'll lock you in the cell at the water gate until it is." The marquis turned grey and cringed.

"I think I've loved you since I first saw you," said Torquil, as they walked down towards the rocks, Emerald's sari tilted away from her ankles to allow her to move gracefully. "I never thought I could tell you, until. . . ." Beneath them they could see Digby, still standing on the rim of the Earl's Chair, haranguing the three others.

"I want you to meet my friends. Let's hurry and hear what he's saying." They began to run forward across the tussocky nardus grass and came to the sea-wrack below the *machair*. They heard Digby end, ". . . vanish like a puff-ball, hooted out of existence," and saw Sheila Strummet murmur something, then they came closer and this time heard her say, "You would be free then, Digby; free from all the past." He jumped from the rock and landed close beside her, and they all began to walk up the beach together, the eternal sand whispering at their feet. His hand was lightly linked with hers.

The marquis watched them from the turret window. Bloody fools, he thought, trying to buck the Establishment. He wondered when the refugee girls would arrive.

The End

STORIES FROM THE ILIAD
AND THE ODYSSEY

TITLES IN THIS SERIES: